About the Author

Miles Hudson loves words and ideas.

He's a physics teacher, surfer, author, hockey player, inventor, backpacker and idler.

Miles was born in Minneapolis but has lived in Durham in northern England for 30 years.

2089

Miles M Hudson

PENFOLD BOOKS

Published by Penfold Books
87 Hallgarth Street
Durham DH1 3AS
England

Author's website:
mileshudson.com

ISBN: 978-1-83812-583-7

In the first instance the publication of this story was made possible by very generous support from those listed here:

Super Patrons

Jen Baxter, Sean Chuhan, Mark Cornwell, Irene Covell, Jason Covell, Kirsten Crombie, James de Winter, Tato Debernardi, Greg Dick, John Ellis, Jamie Glister, Heather Handley, Ian Harley, Laura Harm, Stan Hecks, Keith Herrmann, Carol Hudson, Dougal Jerram, Jane & Jon, Dave & Hannah & Frances Jones, Dan Kieran, Matthew Lawson, Stacy Miles, John Mitchinson, Pat Pauley, Justin Pollard, Matthew Potts, Dominic Stephens, Asa Taulbut, Philip Vaughan, Lee Worden

Patrons

Stephen Atkinson, A. John Chapman, Andy Collins, Julian Emslie, Brioney Euden, Andy Guest, Richard Hall, Robin Hart, Tim Hassell, Christopher James, Nicola Janna, Paul Karamath, Polina Kliuchnikova, Ben Leighton, Emma Less, Tim Lever, Xiao Liu, Samantha Lunney, Clauz Mansilla, David Miller, Diego Montoyer, Christopher Moore, Mark Morfett, Carlo Navato, Charlotte O'Brien, Alice Peng, Larissa Prates, Louise Reid, Sam Ross, Carol Sayles, Mark Scott, Magdalena Skowronski, Quentin Spender, Jason Stewart, Scott Thomson, Kayem Toia, Derek Wilson

Other acknowledgements

The inspiration for this story was a TV interview with Edward Snowden.

Amazing help and support in turning it into this finished book came from: Dominic and Lois for the use of their NZ writer's retreat; Kirsten Crombie for the most amazing proofreading work (twice); all my beta readers, especially my mother and father; all at Unbound; great editing work from Gary Gibson and Philip Purser-Hallard; wonderful cover design work from Mark Ecob; and all those who pledged support up front, especially the ever incredible Stacy Miles.

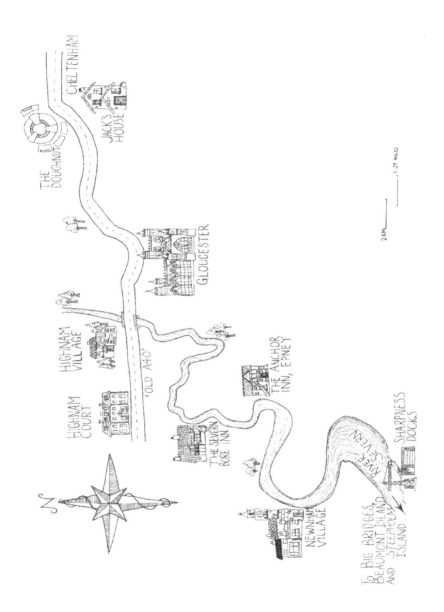

THE DOUGHNUT

CHELTENHAM

JACK'S HOUSE

GLOUCESTER

HIGHNAM COURT

HIGHNAM VILLAGE

'OLD A40'

THE SEVERN BORE INN

THE ANCHOR INN, EPNEY

NEWNHAM VILLAGE

RIVER SEVERN

SHARPNESS DOCKS

TO BIG BRIDGES, BEAUMONT ISLAND AND STEEPHOLM ISLAND

N

2 KM

1.24 MILES

The Covenants of Jerusalem

1. Nothing will be hidden or secret.

2. Everyone will act for the benefit of all.

3. Actions will be judged by everyone.

4. Local population groups will be self determining.

5. No influence over more than 10,000 persons will be permitted.

Signed into law as the new global constitution, 11th November 2040.

Chapter One

Jack Smith hefted his rucksack of 'dummy bombs' to set off for the trial run. Leaving a sack of river cobbles in the basement of the Doughnut could be explained away if anyone found them. If nobody found them during today's work shift, then next time they'd be real bombs, not just stones. Jack expected that, on 10 September 2089, he was going to cause the biggest act of terrorism for fifty years.

Jack did not lock his front door. There would be no burglary; he closed it to keep out animals and bad weather. Because of his work as a sifter, nobody could ever get away with a crime, so people simply didn't bother to try.

He flicked a switch to connect the roof solar panels to charge the battery collection under the stairs inside. The old electricity storage units were more than sixty years old and no longer held charge very well. As with most technology, they needed careful nurturing.

The house was on the outskirts of old Cheltenham, a nice residence that had suffered little from its abandonment in the Times of Malthus. It had originally been in the last street before the countryside, both a city house and a rural house. Now that nature was reclaiming much of the urban areas, this borderline was blurred.

Jack liked his home; the proximity to fields and woods was settling. Grannie Ellie's farm was in the midst of similar woods and fields. A few other farmhouses had been visible as Jack grew up, but he and his grandmother had had a swathe of countryside to themselves. At his garden gate, he wondered if animals and vegetation, or indeed people, had taken back his childhood home in the year since her passing. At the memory that Ellie was gone, the weight of the rucksack made his legs wobble, and he had to steady himself with a hand on the gatepost.

1

Jack's walk to the Doughnut was mostly through derelict streets, the houses dark and mouldering, long abandoned. He crossed the old railway. The metal tracks still lay in perfect straight lines, red-brown stripes running along a grass corridor through semi-ghost town. The route was easy walking in any weather – the roads were fine for pedestrians. Flooding and winter snow and ice had combined to ruffle and pit the asphalt surface. Had any of the rusting cars been started up and driven around the empty streets, it would have been rough going for them, impassable in places.

'Morning, son.'

Jack leapt away from the sound of the voice and hit his thigh against a front garden wall. In the doorway of a house across the road, an old man smiled and gave a brief wave. Jack looked up and down the street. He stuttered back, 'Goo-good morning.'

Jack kept his back to the wall and sidled away, the rucksack's base scraping on the top of the crumbling bricks. The old man said nothing further, and stared.

Here and there, houses were occupied and Jack would normally wave or greet people he saw on his route. He knew them all by sight, but rarely held any long conversations with anyone. With daily twelve-hour working shifts, and over an hour's walking commute each day, Jack did not have much time for chit-chat. Today, he was carrying twenty kilograms of dummy bombs. Chit-chat was definitely not going to happen.

Across the cricket pitch, still well maintained and in regular use, and a footbridge over Hatherley Brook, the route led him onto the tarmac fields surrounding the Doughnut.

All the sifters for southwest England, and the whole of Wales, worked in the Doughnut. The old government had established the ring-shaped building for its spies and information thieves to work in. After the signing of the

Covenants of Jerusalem, numerous communities had repurposed bits of its computing power for their own surveillance sifters.

The glass and steel torus was enormous, and each sifter had a significant space in which to work undisturbed. With the global population crashed to less than 100 million, England as a whole had only 83 Kangaroos – the remaining population groupings. The number of sifters at the Doughnut was far fewer than it could have held, and there was little interaction between them. Most of the roof of the building was now covered in solar panels – the electricity grid had long since been abandoned in favour of small, local, renewable generation.

Jack had a second floor workspace entirely to himself. The Doughnut was constructed in thirds, and his area covered a chunk of the Western Third. Whilst the Northeastern and Southeastern Thirds overlooked parts of Cheltenham, he had panoramic windows that looked out in the direction of Wales. Eventually, although obscured by mountains, the view faced the Irish Sea.

Each sifter could arrange their own workspace as they wanted to, but Jack had followed the example of his mentor and developed a horseshoe of display screens on three levels. These twelve screens half enclosed him when he sat in the black swivel chair, which had moulded over fourteen years to fit his exact body shape. He put his lunchbox on his desk and headed downstairs.

The basement of the Doughnut housed all of the computers that ran the infonetwork and digital records, including all audiopt feeds, for the same region of southwest England and Wales. Although these were all housed in the same building, each village population – or Kangaroo – had a separate computer server for its local infonetwork. The individual systems were each maintained by a pair of engineers, the infotechs. The Fifth Covenant of Jerusalem meant that although the region's various Kangaroos all had their sifters working in the Doughnut, the operations of each were totally separate. No organisation was permitted influence over too many people.

Jack had only been to the basement a few times; he would look out of place if anyone saw him down there. The audiopt surveillance would see his every move, but he knew to avoid looking at anything that might give away his secret purpose.

He had an idea where to place his bombs – around the main server area – but needed to get there without meeting anyone. His rucksack only held imitation explosives this time round. If nobody came down and found them in a day, then he could be confident the real explosions would not hurt anyone, but just destroy the infonetwork, and hence the audiopt surveillance.

Jack placed four packages in the corners of the server hall, hid the rucksack under the stairs and stole back up them to head to work as normal.

As he came up towards the first floor, Jack saw a dark ponytail. Its owner was leaning on the tall window's shiny handrail staring out at the scrubby brown landscape. He had tried to be quiet on the stairs and she didn't appear to have heard him. However, there was no way he could get past without her seeing him. Jack decided quickly that to descend again and cross the basement to the other staircase would look very suspicious, should anyone watch his audiopt feeds.

'Hi Aluen,' he said brightly.She turned. 'Oh, Jack. Good to see you. Where have you been?' She had immediately thwarted his plan to engage her in innocuous conversation. Without looking, he put out a hand to lean on the wall, misjudged the distance and toppled slightly.

'Oh, um, trying to find my infotech. You haven't seen her, have you? Nobody down in the basement at all.'

Aluen shook her head. 'Sorry, no. But actually, glad I caught you.'

Jack leaned further against the wall for support. Was Aluen responsible for monitoring him, as well as her own village of Newnham? Had she come to the stairwell simply to intercept him?

She stared at him for a moment and then continued, 'Have you got a minute to help me with a case?' Jack didn't reply but stared back. 'I'm not at all sure what's going on with it. A second pair of eyes would be really helpful.' She smiled at him.

After a moment, Jack stood more upright and said, 'You know I'm not allowed to decide on matters in another Kangaroo. I won't know the current mores in your village.' What was legal or not in Newnham could vary weekly, as the population decided.

'Yes, yes, it's not that. I don't need an opinion on whether to send it. At least, not exactly. The feeds just have me really confused. Come and take a look.' She grabbed his hand and pulled Jack up the last stair and into her huge workspace.

When her bank of screens had all come back on, they showed the audiopt feeds that his sifter colleague was following to produce her weekly KangaReview. The rolling timestamp on the screen told Jack that this event had happened the previous evening.

The infoservers pre-sifted all the audiopt feeds. Any events that the computer algorithms identified as potentially breaking the Second Covenant of Jerusalem – that 'Everyone will act for the benefit of all' – were fed to the sifters to be examined for confirmation, or denial, of the existence of a crime.

The screen Aluen pointed to showed an image of a child in a bedroom. There was scrolling text at the bottom of the screen to tell the sifter what the algorithms had concluded as the possible problem. In this case, the text was slightly larger than usual and in a shrieking blood red: 'Potential child abuse,' it warned.

The audiopt feed clip was seen through the eyes of the child's father. He entered the room in which the boy was screaming in bed. Jack guessed at four years old and then Aluen clicked for the boy's feeds to be shown on the adjacent screen. This confirmed the boy's identity and that he was in fact five years and two months old.

The boy saw his father come in, and his crying caught in the boy's throat for a second. His eyes were fixed on the approaching parent, and he started screaming again, a little louder and with genuine fear in the cries. It was a disturbing scene. Without a pause in his movements, the father struck the boy on the arm. It was a hard slap, after which he picked up his son, and they hugged each other. The boy continued to cry, but it subsided with each lungful of air until the boy was silent, and the father put him back down under the bed covers. Neither adult nor child said any coherent words during the brief clip.

Jack scowled. The conclusion to the clip was contradictory. The computer had suggested this father might be beating his child, and that was clearly what Jack had seen, but they hugged at the end as if nothing had happened between them. The final view through the father's eyes saw his son contented and ready to sleep.

'What do you think?' she asked.

'Yes, there is something not quite right. It looks obvious, but... that hug. The boy's not subdued by his abuser, he seems genuinely thankful to have been hit.'

'Exactly. Am I missing something?'

Jack leant over to the controller and moved the feeds backwards and forwards several times. The pre-sifting software was good, but it could not comprehend the nuances of human behaviour. A human sifter was always needed to give the final judgement about what should be included in the KangaReview.

There was one brief moment, lasting less than a fifth of a second, where the father's eyes moved from the boy's face to look at the arm he would then hit. The room was quite dark and, in slow motion, there were only three frames of the man's vision that were looking at the arm. However, in those frames, it was absolutely clear that a large house spider was crawling on the son. Jack called up the boy's feeds from the minutes before what the computer had supplied. Playing this through showed the youngster looking at his own forearm and seeing the creature there. It was clear that he then froze in fear, but called out the one word 'spider' loudly and repeatedly before breaking into the screams of terror. Aluen had initially only been supplied with the feeds from the moment the boy started screaming.

'I remember something my mentor told me,' Jack said. 'We are the arbiters of history in this world. Others could also find out the truth, but nobody ever bothers to look. Right or wrong, our submissions to Kangaroo have become the origination upon which everybody's worldview is formulated.' He ran the fingers of both hands through his wiry black hair and looked at Aluen.

She turned her head and stared at him. 'What?'

'Do you really believe we have the right to spy on people all the time?'

Aluen scrunched her eyebrows. 'It's our job.' Her tone became sardonic as she mimicked his language: 'If "we are the arbiters of history in this world", then we need to see everything, in order to make sure we tell the true story.'

Jack realised he had said too much. He took a half step backwards. Had he given himself away? Would she report him?

But Aluen had already turned back to her work. 'Thanks

for helping.' She clicked on the button on the screen's toolbar marked 'Nothing to report'. Both screens changed image to show two new suggested issues with scrolling text explaining the algorithm's thinking in each case.

Jack moved to go back to his workspace. As he looked out of the window on the staircase, he mouthed silently, 'Soon, I'll put a stop to all this.' He thought about the homemade bombs hidden in the cellar of his house, waiting to be used, and felt a small surge of satisfaction. *Soon.*

Chapter Two

Marmaran Truva held the small, white coffee cup to his nose and sniffed briefly. Vicky Truva thought the coffee smelt good, which would be a surprise to her father. He had had to teach the cafe staff in Kangaroo Hall how to make coffee properly, and even then the outcome was seldom palatable to him.

The coffee that now struggled to grow in English greenhouses was a poor substitute for the tropical varieties historically used to make Turkish coffee. Although neither Vicky nor her father had ever actually been to the country of their forefathers, there had been a family line of coffee perfectionists dating back to her great-great-grandfather from the city of Truva, in the old Turkey.

Marmaran sipped at the black liquid and winced. 'Why don't the sifters ever send in the feeds of these people making coffee?' he muttered, ostensibly to himself.

Vicky watched the big, ginger-haired man next to her father laugh and slap the shorter man on his broad back. 'You and your coffee, Marma. You know you'll never get it the way you want it; you need to accept this.' Marmaran cushioned his cup from the physicality of the man's blow, looked up at him and nodded, pushing his closed lips outward.

Vicky smiled and thought of her mother making coffee for him years before. She knew that she had her mother's long, English face, but her darker skin had been handed down from her father and his ancestors. She also had her mother's height and was nose-to-nose as tall as Marmaran. Her mother had been able to produce a cup of coffee that he adored. He would smack his lips in delight at the flavour. Vicky had never been able to emulate the feat, and since his wife's death, Marmaran himself

9

had been the only person who could make coffee he approved of.

Both men looked up to the dais as Lloyd Lloyd, the Spokesperson for Highnam, began the proceedings. His voice projected naturally, 'Ladies and gentleman, welcome to Kangaroo for this day, Sunday 3 September 2089. Firstly, let me tell you that the death of Old Man Jones has been punished, as we decreed last week, with the imprisonment of his son at the Bristol Jail. The Bristol Brigade members came on Tuesday to escort him away. Poor young Derek was ill – there was no way we could have foreseen what he would do. You all saw him here last Sunday. It is so sad, but mental illness happens. Indeed, I think we should be thankful that it is only sick people who cause such tragedy; genuinely profound criminal behaviours never get past the planning stages, as they are caught by the sifters.'

There was a light round of applause from the assembled villagers and one shout of 'Hear, hear.'

'Fortunately, such things are rare. This week's Kangaroo should be relatively brief as we have only a few matters to discuss, and these are all pretty straightforward.'

Truva senior's ginger colleague called out, 'Old Marma here wants to add an agenda item.' The assembled crowd looked round at the pair.

Vicky's father gaped up at the man, almost spilling the coffee himself this time. 'What are you doing?' he hissed. Vicky stared at Marma and wondered what was happening. Her right forefinger traced pensive circles looping the mousy hair at her temple.

The bigger man beamed back a gigantic smile from his round, ruddy face. 'He says the coffee in here is a crime!' The hall filled with laughter. Some people looked towards the small hatch where two ladies made refreshments, but most returned their gaze to Lloyd Lloyd and his floppy, blond fringe.

Vicky watched her father continue to stare at his neighbour. Marma narrowed his eyes to tiny slits. He muttered again out loud, but at an even quieter volume, 'And I'll be able to make my own coffee there too.'

She guessed he had inwardly decided that in future he would attend Kangaroo remotely via his armulet, from the comfort of the sofa in the front room of their farmhouse. Vicky had been only eight years old when her mother succumbed to the snow, but she was certain that her father had become more insular in the years since.

Highnam's Spokesperson, Lloyd Lloyd, was in his thirties, broad and strong, and looked every bit the country boy. He had an assured air, and on the stage, when he moved and spoke to the assembly, this was amplified to a veritable swagger. Above his head, a huge projection of Highnam's marketplace on a summer's day was a placeholder for the programme they would soon scrutinise. 'Before we watch the KangaReview from this week, we have one item of community business. The chimney on the mayor's house was damaged by those winds on Wednesday night, so we need to arrange to fix it up. As you know, the house is nearly two centuries old, so it's not surprising that it needs so much maintenance.' It went unsaid that the 'mayor's house' was the one that Lloyd Lloyd and his family lived in.

A woman close to the front of the assembled crowd offered, 'The old Canelkin house across the A40 is empty. Should we take the bricks from its chimney?'

The old road running along the southern side of Highnam village, known to all by its historical designation, the 'A40', had not seen fuelled vehicles in nearly fifty years. It was still the major transport link for the village, though, to Gloucester in particular. Decades of seasonal flooding had undermined it in places, giving carts and electric quad bikes some trouble, but for horses, cycles and pedestrians, the surface was manageable, if not good.

Lloyd Lloyd pointed at the woman and replied, 'From what I've seen, we only need a handful of replacement bricks. Well, you know what I mean... ' He grinned here, with a deliberate pause. '... A few bricks, maybe more than one hand could hold, but... ' He trailed off to offer the people a chance to enjoy his joke.

'Most of those that fell are fine to reuse, but thanks Mrs B, if we need some new bricks we'll use those. Anybody see a reason why we shouldn't?' The villagers generally shook their heads and looked at each other; nobody demurred. 'OK, that was the easy part. Now, who's going to volunteer to do it, and when? Hands up, please, let's have a working party of six, at least two of whom will need to provide some ladders and tools.'

Two hands went up on the side of the room away from the Truvas. Marma was not paying much attention. He played his small spoon through the coffee. Vicky expected he would pronounce a far-fetched analysis, concluding with what had been done to the grounds to produce it.

Lloyd Lloyd continued to recruit volunteers. 'Thanks Asa and Tony. Who else? Asa, Tony, when are you thinking you want to do it? My estimate is one to two days' work for a party of six. At most. And we have stock of cement to make the mortar – help yourselves from the stores behind Kangaroo Hall.'

By this time, other hands had gone up, including the ginger fellow, who poked Marmaran's arm to engage him in volunteering. He looked into the florid cheeks and copper-coloured stubble, squinted ever so slightly, and raised his hand also. The working party was appointed.

'Now then, ladies and gentlemen, including those of you

attending Kangaroo today via your armulets, what's happened this week? I can tell you that the submission from the sifters is a short one today, so let's see what we need to deal with.'

He turned to look up at the projected picture, which faded to black, before a new video started playing. It was a view that one might see if running through woods. At the bottom of the screen, the name George Kendrick appeared. Thus, the audience knew that they were watching the audiopt feeds from the round-faced, ginger man.

Marmaran immediately took a step to the side, directly into Vicky, trying to push them a little between other audience members and away from George. With others making similar small movements, a space appeared all around the man, whose innately red face had become utterly crimson. He was looking across the room, no longer watching the screen. Kendrick muttered repeatedly, 'Oh, Malthus. Oh, Malthus.'

After a glance at the man, all the audience members returned their gaze to the screens. Vicky followed the ginger man's stare, and the only other person still looking their way, and not up at the projection, was a thin woman with a big head of dark, curly hair. She wore large, dangling earrings that Vicky swore she could hear jangling against themselves.

She looked back at the screen and saw that the very woman had now appeared in the video, looking back at the viewer. She wore the same earrings, and George Kendrick had obviously been able to hear them, as the sounds they heard were coming from the projected show above Lloyd Lloyd's blond head.

It was rendered in a three-dimensional manner, so the audience could see it exactly as if they had been Kendrick at the date and time shown in the bottom corner. The curly-haired woman in the room looked down to the ground, whilst her image in the air above looked back towards the viewers with a smile. She gave a shrill giggle and ran off through the trees. The chase continued briefly, but she was easily caught, and the two held each other in a laughing embrace.

One member of the gathered audience called out, 'For shame.'

The two proceeded to kiss and fondle one another with some considerable passion. The sifters had put together the show of audiopt feeds switching the point of view occasionally, so sometimes the woman's view was shown and the audience could see Kendrick as she had. Increasingly sexual acts followed rapidly. The audience was not spared anything, as the feeds proceeded right through until Kendrick climaxed.

Mostly the lovers had been looking at each other's faces: the KangaReview only briefly showed genitalia, as they had undressed. However, no secrets were maintained, the complete tryst was played out – everything that the audiopt feeds had picked up.

The images froze with a view through her eyes looking at the blue sky. Apart from a small area of his ginger head on the right hand side, a few treetops and a wisp of white cloud made the new placeholder picture a delightful scene to hang in the air above Lloyd Lloyd. He proceeded with the formal court proceedings. 'Well, both George Kendrick and Marisa Leone are in the room today. And, as we all know, both are married to other people.'

The same voice called out, 'For shame.'

Lloyd Lloyd raised his hand to ensure there was no further heckling. He had been Spokesperson of the Kangaroo for long enough to be able to run the show very effectively. Decisions got made, with appropriate contributions from the populace, and in good time. 'We generally have a case of infidelity a little more frequently than once every six months and, during my office at least, our punishments been fairly consistent. George,

Marisa, do you have anything we need to hear? Any mitigation, or anything that the feeds maybe misrepresent?'

Circular spaces had been created by people retreating away from the two of them. It was as if each one stood in a spotlight. Both looked at their feet, and Kendrick responded. He spoke quietly, but the audience was silent so he was heard. 'We had both had a bit of wine and lain in the sun for a while. We weren't thinking straight.' He finally invoked an apology to his wife: 'I'm sorry, Jackie.'

Some of the crowd looked over to Marisa, whose curly locks hung around her head so her face was mostly obscured. Her head was bobbing up and down a little. She was nodding in agreement, but also crying at the same time. She said nothing.

'Well, it's an easy excuse.' The crowd murmured in agreement with their Spokesperson. 'And a common one. If it's not hormones, adulterers always talk of drunkenness. Although usually we hear about both.' The muttering agreements continued. 'It might mitigate, but there really is no excuse. Behaviours like this threaten the harmony of our Kangaroo.'

'Hear, hear,' was called from the back of the room.

'Jealousy leads to anger and violence. We have lived a peaceful life here long enough to know that it is what we want to continue, so we must punish those who would threaten that.'

'Hear, hear,' was repeated, but from nearer the middle of the room this time.

'We have not seen these two causing any problems before, and we know them as fine citizens.' Lloyd Lloyd paused, but nobody shouted support at this point. 'The feeds show that they seem equally culpable. I propose that we deliver our usual punishment: ten days of reparations labour each. Are there any objections, or suggested amendments?' The crowd buzzed as people spoke with their neighbours, but again nobody called anything out.

After he had given them ten seconds to consider, he continued, 'OK, I don't hear any alternatives being suggested, so can we vote now on the punishment, please. All those in favour of ten days' reparations labour by Marisa for Jackie, please raise your hands.' A roomful of arms filled the air. 'So ordered,' Lloyd Lloyd's voice had become stentorian. 'And now, hands up those in favour of ten days' reparations labour by George for Jonty.'

As the crowd again voted unanimously, the decision was made that for sleeping with Jonty Leone's wife, George Kendrick would have to work for the man for ten days. The work was for Jonty to determine, and would be administered by Lloyd Lloyd. Marisa would similarly atone for her crime through a penance of labour for Jackie Kendrick. The enforced labour, although determined by the victim, could not be dangerous, or demeaning. The punishments were reparation not retribution. Their aim was rehabilitation and reconciliation. Lloyd Lloyd would encourage the parties to spend some time talking together during the punishment, or afterwards if a victim's emotions were too strong at the time.

As the audiopt feeds provided stark and damning evidence, it was rare for a criminal not to be chastened and shamed by the experience of their conviction in the Kangaroo court. The punishments were generally undertaken with enthusiasm. Above all though, the crimes themselves were only rarely actually criminal. Usually, the purpose of the town meeting and its punishments was to bring the community together. The consensus developed in Kangaroo meant that the residents generally lived in a peaceful harmony, committed to a common purpose, which in turn engendered strength against external threats.

The adulterous tryst was the highlight of the meeting. After that, the Kangaroo had to point out to arguing neighbours, who had come to blows over a boundary dispute, that sharing was the only acceptable solution. They received no further punishment than this censure.

Vicky watched her father smile at his coffee. She thought about where the line was drawn between sharing and ownership, and she wondered what might have ensued had George Kendrick claimed that in Highnam it was made very clear that sharing was the only acceptable solution. She looked at the ginger beard and the small, round eyes, and knew that the man would never dare to rock the boat like that. She fully expected that such ideas wouldn't even occur to most of the villagers.

Chapter Three

After grandmother Ellie's death, there was no one who knew Jack well enough that they would have been able to spot his strange behaviour in the build-up to his act of terrorism.

However, with the audiopt feeds recording everything he saw and heard, his preparations had been difficult and disjointed. He had travelled the escape route to the Leckhampton Hill bunker virtually, through his armulet – there had been no opportunity to check the escape plan in the real world.

He had practised making the bombs with random alternate ingredients, under the guise of trying to make cement for the cobbles in his little garden. And in collecting the actual incendiary ingredients, he had made every effort to gather them by touch out of his own sight.

As the audiopt feeds picked up only the electromagnetic waves generated by signals in the auditory and optic nerves, they could not read thoughts. Things outside the field of vision and hearing – tastes, smells and touch sensations – were not recorded.

Finally, Jack had twelve hours between shifts in which to make the real bombs, set them, and then cycle to Highnam to stash his rucksack and establish his alibi. He was not certain that his one shot at manufacturing bombs from scratch would actually work.

Jack's fingers traced the outside of the rough hessian sack filled with homemade explosives. His blindfold stopped the audiopt feeds observing what he held. Most of the chemicals had been collected from abandoned warehouses or shops, and one he had dug out of the ground. Gathering them had not triggered any red flags in the pre-sifting algorithms of the surveillance network, as they were all innocent items individually. He smiled at the thought that he had been able to collect some of the electronic parts of the triggering system from the Doughnut's own stores.

He got up from the wooden kitchen chair and carried the sack to join the others in the rucksack by the door. Jack was very familiar with moving around his house blindfold. Even before working on the plan to blow up his workplace, he had often worn a self-imposed eye covering in order to feel free from the audiopts' ever-watchful supervision.

As he closed the pack, he felt a twinge in his stomach. He had completed the physical preparation of the bombs – he would soon destroy southwestern Britain's audiopt network entirely and nobody would need to blindfold themselves to ensure their privacy. He whipped the cloth band off his face with a flourish and observed the apparently innocent domestic situation intently. 'Ooh, look, there's my table. And the stove with two pots. What a calm kitchen I live in.'

Jack grinned and scratched his short dark hair where it itched from the removed blindfold. He imagined his grandmother sitting with him for a cup of tea, and pictured her own deep smile. She would have congratulated him on giving people back the chance to have secrets.

After he left home, they spoke pretty much daily using armulet video communications. With his long working hours, these were usually mundane chats about their respective daily activities. Sometimes the seasonal work in Ellie's fields meant that she was not available much during Jack's free time. Often their daily time together was shorter than he would have liked. The sometimes difficult nature of this arrangement meant that the life stories Ellie shared with her grandson had essentially stopped when Jack moved to Cheltenham at fifteen years old.

It took all his strength to upend the costermonger's barrow. The wooden cart tipped forward away from the unsuspecting grocer and thudded onto the dry-packed marketplace mud. Green and red apples, which had been so carefully piled in little tetrahedrons of four fruits, cascaded onto the floor, streaming away in all directions. Jack's incoherent roar was the thing that most attracted the villagers' attention though. They froze and looked over, wide-eyed and open-mouthed, as the skinny sifter created the most unusual gossip. This sort of thing never happened in Highnam Kangaroo.

Overhearing two middle-aged sisters had finally tipped Jack into action. They met weekly at the Sunday market to trade gossip from opposite ends of the settlement. With a population of nearly 4,000, it had enough people so there was plenty of gossip and few enough so that everybody just about knew everyone else. Or, even better for gossiping purposes, nobody quite knew everyone else. Each tale could begin with a lengthy relationship scene-setter: 'You know Harry's sister's first husband? Well, his mother's cousin... you wouldn't believe it...' Thus the stories were close enough to be interesting, yet just far enough removed to be not personally affecting.

Jack hated this aspect of society. As there was nothing private, he could not understand why people would be interested in discussing the activities of others. It was all available on their armulets, at any time. As soon as anybody saw anything, or heard anything, including their own voice, it was published publicly and could be viewed and reviewed at one's leisure.

Frances had grabbed her sister's arm to distract her from the bunches of grapes laid out on one stall. Whilst Frances was a large woman, Amy was much thinner. They had similar short faces, and virtually identical curly brown hair. With sagging, wrinkly skin, the women looked as though their lives had been hard lived.

'Amy, you coming to Kangaroo this afternoon? I reckon it's gonna be a good one – that Ali Dally has been messing on again, this time with a married woman from Wessex Road. Two adulteries in two weeks!'

'He's a queer one that Ali Dally. They're all the same, mind. And last week, George and Marisa at it. And them getting ten days' labour. Can't wait to see what happens to Ali, second offence this year. But nah, I'm just gonna watch on the armulet today. Harry's not been so well, so I figure best to keep him out of the afternoon sun walking there.'

'It's not been too hot this week, but I guess you're right. Best not to tempt things. Who'd have expected mid-September and only twenty-six degrees?' She looked at the small armulet screen strapped above her wrist and its temperature reading in one corner.

Nobody recognised the boy they had voted to be their sifter fourteen years previously. His hair was darker than the common brown of the others, but his pale skin was different.

With the eyes of the square then on him, a distant booming sound floated through the throng, and smoke from several miles away rose into view above the mayor's house behind Jack Smith. 'Vive la revolution!' he croaked, merely to himself, before turning to flee down the alley between the mayor's house and the wall edging Highnam Court's gardens.

Kangaroo Hall was located within the oldest surviving building for miles around. Constructed originally in the 17th century, Highnam Court had been commandeered by the populace almost immediately after the signing of the Covenants of Jerusalem.

The most recent generation had worked hard to restore their village's grand meeting place, including returning the sumptuous gardens to their early 21st-century glory. From a distance, it looked bright and new and, as Jack trailed his fingers along the rough red bricks of the alley wall in the village, he felt like he was touching the court building itself. Emerging from the rear alley onto Lassington Lane brought him back to reality.

Jack kept looking back, but nobody chased him. With the audiopt feeds, nobody thought there was any need to chase him. People helped the grocer to rebuild his stall, set in their knowledge that the vandal would be rounded up for Kangaroo.

However, Jack had been keeping an eye on the time and had waited until just moments after the explosion at the Doughnut knocked out all the audiopt feeds for 200 miles. At the instant of his act of violence, there would be no digital record of sights or sounds. The townsfolk would have their memories though, in case he needed an alibi. Highnam's Kangaroo court might believe he had something to do with blowing up the infoservers, but, with no digital record, they'd only be able to prove that he was seen in the marketplace when the bombs went off.

Justice for Dummies, his grandmother had called Kangaroo. Or sometimes, when she was most hacked off with it, she had changed the epithet to No Justice for Dummies.

After less than fifty yards, Lassington Lane swept around to the right into a double-width boulevard where large carriages could easily pass on both sides of the central grassy space. Jack, though, continued straight on along the much narrower byway. This was still a fairly busy thoroughfare, especially on market day, and he had to weave past pedestrians as he jogged north on the old, broken tarmac. After 200 yards up the narrow road, Jack was wheezing heavily.

He turned left onto a footpath between fields, a path with no other walkers on it, but where the dark green hedge was lower, a little lower than Jack's shoulders. Looking back over it, across a fallow field, there was a view to the market. That was some distance away, and the activities of the villagers were not entirely clear.

Jack half lifted his arm to get a marketplace view on his armulet, before remembering that he himself had just destroyed all network service. The electronic part of any armulet was sealed and waterproof. Jack rarely bothered to take his off. Its strapping brace was black leather, and with his sweat and exertions, it felt tight and itchy.

One of the main thrusts of Jack's escape plan was misdirection. His current route was headed in almost exactly the opposite course to the one he intended to take. His idea was that he would be seen passing mostly westwards, and then secretly return on a large arc to end up heading off to the east of Highnam to hide out in the old bunker he had researched.

To exaggerate his furtiveness, Jack walked the path with a slight stoop and occasionally popped his head up over the hedgerow to look over to the market. His intention was that anybody watching would remember him behaving strangely, and be able to advise his pursuers exactly which way he had gone.

The end of the footpath entered into a narrow but long thicket of trees bordering the edges of the fields. This copse, Rodway Hill Covert, extended for a half-mile to the northeast and formed the beginning of Jack's secret escape route. From this point on, he could not risk being spotted. Pushing aside the thick branches and leaves and undergrowth, whilst making as little noise as possible, he sat down beside the grey rucksack he had secreted there just before dawn, six hours previously.

Jack had exchanged bombs for provisions in his rucksack. He pulled a water bottle from the side and took a long drink from it. The dust mixed into the sweat on his blue and white checked shirt made it itchy again. His armulet read twenty-eight degrees; some armulet functions were built into it without the need for an infonetwork connection.

Jack intended to rest and wait until dark before proceeding, so he took off his shirt and hung it over the leaves of a shrub. The hideout was small, as the vegetation of the copse grew tight and compact. At this point, the ground was steep, dropping away to the west. Lying down, with his head on the rucksack, Jack had a good view through the tree canopy into the nearest fields. He had previously cleared away the leaf litter, and, in the daytime heat, the earth had dried out. Thus it was relatively pleasant, and above all quiet, as long as he was happy to lie down in essentially the same position all the time.

With another swig of water, Jack started to eat one of two soft plums from the uppermost pocket on his rucksack. The trees within the thicket were all naturally occurring, and none offered up any fruit that would be good for humans. The whole place was alive with insects, small birds, and the occasional rustling in the undergrowth, which Jack assumed to be a small mammal. He was starving, and after the plums, he also ate nearly a whole bunch of red grapes and a bread roll.

Leaning his head back on the rucksack to finish the last mouthful of bread, Jack realised that his planning of food resources was likely woefully short. The notional four days of meals he had packed were only enough for a man who on most days sat for twelve hours and slept for eight.

Jack scrolled through a number of photographs stored on his armulet. The photographs appeared as three-dimensional images just beyond his feet as he lay flat. In places, the immediate plant life interfered with the images, but he was not in need of a detailed study. The pictures were of the areas immediately outside his hiding place.

Southeast from his current location, beyond a number of vegetable plots and fruit trees, was a big, dilapidated building. It looked like it was lucky to still be standing, as numerous holes weakened the walls, whilst others had rusted through the metal roof.

A noise came to him through the trees. He froze and peeked between the trunks, out of the copse. Sitting up on the rucksack, Jack's line of sight over the lowest level of shrubs allowed him to observe the closest of the vegetable plots. He saw a woman a short distance away, in the open, laughing out loud.

Perhaps in her mid-twenties, she was kneeling side on to his view, and he could see a broad smile in profile. It wrinkled the smooth skin of her face. The skin was an olive oil brown colour, but the wrinkles looked very dark in the grey afternoon light. He remained stationary, watching his childhood friend. She tucked a lock of stray hair behind her ear and Jack's memories of her flooded his mind.

Vicky Truva held a muddy, uprooted beetroot in her left hand and leant forward to grab the next beetroot stalk. Jack decided he should watch the harvesting carefully so that he could learn how to gather each type of food. He was mesmerised.

Chapter Four

A good speech should be like a woman's skirt: long enough to cover the subject and short enough to create interest, Major Frank Halthrop recalled to himself whilst waiting alone in the lecture theatre.

He insisted they use the old Bristol University building for his Brigade meetings; the blackboards had been in place for more than a hundred years. The chalk sticks had run out even before the Times of Malthus, but it was still possible to use the boards for presentations using some of the soft rocks that had been left as ornamentation in the old churchyard opposite the lecture hall. Plenty of cloth rags lay around the building that could be used to clean the blackboards each time.

Darren and Terry clattered into the room, shoving each other and laughing. They nodded and muttered 'Frank' in greeting to their boss. Halthrop looked at his armulet to see how late they were. In 2089, people lived very much by the rhythms of nature: dawn, dusk, new moon, full moon, and the growing cycles of their crops and livestock. Time had not been forgotten, but there was little incentive or need for people to pay much attention to it. Life was durative, and the very notion of time-linked self-discipline was alien to the youth that joined the Bristol Brigade under Halthrop. Sifter was about the only occupation left that had a timed shift pattern.

It was another ten minutes before Jane entered. She was well turned out in the simple uniform that Halthrop himself had designed. Despite trying twice as hard as the boys to impress him in most areas, she still arrived after them on most occasions. She sat in a seat adjacent to Darren as they all said their greetings to her. Jane's posture was quite military in its bearing – she copied the pose that Major Frank took in his chair, and her eyes followed him as he stood and stepped centre stage in front of them.

When they settled, Halthrop began. 'Good evening. Thank you for arriving nearly on time. I am sure that your punctuality will continue to improve as it needs to do.' The three were from farms around Bristol, which had enough family members that they could be spared to take on some militia work.

Halthrop looked along the line of three. Terry smiled a little. The ruddiness in Darren's cheeks led down to the corners of his mouth, which was slightly agape in anticipation of the briefing to come. With his bright blue eyes and fine blond hair, Darren had a very healthy appearance. Jane was agog. Her forearm was held in front of her stiff, vertical body, armulet video-recording the entire scene, should she need a reminder of anything that was said.

'You will have found that your armulets have no infonetwork connection at present. This is the result of an explosion at the Doughnut in Cheltenham. The infotechs there have sent word that the explosion was an act of sabotage by person or persons unknown, a little over eight hours ago. A few aged, rudimentary, but functional electrical communication cables have been returned to temporary service, but to all intents and purposes, the infonetwork connection has been severed throughout the southwest of England. Many Kangaroos have set up local posses to catch the saboteurs.'

Halthrop stopped for a moment to allow this to sink in to his three young soldiers. Nobody spoke, and the major was unconvinced that they fully comprehended the enormity of the situation.

'For the last fifty years, fugitives for whom a posse was mobilised have been easily caught by following their audiopt feeds. Occasionally, a criminal has thought to destroy the audiopts in order to evade capture, but they have always been caught beforehand because the sifters have spotted their activities in advance. This was not the case here. So, not only are we dealing with an extremely sophisticated saboteur, but we do not have the feeds to use to chase them down.'

Silence ensued again.

Major Halthrop did not elaborate, but continued briefing. 'In this case, one of the sifters at the Doughnut did not arrive for work today and is not at his home in Cheltenham. He's currently the main suspect, and so we have been charged with searching for him.

'Jack Smith is originally from near Highnam. We have no actual images of him, with the infonetwork down, but one of his neighbours has drawn this sketch.' Halthrop waved at his armulet and a childlike drawing appeared in the air, showing a very white face, inset with dark eyes, dark eyebrows, and short, dark hair.

'The infotechs reckon they will hopefully have something back up and running in anywhere from forty-eight hours to six days, so the task should become easier then, but of course the closer we get by then, the more chance we have of being the ones to catch him.' The major let this last point sink in.

All the Kangaroos would have contracted a posse, or organised one themselves, but he did not rate the other militia leaders highly. Those he had met were lazy and ill disciplined, and a posse made from inexperienced villagers would never find a fugitive without their armulets for assistance.

Terry said, 'So how much will this job be worth?'

Major Halthrop scowled. 'You know what I keep telling you about questions during briefing, Terry.'

Terry frowned and then raised his arm. Halthrop shook his head. 'NO! All questions at the end.' Terry lowered his arm again at looked at the other two. 'Now, where was I?' Jane rewound her recording a few seconds and they all heard the major's disembodied voice repeating, '... chance we have of being the ones to catch him.'

Halthrop scowled at Jane and remained silent.

After an uncomfortable pause, he carried on, 'You have training in martial arts, so now is the time that you may have to use these. And I mean for real, not just to knock a man down; this could be as much as saving your lives.' Halthrop paused. Nobody dared to speak, but Darren and Terry looked at each other. 'There are many militia men and women around the country who will be ill-prepared to take on a dangerous adversary, but I am convinced that you have trained well enough to be able to capture Jack Smith, and any accomplices of his, safely.'

Halthrop and his young novices were being presented with a reality that had only previously existed in the videostories of history.

'Are there any questions now?'

Terry piped up, 'You made it sound like we're competing against other posses to catch this fugitive. Shouldn't we work with them?'

Halthrop's lips flickered slightly, almost a small smile, but it was quickly gone. 'All for the benefit of all?' Half quoting the Second Covenant, he looked up a little, over them towards the back of the room. 'Yes indeed you're right. However, I really do think that we are the best outfit, and that too much collaboration with others will hinder our progress. Especially as the armulets aren't functioning – the time that we would have to spend liaising in person would be wasted. We aren't in competition with other groups, but I think it would benefit all for the Bristol Brigade to go for capturing Smith without those distractions.' Jane nodded vigorously throughout this answer.

The major asked, 'Anything else?'

'Where are we going to start? And when?' Jane was poised to type on her armulet screen.

He nodded and turned to point at the blackboard. It had a chalk map outline of the area from Bristol up to Cheltenham, including Highnam village marked on it. The old road connections and Gloucester were marked, along with some points of particular interest. Using a one-metre wooden ruler that he had found in one of the building's science laboratories, Halthrop pointed to a star marked near the circle he had drawn to represent the Doughnut then slid the pointer down slightly.

'We'll go to his home first, edge of Cheltenham, and see if there are any clues left there. Unfortunately, as there are several posses engaged on this, I suspect at least one of them will get there before us but we don't have a better starting place. The only other link we have is Highnam itself. He is their sifter, and he grew up in his grandmother's farmhouse.' The metre ruler rapped the blackboard at a picture of a house. The three jumped in their seats at the sudden sound.

Darren came to life. 'I've never heard of Highnam, where is it?'

He slid the pointer slightly to the word Highnam and looked at Darren. 'You can see I've marked it on the map here. It's a farmland Kangaroo to the west of Gloucester. It's about sixty kilometres from here up the old M5. Population of about four thousand, and pretty fertile land, I believe. If you think back ten days, you may remember that we went there to get that boy to take to prison.'

He looked to Darren for recognition of this memory. The young man's face was red, but Halthrop could not tell if it was any different from his normal appearance. He was always rosy cheeked and sported a rustic, haymaking countenance. The major hoped Darren was blushing with embarrassment.

'From Smith's house, we'll probably follow the old railway line, which I've marked here. The old A40 is shorter, but the floods have washed it away in some places near Cheltenham.' He waved the ruler along a line drawn with hatch marks to indicate railway line. Darren was looking at the board, eyes flicking back and forth across the symbols, but did not appear to be comprehending.

Jane's arm was vertical again. 'When is departure time?'

'We will meet at 0800, at Brigade HQ, where I will issue kit. You will need to bring your bikes, and your rucksacks, plus a change of clothes. We may be away for several days, so make sure that your families are aware of this. And remind them that communications are currently not functioning, so you will not be able to update them on your expected return date and time.'

'The reward money must be pretty big for this guy?' questioned Terry again.

Major Halthrop scrutinised him for several seconds. 'All for the benefit of all, eh Terry?' He paused, and his audience shuffled a little in their seats and looked at the ground. 'We will get paid our normal stipend. We have been contracted by three different Kangaroos though, and they will each pay if we capture Jack Smith. Actually, I should say that they will pay when we capture the actual bomber: at the moment Smith is simply our prime suspect, albeit our only suspect. But also, all acting for the benefit of all means that the other posses will get paid by their contracting Kangaroos whenever the bomber is caught, be it by us or somebody else. As will we.'

'Very nice,' Terry commented, and the three junior members looked at each other, nodding and pushing out their bottom lips.

Chapter Five

Vicky walked slowly from the small vegetable field, a casual stroll. Her hand remained at her forehead, the index finger moving in a small slow circle, winding her hair. This idiosyncrasy was Jack's strongest memory of the girl he had once known. She appeared to sashay away towards the Truva family farmhouse. Jack could make out the building but it was mostly obscured by woods.

Jack crept out from his hiding place and moved to where she had been sitting. He had watched Vicky pull up a radish and mimicked the actions she had used to do so, finding a radish that was also so beautifully formed that it could have been entered in a competition at the Highnam summer fair. The small area also offered up tomatoes and a beet, and he doubled his collection of carrots. At that point, Jack decided he had enough to eat and some spare to carry away, but would not have room to carry any more.

He collected his rucksack from the dense bushes at the eastern end of the Truva farmland. The sun had disappeared below the horizon. It would be dark in less than thirty minutes, and Jack had changed his original plan, deciding that he would spend the night in the rusting barn that towered over the field to the southeast.

Decades earlier, the building had been an industrial milking shed. It was now derelict, and the doorway, wide open at the east end, had a pair of trees growing out of the threshold. They were at an angle to the vertical, leaning towards the outside, reaching for the sky. The barn stood thirty feet high, and in places the metal roofing sheets had fallen through, leaving large, rectangular openings.

Inside, one half was an open space with a mud floor. The centre had a raised platform running the full length, and against the north wall were a number of open rooms that reminded Jack of large stable booths. Everything was made of metal, some galvanised and still quite shiny, but most parts pitted and holed with rust. One strong wind-storm might cause a collapse.

He started a fire in one of the side rooms. Jack chose one that did not have a hole in the roof above, in the hope that the smoke would disperse more diffusely if it had to find its way out of the roof some distance from the fire. He was unsure how well the vegetables would cook on an open fire.

During the cooking procedure, Jack determined that he would stay in the barn for 24 hours and make for Leckhampton Hill the following night. He told himself that this delay would give any pursuers more time to follow him in the wrong direction, before he made his real getaway.

He also decided that he should talk with Vicky Truva to gauge another's view of the revolution he was starting. He had always found that she could be relied upon to think intelligently. As Ellie had died before he had come up with the plan to reintroduce privacy by destroying the audiopt feeds, Jack had not had an opportunity to discuss the idea with anyone.

Jack had picked up a survival knife from an abandoned shop in Cheltenham almost three months previously, in preparation for this moment. In spearing a carrot with it, he felt like an action hero from any number of old Hollywood videostories. He aped what he had seen in them, hunkering down in a corner and giving furtive looks around the space, before biting into the carrot from the knife. Jack grinned at his own parody. 'Who says I'm just a crazy idiot?'

The night's sleep was marred by discomfort from lying on the hard soil, and frequent short dreams. Vicky smiled at him, her finger stroking circles at her temple. He attempted to vanish the hallucination by closing and opening his eyes again. Vicky did not disappear.

'Good morning,' she said in a singsong voice.

'Um, yes, morning.'

'Looks like you slept well after a fine dinner.' She waved her other hand toward the fire and the pile of vegetables next to his rucksack – vegetables Jack had stolen from her field.

'I'm sorry, I was very hungry. I had travelled far and... '

Smiling, Vicky interrupted him, 'It's OK. Don't worry, not a problem, we're happy to help.'

'How did you know I was here?'

'At night, the fire in here makes a bright light. You can see it from our veranda.'

Jack felt stupid. He was a fugitive on the run, and at the first opportunity, he had managed to give away his location. 'Why didn't you come for me last night?'

Vicky's eyebrows furrowed slightly. 'This barn is often used by travellers. It's them who made the fireplace you used.

'Like I said, we're happy for people to use this place to shelter. They don't usually take our vegetables without asking, but I'm sure your theft will be on the video feed at Kangaroo this Sunday.'

Jack looked at her. He was not sure if she had made a straightforward statement, or if he needed to interpret hidden commentary. He chose to assume the best scenario, that she had come to visit a stranger on their land, rather than catch the most wanted man in England. 'I doubt it. You know the audiopt feeds are down.'

'Oh yes, course they are.'

Jack nodded. 'No armulet connections means no audiopt feeds – if the servers aren't communicating, any of your brain's signals that the masts might pick up won't be recorded. You can say or do what you like and nobody will know.'

'And you decided that would be a good moment to steal some vegetables.' Vicky's tone was light and teasing; she smiled slightly and watched his face.

'I don't want to steal things. I will pay you for them. But it's an interesting idea though, isn't it?'

'What is?'

'That we are not being monitored at the moment.'

Vicky looked at the metal wall above his head and shrugged her shoulders. 'Does it make any difference?'

Jack glowered. 'Of course it does. We're free. Nobody is watching everything we see and hear. Our actions are our own, without the cowering influence of the sifters always watching us.'

She reiterated the shrug, somewhat less exaggerated, and said, 'I can't say that I particularly care about people watching what I do. I'm happy with my actions, so let them watch. I reckon it'd just be boring for them. Anyway, you're a sifter.'

He tried to breathe, but struggled. He had given away his hiding place by lighting a beacon fire to the authorities, and the first person who had come to find him knew the full story. 'How do you know that?' he finally croaked.

'Jack, we were friends for ten years, and you haven't changed a bit. I haven't forgotten you. On your last day here, we spent the afternoon together. Surely you haven't forgotten? I'm Vicky Truva.'

His heart's pounding settled down slightly. After a moment spent regrouping his thoughts, trying to estimate how much she did or did not know of his crimes against society, Jack responded. 'Sorry, of course I haven't forgotten. I just didn't think you had recognised me.' He blushed. 'That was a really good afternoon we spent by The Lake.' He attempted to smile at her, but it was weak. He looked more like he had an itch on his cheek and was trying to shoo it away without scratching.

Vicky smiled, and it was quite the opposite of Jack's effort – a twinkling grin; she seemed to have internal illumination. 'It sounds like you don't like your job?'

He coughed and inhaled a huge breath as if he had just surfaced after too long underwater. Jack had slept in his clothes and spent a moment spreading his hands along his trouser legs. 'It's more than just my job; there is something rotten in our society.'

'What on earth do you mean?'

'The way we live, it's unnatural. Being watched all the time. This is not how humans evolved. We've only had the technology for fifty years, but we've had human societies for thousands of years without any audiopts. This cannot be the right way to govern our society.'

'I'm not sure that "govern" is exactly the right word.'

They looked at each other for a few moments. Jack shrugged and climbed down from his high horse, deciding it was better to avoid a contentious discussion. Their friendship had been years ago, and she might not be willing to hide him on the strength of it. 'Maybe you're right. Let's talk about simpler things. How have you been? Are you married? Children?'

Vicky gave a small smile and answered with a drawn out tone, 'Nooo, no husband or children. My brothers keep trying to encourage me to find a man to carry on the family line. Did you know they're both gay? That means that it's down to me to have kids if the Truva family here isn't going to die out.'

Truvan and Bailey Truva, Vicky's brothers, were twins and the same age as Jack. 'Oh, no. I hadn't learnt of that. They would have been fifteen when I left, so probably hadn't worked it out themselves by then. Had they?'

Vicky looked straight up to the rust-spoiled roof. 'I don't actually know. It was an accepted thing in our family once we all got to the stage where you might start talking about finding a husband or wife, but I honestly have no recollection of when it entered into my own consciousness, let alone theirs.'

They caught each other's eye, and there was a long silence. Vicky's eyes flicked down to his feet and slowly back up to meet his gaze again. She looked as if she was assessing him like one of the cows that might previously have occupied the room, evaluating his stature, the shininess of his coat, the symmetry of his horns.

'Well, I've got to head into the village, so I'll say goodbye for now. How long will you stay here? Do you know when you have to go back to work?'

'I think I'll be moving on tonight, when it's cooler,' he said carefully.

'I was so sorry to hear about Ellie last year; she was such a wonderful person.'

The sound of somebody else saying his grandmother's name made Jack tremble, but he hoped it was outwardly imperceptible.

'Hopefully, I'll catch up with you before you go. It'd be nice to chat some more.' With that, she walked over to where he still sat leaning against the dirty, metal wall, bent forward and gave him a kiss on one cheek, with a hand on the other. Jack raised his own hand to touch hers. He barely grazed it before she turned and walked out.

Chapter Six

Despite Jane arriving last, at just before nine, they were loaded up and ready to go within another hour. Darren and Terry each had a small trailer attached to the back of their bike. Jane and Halthrop rode unencumbered.

Usually, they would use electric all-terrain vehicles but Major Halthrop had decided that on this occasion, there was no certainty as to when they would be able to reconnect them to a solar panel battery array. The ATVs could generally last for about fifty kilometres between charges, and the distance to Cheltenham alone was more than that. Halthrop was against reliance on them anyway. He often quoted the ancient Indian strategist Chanayaka, who said that 'Willpower is more important than material power,' on the perils of failing to be self-sufficient in all aspects of any military operation.

Terry commented, 'Everywhere we go, people will want to help us catch this guy. We'll be able to plug in whenever we need to. We'll be so much slower if we insist on being self-sufficient.' The last word was scornful.

Halthrop listened, stroked his moustache, and explained, 'Preparations should always be made for a worst-case scenario. Whilst we're not fighting a straightforward military campaign, the situation is perhaps worse; the degree of violence we can expect is not known.' The major was then equally sardonic. 'If you're not up to it, I'm sure we can relieve you of the weight of the trailer.'

Terry shook his head and started slowly towards the compound's gate.

'Wait, wait, you don't even know where to go yet,' Jane called to him.

Only two GPS satellites remained functional, too few for any navigation system to operate using their data. Navigation features on the armulet worked by triangulation from the radio masts that made up their network. With the network down, the posse would have to navigate using paper maps. Halthrop smiled broadly as he issued each of them with different formats of map for the region. One emphasised the old road network, one was better for topography, and to Jane he gave half a dozen smaller ones showing old street plans of the towns he anticipated they might possibly find themselves traversing.

Halthrop emphasised, 'We need to record the details of all the legs of the route. Remember, your armulets aren't recording anything for you at the moment. Jane, you're responsible for reminding us all to make these records at every stop.'

The posse set off along the Gloucester Road until they got to the M5 motorway, known locally since the Times of Malthus as the Big Road, which was the quickest route until they were very close to Cheltenham. The going was pretty easy as there was a continuous, generally smooth surface for the first long stretch.

The entire width of the road had been washed away by flooding in two sections, the first after the nearby old Cam and Dursley railway station, and then another four kilometres north at the River Frome. Walking their bikes past these obstacles added some time. The first one in particular took more than half an hour to bypass. A fifty-metre section of the entire embanked roadway was missing, so they had to descend, cross the rough gap and climb back up on the other side of the fissure. In 28 degree heat, and with their legs tired from the cycling, the climbing back up went particularly slowly.

Beyond the second flood destruction, the road again proceeded with a continuously navigable route to the point where it met the smaller road leading into Cheltenham.

This was only two kilometres from Jack's home, and Jane navigated them with aplomb using the small street map. They parked up the bicycles in front of the house a little before 3pm.

'Wait here,' Halthrop instructed.

'What if he's in there?' asked Terry, still breathing hard from his exertions. 'What if... '

The major shot him a look and Terry fell silent. 'Wait for my order,' he told them all, then turned to Jane. 'Jane, make sure no one enters until I tell you.'

As with most places, the door was unlocked, so the major slipped through silently. Frank Halthrop had only ever read about booby traps and was not experienced at searching for them. When he was convinced that the place was empty, he called for the other three to join him. They boisterously entered, pushing and shoving through the doorway, vying to be the first to find a clue.

'He's a messy one, isn't he?' said Jane, pointing towards open drawers and objects scattered all around.

After a quick look through three doorways, Halthrop responded. 'This isn't how he lives, another posse has been here already.'

She picked up a photo of an older woman with a strong smile. 'Why doesn't he just have this on his armulet?'

'Good point.' Halthrop nodded, looking at the old woman's framed picture. 'She must be pretty important to him. Probably the grandmother with the farm in Highnam.'

'There's no writing to identify her.'

Darren appeared from a bedroom with a pair of boots, encased in dried mud. Terry and Jane looked at him and the boots. Frank held up his palms in a questioning gesture but said nothing. Darren looked at each of them in turn, and then to the boots. He turned and threw them back in the room. 'Nothing of use in there,' he said.

Terry had pulled a paper map from the wall of the other bedroom, which appeared more used as a study. It covered a region about fifty kilometres on each side, centred on Cheltenham. There was nothing marked on the map beyond what had been printed by the cartographers years before – no escape routes or hideouts annotated. Terry commented, 'How many people have paper maps? You'd kind of have to be expecting the armulet connections to go down.'

Jane replied, 'My mum and dad have got two maps on the wall in our hallway. One's around Bristol, and the other's London, and they're quite a bit older than that one.' The map Terry held was likely to have predated the Times of Malthus. He shrugged and turned to follow Darren's lead in throwing it back in the study room.

Halthrop interrupted, 'But Jane, I bet your parents' maps are framed and mounted with pride, aren't they? How did you find that one, Terry?'

'Yeah, it was just pinned up on the wall. No frame; and I don't think it was even straight.'

The major continued by showing his search evidence: he took two textstories at random from a narrow but tall bookcase in the main living room they were standing in. He held the paperbacks aloft. 'I'm sure you all know what these are, but have any of you ever seen a real one?'

Darren jumped in first. 'They're books, and you're usually carrying one.'

Halthrop nodded, looking at the floor with a smile. 'Well spotted, Darren. Anybody seen any other than the ones I have?'

Jane and Terry looked at each other briefly, his eyes wide. She turned back to the boss and replied, 'My parents have maybe ten on a shelf at home. I don't think they've ever taken any of them down, but my mum's very proud of them.'

'These have been well read, the page corners are all worn

41

and creased.' Halthrop flicked the pages, showing them to other three, and then replaced the books. 'And yet this is the home of a sifter who is, by trade, an electronic researcher. The man obviously likes to make connections with the old days. Anybody got anything else?'

There was a shaking of heads and mumbled negative answers. Terry piped up, 'Actually, look at this place. I know it's an old house, but everything's old. All this furniture must be antique. It's like it was frozen when the Times started.' Each of them stared around, absorbing the history. Terry was quite correct, it was as if they had stepped into a museum exhibit, 'Life in 2025'. Any recent objects remained hidden in cupboards, and the posse left the house quite sure that it even smelt old and musty.

They mounted their bikes, intent on making Highnam before dark.

It was a small detour to travel to the Doughnut, before turning due west out of Cheltenham for Highnam. An infotech was at what remained of the entrance to the building nearest the main route from the town.

'Good to see you, Major. There's half a dozen more infotechs down in the basement working full steam to bring the network back into action.'

'How long do you think it will take?'

The man shook his head. 'Given that all the Kangaroos work separately, we've never really had to deal with the entire network together. We're not even sure we actually know how to make the whole lot work together.'

He showed them along a ground floor corridor and into a small office. Halthrop quivered when the man produced conclusive evidence that Jack Smith was the bomber they wanted. The infotech handed over a printed greyscale picture of a man: light skin, dark hair, and wearing a black blindfold.

'How did you get this?' Halthrop asked. 'Is some part of the infonetwork working?'

'No. Quite bizarre, actually. Although we don't monitor them, the Doughnut has always been protected by closed circuit cameras. As with everything on the site, they're powered by solar panels cladding the upper surfaces of the circular building. With the audiopts online, nobody ever considered watching the camera feeds. This is the first security incident here since it was reconfigured for use by the sifters. I've never even been in the CCTV monitoring room in my whole life, until yesterday.'

There were more photos showing the bombs being placed in the basement. However, as they ran entirely separately from the main infonetwork, the servers for the camera system were in this upstairs office. He leant against the chest-high computer and said, 'These beauties have been overwriting their own data on a seven-day rolling recording, unwatched, for fifty years.'

The footage showed Jack installing the bombs during a four-hour period after his last shift. The infotechs had watched the tapes over and over again, astounded that he had managed the task silently, and blindfolded. 'So the audiopts didn't pick up anything,' the major mused out loud.

'Thank Malthus he put the explosive materials in sections of the underground server rooms that were unmanned. Gotta be grateful for small mercies,' the man concluded.

'I'd say that was a pretty big mercy,' Halthrop concluded in return. Frank held up the picture for all to commit to memory, and inwardly mulled over how bandits, historically, had often swathed the lower and upper parts of their faces so only the eyes were visible. This picture was the inverse – Smith's full face showing, with only the eyes covered.

Although legs were tired, the ten-kilometre journey to Highnam took much less than an hour. As Frank had anticipated, the railway line was an easy and level route. If anything, it went slightly downhill. They went straight to the Kangaroo Spokesperson's house. Some forty red bricks were piled randomly in a little heap at the gable end of the house. Other than the bricks, the place was very neatly kept, a tidy garden and the building in very good order.

Lloyd Lloyd opened the door to the visitors before they had all dismounted. He walked out into the bright afternoon sun and welcomed them with a booming, 'So good to see you again, Major Halthrop. And posse.'

The major stepped forward and shook Lloyd Lloyd's outstretched hand. The other three troops nodded a greeting in unison. The Spokesperson wore no sunglasses and held his other hand to shade his eyes. 'Thanks again for your work with Derek Jones. I trust that all went off according to plan? Actually, sorry, more important matter.' Highnam's representative wrung his hands. 'We're all in a bit of a tizz as I'm sure you can imagine. I've already sent the Cirencester posse to Ellie Smith's old farmhouse. The late Ellie Smith, that is – been dead more than a year. Place has been empty since then. Jack came back for the funeral but only stayed a couple of days. And he disappeared the next day. Without a word of goodbye. Been shut up since then.'

Major Halthrop held up a hand to halt Lloyd Lloyd. 'Just tell us the way, and we'll go and have a look for ourselves.' He looked over his shoulder, but Jane already had the plan of the village open and resting across the top of the trailer behind Darren's bike.

'I remember this place,' Darren almost shouted. Halthrop's hand of silence swung round to hush his charges. Jane nodded at each instruction and, when he was finished, she looked up to the major and nodded several times quickly, without speaking. Halthrop's reply nod was barely perceptible, but she caught it and folded the map away.

He proffered his hand to Lloyd Lloyd. The man shook it strongly but still sounded nervy. 'Please catch him. The last thing we want is to go back to the dangers of the Times of Malthus.'

Major Halthrop nodded, and said, 'I think the security of your village is beyond the catching of Jack Smith. It's the infotechs at the Doughnut that we're all relying on now.'

The bicycle convoy was a strange sight for the villagers in Highnam. Bikes were common; it was the uniforms that were unusual. The Fifth Covenant of Jerusalem disallowed mass influence. The upshot was that uniformed groupings of people had all but disappeared. The few militiamen across the country that remained ready for activation for posse purposes were all part-timers. Only about half the militias still used any sort of uniform at all.

Boots were highly coveted in 2089. The remainder stocks in warehouses around the country were being depleted. Common sizes were extinct and had to be handmade or repaired. Military boots were less popular than work boots, but one of Frank's forward-thinking predecessors commanding the Bristol Brigade had taken a large collection into store at HQ for future use.

Ellie Smith's farmhouse had been built halfway up a slope that descended from the centre of Highnam. The land met the River Leadon as it completed a large meander before turning east to join the Severn a little over a kilometre away. From her house, the grassy fields continued down a slope for about 200 metres before flattening out for another 200 metres to the river. She had only ever worked about half the land, and the property was not assiduously protected. The vegetation had not run wild, as the lack of fencing encouraged the animals of other Highnam residents to graze there freely.

The evening remained hot and humid. The Bristol Brigade

parked up their bikes on the large patio, which was enclosed on two sides by the L-shaped farmhouse.

Darren sniffed the air and commented, 'It's gonna rain, Frank. I'd say a lot of rain.' The party stood by their bicycles and, at Darren's forecast, looked up at the moody clouds.

The house itself was old, more than a hundred years, of brick and wood construction, with red roof tiling.

Inside, the rooms were darkening quickly as the sun had just set. The main solar panel array had been disconnected – some of the panels had been removed. The posse all had rechargeable lantern torches, and the three younger members were eager to use some of the equipment they had brought along. Even just using the lanterns was exciting.

Again, another posse had been through the place already, although they had treated this house with rather more respect. Major Halthrop wondered if it was even the same team that had ransacked Jack's house.

Jane pointed to a spot on a table at the end of the main living room where, amongst pictures and ornaments, there was a gap. 'Look, Frank. I'd guess that the other posse took a photo of the fugitive.'

The boss nodded and they continued looking around. There was nothing of obvious interest; it all looked just as one might expect for an old house whose only occupant had died a year previously. A layer of dust covered most surfaces, albeit disturbed in places. If there had been any clues, they were no longer there.

Chapter Seven

Vicky glided across the lawn to the old farmhouse. The ranch-style architecture had been copied from the original family farm when Grandfather Truva settled near Highnam, after fleeing Turkey's civil war. Bailey and Truvan stood together on the edge of the long veranda. Both brothers, thumbs hooked into their front pockets, looked at their approaching sister.

'Who's our guest?' Bailey almost shouted to Vicky, although she was by then only three metres away. She just smiled and shook her head, eyeing up the matching floppy, brown haircuts.

Truvan stopped nodding and followed up with, 'Have we finally discovered some husband material?'

Vicky stopped at the first veranda stair and looked up at the twenty-nine-year-old twins. She broadened her smile. This did not so much have the effect of lighting up her face as giving it a backlit glow. 'I don't think so,' she replied. 'It's Jack Smith. Do you remember old Ellie Smith who died last year? He's her grandson.'

'Ah, you mean Beautiful Ellie,' said Truvan, as Bailey looked at him and nodded with a smile.

Bailey continued, 'Distant Beautiful Ellie. Even at over eighty, she had a... ' He paused, choosing the right word.

'Majesty,' concluded Truvan, and they both stared at the line of poplars at the front end of their land.

Vicky strode up the stairs saying, 'If I didn't know you two were gay, I'd swear you'd given something away there.' The brothers brought their eyes back to her, stood between them. Vicky's caramel face was only two centimetres lower than their stubbly complexions.

'He left town though, years ago. To... ' Again Bailey paused, looking above his sister's brown hair.

'Become a sifter,' Truvan stepped in.

Vicky's mouth became a tight straight line, and her glow had gone. 'Yes, he left fourteen years ago.' It was Vicky's turn to stare ahead. She looked between her siblings, through the open front door behind them, into darkness. Her hands rested on their little backpacks.

'A sifter?' Bailey's tone was rhetorical.

'What's he doing here then? Don't they have to work every day? I'm sure I remember that they are working on computers for twelve hours every day of their lives. Has he quit?' Truvan asked with crinkled eyebrows.

'But sifters never quit.' Bailey continued to use a loud questioning voice that expected no answer.

'I don't know,' Vicky answered the questions quietly. 'He's just as enigmatic now as he was before.' She pushed on them, turning her brothers like saloon doors as she walked forward past them and into the interior gloom. Now facing each other, the twins made one slow nod in unison.

Inaudible out on the veranda, her words lost in the dim front room, Vicky added, 'I held his hand the day he left.'

Truvan and Bailey remained on the porch and, discarding their packs, sat down on the veranda sofa. Bailey started tapping on the screen of his armulet, increasingly rapidly and hard. It was working, but would not respond to some of the things he asked it to do. He tried shaking his arm. An armulet's energy source was the movement of its wearer, this kinetic energy being converted into electricity and stored within the bracelet battery.

Successive generations of armulet technology had reduced power consumption and improved the sensitivity of their radio communication, to such extents that they could be used even when a person was underwater, up a mountain, in a crowd, or an old stone building with thick walls; or even several of these circumstances at once. Scientists had proven that the audiopt feeds were a more accurate record than the visual and auditory perceptions of the actual person involved.

Bailey shook his arm violently. Truvan put his hand out and gripped his brother's forearm, right over the armulet. 'They're offline. All of them.'

Two hours later, the sun had set and rain had come, heavy and noisy on the dry ground. Bailey left the veranda sofa, and his brother and father, and went inside. Closing the door behind himself against the noise of the water streaming down outside, he saw Vicky looking in the small mirror beside the downstairs toilet room. She was adjusting her hairband, tucking the odd stray locks away. She finally stretched her cheeks with a large jaw movement and stroked her fingers across the tense skin, turning her head slightly to left and right. Smiling, Vicky then turned to the room and saw her brother, hands on hips, shaking his head.

'Do you really think you know what you're doing?' he asked, pausing briefly before launching on. 'That guy's a sifter but he's not at work. I know the building has been blown up, but surely he should be there waiting for the infotechs to fix the servers. You're getting yourself involved with a likely terrorist, just when you should be out looking for a husband. You know what a "terrorist" is?'

'I know,' she replied quietly, looking straight at Bailey.

'This farm has been the Truva family estate since the Times of Malthus. Like your ancestors did in Turkey for over 300 years before that, you should be looking to continue the family heritage into the future. Truvan and I clearly will not be producing heirs, so that falls to you. Like it or not, you are the one that holds the family's history in your grasp. Don't throw it away casually.'

'I won't.' She was barely audible.

'You should be looking for a strong, healthy man to start a family with. I remember Jack Smith. That sifter is weak and small. What does he know about growing crops and raising animals?'

Vicky found her voice again. 'Stop it.'

'You should be looking for a real man, so this land can support generations of Truva children. Otherwise who will look after you when your back is too old to pull up vegetables, or your eyes can no longer see clearly enough? Father is desperately worried. You will break his heart if you get sucked in by that weakling.'

'I said stop. You don't know him.'

'You are behaving like a spoilt child, thinking you can throw all of this away without a care.'

Vicky lifted her face close to her brother's and hissed, 'You are the spoilt child. You are perfectly capable of fathering children, our family is not only down to me. You're just scared that you're going to lose control over me.' She pushed her brother aside and zipped up her raincoat as she stepped out on to the veranda.

Truvan and Marmaran watched from their seats as she strode away without saying a word.

Chapter Eight

Jack watched Vicky touch the ground with her flat hand before she sat down. He had worked indoors for so many years that she had to explain to him that she was checking whether it would dirty her beige cotton trousers.

Jack Smith and Vicky Truva sat at the east entrance to the barn, each leaning against one of the sentry-like trees, where barn doors had once closed. They faced each other, stretched out on the moist earth, legs side by side. Although it had rained heavily, the combination of overhanging foliage and the end of the barn roof had restricted the amount of water landing between the trees. The ground was damp, but not muddy.

Vicky's lantern, placed beside them, created a cone of light that emerged through the large doorway and between the trees and then faded across the large field. There it merged with the light coming from the heavily gibbous moon, which had come up a little before sunset. The giant, orange harvest moon would emerge the next day at sunset.

The silhouettes of several giant stick men stretching six skipping ropes each led Jack's gaze away over the countryside. The metal pylons and cables of the pre-Malthus electricity network remained standing against the elements.

Vicky interlaced her fingers across her chest and leaned back against the tree trunk behind her. 'It seems like you're going to take us back to the Times of Malthus.' She moved to her left. Jack could see her wiggling slightly to make a ridge in the bark more comfortable against her spine.

He had not yet told her that he was responsible for the explosion that had destroyed the audiopt and armulet connections. Jack narrowed his eyes slightly and moved his face barely ten degrees to the side. 'Do you know the history of the Times? Are you sure you really mean that?'

She shrugged without moving her hands. 'Everybody learns it as a child. But it was more than fifty years ago, I'm not sure anyone really understands it all now.' She leant her head back and used the pile of her nut-brown hair as a pillow against the tree.

'My grandmother lived through it all. She told me detailed stories when I was a young boy of how life had been before, during and after them. I still can't believe how radically the world was changed, but I've looked up loads of history during my time as a sifter. Hers was obviously just one story, but the whole essence of it is absolutely true. You really have to study a lot to be able to get an understanding of how people lived before 2030.'

Vicky stared away, across the clearing. 'Like what?'

'Well, I've watched a lot of the videostories from back then. Sometimes crazy, outlandish, imaginary things; sometimes fictional stories that could have been real but just happened not to be. Plus, a lot of news and history, real-life things. It takes a lot of time to watch enough of them to understand life in Elizabethan times, but they give you the context to see how all the wars could have come about. It's pretty hard to think about why people would have fought so much, unless you understand how overpopulated the world was, and how all the food and other things were unequally shared out.'

'Is that what Hitler was trying to do? Reduce the population so there was less pressure on things?'

'Um, I'm not sure – I haven't really studied much history from before when Grannie Ellie was born.'

'When was that?'

'Two thousand.'

Vicky's hazel eyes focussed on Jack's face. She spoke

evenly. 'OK, tell me how things went from then. Help me to understand what you're trying to achieve.' She closed her eyes.

Jack the sifter shifted on the stone slab he had as a seat. 'Um, OK. Let me see. When my grandmother was a young girl, she lived in a town with a quarter of a million people in it. And that was a relatively small town. London had seven million, and there were some places in the world where twenty million people tried to live together within a few square miles. Many people living right next to each other were strangers. This made them wary of their neighbours, and often people were jealous of each other.

'Food had to be brought from the regions where it was grown into the cities, and the amount of things that were made for the city people far exceeded what they actually produced in those huge populations.

'The people in the cities then had to have a way to pay for it all. This meant there were whole economies based on trading only. Nothing was actually produced, things were just transacted. Money was everything. And because people never saw what was needed to grow and transport the food, or to get the materials for manufacturing, it made making comparisons of the value of different things impossible.

'And that was compounded by everybody living so closely packed together. Every moment, the men and women, even the children, would be comparing themselves against each other to see who was best. And the ones who had most things, or the rarest foods, or the largest items, were considered the best. That's where the envy came from.'

She had separated her hands. The left remained on her bosom, and the right index finger was slowly twisting up her hair. Her head leaned a little towards the finger like a cat towards a stroke.

'Now, remember there were no audiopt feeds then. They

were invented in about, um, 2035. So, those people with more money or power were able to manipulate things so that they got even more money and power.'

Without opening her eyes, Vicky interrupted. Her lips barely parted to ask, 'How could they manipulate things?'

'That's why I mentioned the audiopt feeds. In those days, it was much harder to find things out about other people. This meant that they could cheat each other, or not tell the truth, or hurt people, and you couldn't find out who had done it. Or often, you wouldn't even know what had been done.' She scowled a little.

Jack went on, 'So the rich and powerful could manipulate everything so that they got even more money and power, but without you really knowing that it was going on. Now, how that worked out in the end, meant that a few people had virtually everything, and the vast majority of the world's population had virtually nothing. Eventually to the point that they didn't have even enough food and water.

'Towards the end of the twentieth century, many people in the world had too much food. But that then went completely the other way. My grandparents got married in 2027, and by then, food was so expensive all over the world that many of those city dwellers were very hungry. The way economics worked at the time allowed, or even encouraged, large farms – and I mean enormous, the size of several Kangaroos – to be the only producers of food, and they charged much more for the food than was necessary. A continuously increasing world population, it was nearly eight and a half billion people by 2027, combined with the change in climate, which caused a lot of crops to fail, exacerbated the food problems.

Vicky asked, 'Why didn't people grow their own food?'

'Most people didn't know how to grow their own food, or even where to go to find land to use to try and grow it.'

She gave an unbelieving look.

'Hunger is a powerful thing, and desperate people will do anything. Eventually, they went on the rampage, killing the neighbours they hadn't known. This was the start of the Times.

'Early this century, communications expanded suddenly. The Bitness Revelations showed the poor and oppressed how the rich had been cheating them for so long. There was a series of publications of dealings that governments and corporations had wanted to keep secret.'

'Hold on.' Her hazel eyes were bright and eager. 'What's a corporation?'

He smiled back at her. 'OK, sorry. You're happy with the idea of a government, yes?'

'Yes: a Kangaroo but before the Covenants of Jerusalem, so one that breaks the mass influence Covenant, right? A group of people leading a really large population, like all of England having only one Kangaroo to decide on all matters for the whole land.'

'Yes, exactly. So, a corporation is a similar kind of mass influence organisation but for making and selling things. But all the people making things got very little in return for their work. All the benefit went to a powerful few. Those powerful few controlled the lives of thousands and usually did not act for the benefit of all. These corporations were the main reason for the Fifth Covenant, so there could never be elite controllers again.'

Vicky was smiling. She had moved her hands into her lap, one holding the other. 'And what about their secrets? I can see that it would be possible without the audiopt feeds, but why would you?'

He raised his eyebrows and stayed silent for a whole minute. She stared back at him, defying the unspoken challenge to speak. 'Sometimes a few people would know a secret together, but it's basically a thing only a few people knew, and others couldn't find out, unless one of those who knew about it told them. People's lives were better when they could have some memories or knowledge that were for them only. But the corporations used secrecy to stop people discovering how they were being exploited. With the Fifth Covenant, there's no motivation, or chance really, to exploit people. Thus we don't need the First Covenant. The First and the Fifth both serve to generate the same ends.' Jack gave a beaming smile.

'How strange.'

'When you study as much history as I have, it's amazing how many different types of society you find that humans have lived through. But the Times of Malthus was the first crisis truly to affect everyone on the planet. We've all seen the videostories of the huge piles of burning corpses. Everyone lost people, it had to stop.'

'So has life been just the same, continuously, ever since the Times?'

'The arrival of the audiopts opened the eyes of those who would be bandits and raiders to the fact that the Times were over. They could follow a simple life path and always have enough to eat and drink and easily protect their families. Codifying and securing this newfound safe existence was paramount. The new way of life, emerging from the shadow of the Times of Malthus, led to the signing of the Covenants of Jerusalem.'

Vicky sat up, aligning her spine close to the tree trunk again. 'OK, that is more detail about history than I remember ever reading before, thank you. But, I ask again: what will be achieved by taking away that audiopt security?'

Jack turned his head to look across the field following the cone of light. He had not attempted to deny his involvement in the destruction of the audiopts, and she had not directly accused him.

The moonlight gave the wider landscape a dim brightness. Through a thin screen of trees, he could see into another narrow field, which was then bounded by the river, with a steep bank up its far side. His eyes traced along the contour of that bank moving to the left, away from Vicky, as far as he could make it out. Finally, the trees became thicker and he could only see forest. Without turning back to her, he answered, 'This isn't the same world as fifty years ago. Everyone now has grown up in peace. We know how abundant food and other things are, so there's no need to cheat or steal. And it's unnatural for people to be unable to have privacy.'

'What's "privacy"?' Vicky questioned.

Her eyes had not left his face, and he now turned so that they were looking directly at each other. Jack's expression lifted, with a slight smirk. 'Exactly.'

Vicky's hand went instinctively to her armulet. She had only touched the screen two times when she stopped and looked at him.

He was still staring straight at her. 'It's a very powerful thing. It's also the way humans lived during our entire existence, *except* for the last fifty years. And there were plenty of peaceful times before that.'

Vicky lowered her arm and held his gaze. 'Tell me a secret,' she requested.

Jack smiled, tapped her on the leg and stood up, shaking his own legs into action. 'Maybe one day.'

'Maybe tomorrow?'

'Maybe.' They stood facing each other. To depart, Vicky needed to head around the building and back to her house. It had already been dark for over four hours. Jack needed to go inside the barn and gather his belongings to set off. Neither one moved. 'But I'm leaving now, so if you want me to tell you a secret tomorrow, you'll have to come with me.'

'Where will you go?' Little of the lantern light illuminated Vicky as her back was towards it. Jack surveyed her face, the moonlight dappling through the leaves overhead. Her question had implied that she expected he would not be returning to Cheltenham and back to work at the Doughnut. The darkness made her features inscrutable.

'I'm going to the old bunker at Leckhampton Hill. Have you heard of it?' He could make out the shaking of her silhouetted head. 'Well, your armulet can't help you with finding that any more, so come with me.'

She continued shaking her head. 'Jack, I can't just up and leave the farm on a helter-skelter trip across the countryside with you.'

'You can do anything you want.'

'Sorry.' He couldn't tell if she was actually apologising, or merely explaining that she had initially misrepresented herself. 'I don't want to leave the farm and come on some helter-skelter trip across the countryside with you.'

Jack shook a little, a shudder that travelled right down his body. He took a deep breath. 'I understand.' He held her hand, with her twisted little finger escaping sideways in the darkness. 'I trust you, Vicky.' There was a moment of silence; she picked up the lantern and walked away towards a field of waist-high, sparsely planted wheat.

Chapter Nine

Vicky's short walk brought her home at midnight. She was met by her father on the veranda. 'How is he these days?' The light hanging from the roof combined with the lantern light to highlight his small coffee cup, white against the dark of his clothes and skin. Vicky stopped in front of him, looking straight into his eyes.

'He is his grandmother's son,' she answered. Marma did not speak, his silence entreating her to elaborate. 'He's still the most interesting man I've ever met.' She paused and turned to look through the night in the direction of the old barn, invisible through the darkness. Vicky shook her head briefly and continued, 'But for all his learning, he has a strange view of the world.'

Her father touched her on the forearm. 'His grandmother's son.' He paused. 'Ellie was a great woman, there's no denying that, but she could be wayward. As you say, a strange view of the world at times.' They both reflected for a minute. 'The boys say he is responsible for the armulets not working. They say there is word of a giant explosion in Cheltenham that has destroyed all the infoservers.' Marmaran again left his statements hanging so that they became questions.

Still staring into the night, she murmured, 'I don't know, father. He isn't going back to Cheltenham. He says he will head to some old bunker somewhere around Leckhampton, but I honestly don't know what he's done, what he's doing or even, really, what he thinks he's doing.'

'Her death was a real blow.' Vicky looked back at her father, who was himself staring into the distance.

'He asked me to go away with him.'

Marma refocussed on her face. 'You're not thinking of going?' She didn't reply, so it was his turn to fill the silence. 'Vicky, your place is here. When you find a man that you want, we'll support your decision, whoever he may be. But you must stay here. Not only is this your home, but it is the Truva farm. You will not find so much love and support as you have here. Bailey and Truvan and I may seem like male brutes, but we only have your best interests at heart.'

She interrupted his address, 'Father, you have your own interests at heart. I am sure you will love and support me and a family of my own, but your love of Truva heritage is positively Turkish in its closed-mindedness.'

He stuttered, 'But... we are Turkish.'

Vicky put her own hand on his forearm. 'Yes. And we need to think more widely. How long would you have it continue? Should the Truva family stay on this land for another hundred years? Two hundred? A thousand?'

She could see her father was flustered. He could not argue with her, as she had not posited a position. 'We're talking about you – I don't have a crystal ball for the future, but you are the only one who can really keep our family alive. The boys will work the farm until they die, but they will not have any children. And I will not marry again. Only you can continue the Truvas into the next generation. And that should be here on the Truva farm.'

Vicky struggled to keep her voice calm. 'Father, you're as bad as them. There is no reason why Bailey and Truva should not have children. If our bloodline really is that important to you all.'

Marma smiled slightly, shook his head and tapped her hand with his.

She lost control and shouted, 'I am twenty-seven, I can decide for myself.' Vicky let go of his arm, turned and stormed into the house. As she crossed the threshold, she could hear his breath soughing. It was unclear whether it was anger or sorrow, but she did not turn back.

Vicky headed upstairs and stopped at the narrow table on the landing. A picture of her mother was kept there. In the image, she looked serene – although her face gave away little expression, there was clearly happiness there.

She had died nearly twenty years earlier in a blizzard on their farm. Even the armulet alarm of her falling body temperature, transmitting her position to the rest of the family, had not allowed them to save her. She had been injured when she fell in the snow, knocked unconscious. Vicky was eight years old and the twins only ten. It had taken Marmaran more than an hour to reach her, in driving winds with snow a metre deep.

She held the picture up and stared into her mother's eyes. 'I wish you were still alive, Mama. You would tell me what to do. And you would know how to still father and the boys.' Just for an instant, Vicky thought the picture of her mother smiled at her. It was the briefest of flashes, and the tiniest of smiles. Just a little raising of the corners of her mouth, and a twinkle in the eyes. Vicky stared closely but it was gone. The picture was as it had been every day. She kissed her mother's cheek and replaced the frame on the small table.

In her bedroom, Vicky packed a handful of things into a small rucksack. She did not gather important possessions – she packed as if for a weekend away camping: spare knickers, hairbrush, a small towel, quotidian trivia. She appraised the contents, gazed up at the ceiling, looked back into the open bag, shook her head and clipped it closed. Downstairs, Vicky gathered a similarly everyday handful of provisions: a bottle of water, two apples, half a loaf of bread and some cheese.

From raiding the larder, she slipped quietly out of the

back door, and into the dim night. The moon was bright, but the sky was veiled in wispy cloud, as well as tears that blurred her vision. One day from full, the moon was luminous enough that, away from the beacon of the house lights, the night was not even near to complete blackness. However, Vicky knew that she could follow the rear path around the small ornamental garden and head back along the track by the stream, without being visible from the house. She left the lantern behind.

The path she walked would follow between the Rodway Hill Covert and the River Leadon. After about two kilometres, the trees there gave way to open fields. Vicky had often walked the riverside, and it followed a large semicircle right around Highnam. She only had a vague idea as to where Leckhampton was – somewhere south of Cheltenham – so she needed to catch up with Jack before he left off following the Leadon.

On the other side of Highnam, he would need to carry on southeasterly, whilst the river cut back to go due east. This was the point where Vicky knew she could not guess what his route might be. The quickest would be to follow the old roads, probably the A417 if she was right about where she thought Leckhampton was. 'But he'll travel off the main routes,' she muttered to herself, increasing the pace. Her eyes had accustomed themselves to the vague moonlight, so that her footing could be assured on the path itself, but only up to a brisk walking pace. She did not dare to try running.

She estimated that Jack had set off 45 minutes ahead of her. Even if Vicky travelled at twice his speed, he should have left the route she could be sure of within a few minutes of her departure from home. On making this calculation, she did not hesitate. She changed route entirely, cutting a right turn to the path across the fields edging Highnam, and would walk straight through the village itself.

Even if Jack was responsible for the explosions that

people were talking about, she was not connected, and nobody would say anything more than 'Hello' to her. Her fellow villagers might inquire where she was off to in the middle of the night, but nobody would hinder her progress.

Jack would have to cross the River Severn, and this gave her a bottleneck in which to catch up with him. There were two adjacent crossings east of Highnam: the old railway bridge, and the A40. She assumed – hoped – he would not be taking some terribly circuitous route that might offer an alternative crossing. There were also the remains of an old stone bridge between the other two. Glorious giant pillars on each bank, with stone splinters starting out from each one towards the other, were all that remained. Below, there was an island of rubble in the centre of the water flow. The third crossing had fallen in, or been destroyed, before Vicky was born.

She chose to go on the road bridge. Standing on the wall in the centre, she could look through the broken stone span, down to the silhouette of the railway bridge a hundred metres away. Unless Jack was going to crawl across the railway bridge, she would spy him whichever crossing he chose. She hoped that she was well enough lit that her own silhouette did not frighten him into hiding.

As she stood on the wall, and gazed towards the other bridge, Vicky's index finger massaged her crow's feet. After an hour, she was still doing it, but the finger made the lightest of touches and was moving at a snail's pace. She sat down on the concrete wall. Not a single person or animal had passed in the whole time. She looked right and left along the old A40: nothing but shadows. The heavy rain in the early evening had given way to a still, cool night.

She heard a noise on the Highnam side of the bridge and looked back again. There she could see, unmistakably, the thin figure bulked out by the large rucksack on his back, wandering towards her. She sat still and he did not notice her at all. As he stepped level, Vicky shocked him, 'You took your time.' She saw him stagger and leapt to hold him up. Jack made to run off, but she held his arm fast. 'Idiot, it's me.' He stopped pulling away and turned to face her.

He finally replied in a quiet voice, 'I've been walking slowly. And it took me about an hour to pack up my stuff in the barn.' She let his arm go, and he asked in the same whisper, 'What are you doing here?'

'You invited me to come along. Or did I misunderstand that?'

'No,' he immediately answered her. Although his tone had sounded like the start of a sentence, no more words followed.

She paused a little to see if he had anything to add. 'OK, I've come as far as I know where I'm going. You're going to have to show us the way.'

'Did you tell your family you were coming?'

'I spoke to my father. He doesn't really understand – and in fact I'm not sure I really know what we're doing – but he's a good man, I'm sure he'll come to terms with it. He knows I can make my own good decisions about things. My brothers will be noisier about their dislike of the idea, but I didn't see them, thankfully. And I'm sure none of them will come to Leckhampton looking for me.'

'What do you mean?' There was distress in Jack's voice, and it was much louder than a whisper. 'You didn't tell them where I'm going, did you?'

Vicky put her hand back on his arm. 'I told them that you had asked me to go with you, and I did mention Leckhampton. I didn't tell anyone I had decided to come... although I guess it'll be pretty obvious when they find I'm not at home. But like I said, they will leave me to work things out for myself. I'm still not sure why I'm coming with you, but I'm sure it'll be fun.'

'Fun?' His tone sounded outraged. 'I'm a fugitive, Vicky. I thought you understood that?'

It was her turn to be at a loss for words. Vicky's free hand went to cover her mouth and she held it there for some time.

Jack sat down on the concrete wall and looked into the charcoal sky. A few gaps had appeared in the cloud cover, and she watched his head wander from star to star. 'That's it, I'm done for. My whole plan is blown, they'll probably catch me before I even get to the bunker.'

Vicky's voice wavered. 'I didn't mention the bunker.' She paused and then remembered and admitted that in fact she had told her father about it.

'I don't believe this,' he said, as he stood up and walked along the bridge.

She had not moved position since her indiscretion had been exposed, and she watched him walking away. Finally, she grabbed up her small pack and chased after him. 'Jack, I'm sorry.'

She caught up with him and reached for his hand. He pulled it away and changed direction so that he was still crossing the bridge, but attempting to walk away from her at the same time. This only lasted until he reached the railing at the edge of the roadside, and then he had to continue straight forwards. Vicky walked a step behind and to the side of him all the way, watching the shadowed face.

With a few metres of the bridge span remaining, she ran a few steps to be in his path, facing him. 'Stop. We can solve this. There must be a way. Stop and think it through with me.' He stopped and stood silently looking over the parapet at the flat black water below. She continued, 'My family will not give us away. We can still hide out in the bunker as you planned.'

His face whipped back to looking straight at her and he

65

almost shouted, 'That's rubbish and you know it. They don't want you coming with me – I'm a fugitive, which puts you in danger, and they didn't even like me fourteen years ago. They will tell anyone who will listen, at the first chance they get. There will be a lynch mob waiting for me at Leckhampton.'

Tears were pressing to be released from Vicky's eyes, but she held them back. 'It's not true, Jack. Why do you think they didn't like you?'

'I could see the way your brothers looked at me. They never thought I was even good enough to be your friend, let alone anything more.'

'Stop, please. You're wrong.'

'It doesn't matter.' He shook off her attempt to hold his hand again. 'We can't go to Leckhampton and that's it. It's just not safe.'

'So let's work out a different plan. I know you, Jack, you don't just give up.' They were both silent, and he stared down again at the silently flowing river. Vicky continued to look at him, but eventually followed his gaze down from the bridge. She then lifted her view to follow the river past the broken-down bridge and over the railway crossing. In the further distance, the moon illuminated the river, and its course contrasted quite obviously against the darkness of the landscape. It wiggled left and right slightly before the various shadows merged together. She grabbed his arm and pointed at the river's vanishing point. 'That's it, look!'

'What?'

'We'll follow the course of the river right down to the estuary – I took a flightview on the armulet one time. When we get to the abandoned docks, then we can take a boat to one of the islands in the estuary. Most of them are uninhabited, and they're covered with vegetation, so you could hide out there.'

Jack strained to see far downriver. The furthest Vicky

could see was where a tributary joined from the left, 500 metres away. She wondered if she actually could make it out in the darkness, or if her mind simply delineated between identically dark patches, having seen it often in daylight.

He began to nod slowly. 'Hmm, that might just work, you know. Plenty of drinking water. And we could catch fish. And if it's already overgrown, the island might have some fruit. Well hidden, no tracks to follow.' He turned to her and held both her arms. 'You're a genius, Vicky. It's better than my plan, anyway, because we will have a ready supply of food.'

'We will have to steal a boat, though, which is a problem.'

'Needs must. It is a shame, but we've already committed a bigger crime than that.' He was still gripping her upper arms, and she could feel him shaking slightly from side to side, as if they were dancing an awkward jig. 'And no audiopts, so they won't know it's us, or where we've gone.'

'We could try and find an abandoned one that nobody uses.'

'Let's go back this way, and take the west riverbank,' Jack said and pointed back the way they had come onto the bridge.

'Why?' She paused a moment. 'Surely it'll be easier to catch up with us if we're on the same side we started?' Vicky looked back across the bridge.

Chapter Ten

The Bristol Brigade had spent the night at the house and sat around Ellie Smith's patio table eating breakfast. Halthrop had instructed that, in the absence of obvious clues, they would have to go through the place more thoroughly. After several hours searching the remains of an old woman's long life, they were no further forward.

Tea had been grown in parts of Britain for hundreds of years. It was poor quality in comparison to that previously imported from better climates, but with little international trade by 2089, few people knew any different. Home processing meant that England's traditional brew was now much more akin to green tea than it once would have been. Darren nearly dropped the dead woman's teapot when Truvan Truva called over the fence to greet them. 'Ho there!' Bailey was with him and waved.

Halthrop stood up and went to intercept them. He had hoped that they would not have to deal with any curious locals, but once they decided to stay the night, he had accepted that it would probably happen. They were paying the posse's reward, so he intended to be polite and positive.

'Good morning,' the major was smiling broadly, casually holding a Brighton Palace Pier mug. He met them at the fence bounding the garden so they did not need to come in.

'Lloyd Lloyd told us we could find you here.'

'Yes, we had to stay the night as we haven't got much to go on, unfortunately.'

'That's why we're here.'

Truvan had done all the talking initially, but Bailey took over at this point. The brothers looked identical – even their beards were trimmed to the exact same round shape – and, as Frank Halthrop switched his gaze to the other twin to follow the conversation, he could not identify any difference, including in their clothing. 'We have information about the guy you're chasing. He's taken our sister.'

Halthrop frowned and said, 'Go on.

Bailey continued, 'He was hiding out near our place yesterday and took her with him when he left last night.'

The major was now standing straight upright and was several centimetres taller than the twins. 'Are you saying he's kidnapped her?'

Truvan and Bailey looked at each other, did not speak, and then turned back. Haltingly, Bailey carried on, 'We don't think so exactly. Vicky knew him when they were children.'

'We all did,' Truvan followed up seamlessly, before turning back to his brother.

'Yes, so they spoke at length in the old barn that's off one end of our fields. Then she came home and argued with our father. This morning, she's not on the farm, and he's gone as well.'

'This is troubling,' Halthrop sympathised. 'However, you may well know a lot more than you think.' He moved his hand in a large arc to indicate where the Brigade members were sitting. 'Come and sit down and we'll talk through some of what you know about Mr Smith, and see if we can work out where he might be headed with her.'

'We know where he's going,' Bailey responded abruptly.

Major Halthrop looked carefully at their faces. He said, 'OK, that sounds excellent. Do come and sit with the rest of my group and you can tell us what you know.'

'No,' Truvan retorted even more abruptly.

Frank was fiddling with the now empty mug in his hands. 'I'm sorry, I don't understand.' His tone was questioning.

69

Bailey nodded as Truvan went on. 'We want to find Vicky and bring her back home. So we're coming with you.'

Bailey spoke up, 'We'll only tell you what we know if we can join the posse.'

Halthrop did not answer immediately, so Truvan said, 'We don't want any of the reward money, we just need to get her away from him and back home.'

He shook his head. 'I'm sorry, gents, I can't do that. My troops are properly trained for the potential dangers involved in a manhunt.' At this, he looked across to the breakfast table where Terry was poking Jane in the ribs, and she was smacking his hand away playfully.

Major Halthrop quickly turned back. 'I can assure you that we will do our utmost to find your sister, and if she's with Jack Smith, she will come home to you when we apprehend him. It might not be dangerous at all, but I simply cannot take any risks with members of the public. We have procedures and systems for these things and, to be totally honest, if we have to take along two untrained additional team members, you'll just slow us down. And I'm sure you can understand how that might be the difference between finding them or Smith's getting away.'

The brothers looked to each other. Bailey answered, 'I'm sorry, Mr... um... '

'Oh, apologies, I'm Major Frank Halthrop, Bristol Brigade commander.'

He extended his hand over the upper horizontal fence wire. Bailey shook first, after which Truvan took hold and gave their names. 'I'm Truvan and this is Bailey Truva. Bailey was about to say that we're not asking to join. We're telling you that we're going after them ourselves, and if you want to come along we'll share the information with you.'

Halthrop bristled. This was not even an attempt at

blackmail: it was almost a taunt. 'I really would advise against that, gentlemen. Jack Smith caused the first significant explosion in this country since the Times – there's no telling what he's capable of if threatened.'

The twins both shook their heads, and Bailey spoke. 'He threatens our family. I don't think we're even sure what we might be capable of in this situation. So, we are definitely going, but we know you'll be better at tracking them, so we'd like to team up.'

Major Halthrop half closed his eyes and continued thinking in silence. After a couple of minutes, he eyed up Bailey and said, 'Firstly, be aware that I cannot allow any criminal behaviour. We are going to capture Smith and return him to Kangaroo for trial. And that is all. There is no room for any violence, and we will arrest you too if we are witness to anything that should go before Kangaroo. Sec... '

Truvan interrupted him, 'No, that's not what we're after. We just want to get our sister back and bring her home.'

'OK. Secondly, if we do take you two along with us, you must follow my instructions. No question, no arguments, what I say goes.'

Truvan and Bailey had been nodding throughout and Truvan answered, 'Understood, and agreed.' He pointed into the trees behind where they stood. 'We've got horses, so we won't slow you down at all.' Only the woods could be seen, so Frank had to assume that the horses had been left to graze out of sight.

The major then pointed behind where he stood. 'Perhaps you should come and meet my team. Have you had breakfast yet?'

The twins were a few years older than the other three, and when Major Halthrop introduced them as joining the posse, Darren and Terry greeted them with clear detachment. Jane, though, welcomed them vigorously.

71

There was some discussion about why the twins were joining the posse. Jane was particularly sympathetic about Vicky's kidnapping. Terry was more sceptical, asking if there was any evidence that she had been kidnapped, rather than simply leaving with Jack.

Before anyone had time to respond to it, he asked additionally how they thought Jack might have managed to make any sort of escape with an unwilling kidnap victim. Even if he had threatened or assaulted her, the going would be very slow. If he was carrying her, it would be even slower.

Bailey responded but did not answer any of the specific questions. 'If she's with him, it's bad news whatever the scenario. Even if she's got some idea into her head about wanting to go along with him, he's a terrorist, and so she won't be safe. We're going to get her back regardless of the situation. It's what's best for her.'

Terry folded his arms across his chest and leant back, and Darren followed suit, mirroring his friend. Jane frowned slightly but said nothing. There was a long silence and everyone sat still.

Major Halthrop looked at each face around the table, finishing on Bailey. He asked them to reveal what they knew of Jack's escape plans, and if they had already thought about how they might intercept him.

The twins looked at each other and Truvan asked if they had a map of the area, including Gloucester and Cheltenham. Darren went over to his parked bike and started rifling through the trailer. He finally pulled out the road map he had been issued with and gave it over to Truvan. He laid the map onto the wooden table as everyone cleared a space amongst the breakfast things.

'Our father says Vicky mentioned an old bunker at Leckhampton. That's all she said about it. Father says Leckhampton is the other side of Gloucester somewhere; quite dense forest he says.' All except Halthrop leaned forward, fingers tracing across places on the map trying to spot something that related to this information.

'Here's a place called Leckhampton Hill,' Darren held a fat forefinger on a point near the right hand edge of the map. He looked at the major and asked, 'Do you think that'd be it, Frank?'

A finger stroked his moustache, offering a moment's pause for thought. Halthrop answered that the only Leckhampton he had ever heard of was a southern area of the town of Cheltenham, above where Darren was pointing. 'I've never heard of any bunker though. I wonder what that meant exactly.' He looked at each of the twins in turn. They also looked at each other.

'Sorry,' Truvan said. 'We didn't get any more details about it.'

Terry joined in. 'Well, following the roads on this map, all those things with Leckhampton in the name have got to be at least fifteen kilometres from here. Should we get going, Frank?'

Everyone turned to look at him, and Halthrop paused momentarily. 'The chain of destiny can only be grasped one link at a time.' He paused, but there was no recognition from any of them. The twins looked confused and glanced to each other. He did not expect any of them to know the source of the quotation, but he had hoped that somebody might understand that it was a metaphor, and at least endeavour to think it through.

'Unless you two have anything else we should know, let's pack up and head off for the general area. As we get closer, hopefully there will be some sightings, or at least the locals will know about whatever the bunker is.' He looked at his armulet. 'Departure at 1030.'

The Truvas trotted along at the back of the convoy. They

settled on a gap of about twenty metres behind Jane. She confirmed with each of the Brigade members that they had made their navigation recording, and the group finally set off ten minutes late.

The track from Ellie Smith's old place met the A40 at the point where it was closest to the railway line. So they crossed the road and a muddy farmyard to rejoin the route from the previous day. Within 400 metres, they were clattering over the railway bridge that Vicky and Jack had looked beyond in the small hours of that same morning. The boys with the trailers found it much easier work if they walked the bikes across. The horses too were unhappy about the gaps in the deck of the bridge.

Just as Bailey was about to dismount, a man popped up from beneath the safety railing on the downriver side. His sudden appearance gave the twins a start, but they recognised him as Big Bearded Bill from Over Farm.

The man was not only large, but he sported a giant and unkempt dark beard. He took a rein and cried a greeting to both of them that was at the same time gregarious, but also unnecessarily loud. He offered to walk the two horses across so the twins could stay riding.

When they reached the east end of the bridge, Truvan called to the convoy in front, which had extended further ahead of the walking horses. The bikes stopped and waited for the locals to catch up. 'You need to hear this, Major.'

The three younger militiamen stared at the approaching bear of a man. Halthrop greeted him, 'Good morning, sir. Who are you?'

'I'm Bill. From that farm back aways.'

Halthrop looked up to the Truvas for a clue and they both turned their gaze down to Big Bearded Bill. The major followed suit and asked, 'You have something to tell us?'

'I was just asking the lads here where you lot were off to with your fancy bikes, and they told me you're the posse for the explosions guy.' Halthrop did not speak, so Bill continued, 'Well, my brother seen Vicky and a fella what sounds like your man walking along the riverbank this morning.' He pointed over the neck of Bailey's horse back towards the nearest bank of the River Severn.

'You sure it was them?'

He looked back to Halthrop and brought his hand back down to the rein. 'Sure. Harry knows Vicky well. I doubt he'd remember what Ellie Smith's grandson might ha' looked like, probably wouldn't recognise him at all now, but if he says it was Vicky, then it was definitely her. And he said a man with dark hair. He had a big rucksack on, and she had a little one.'

Halthrop demanded, 'What were they doing? Which way were they going? Was there anybody else with them? Could he hear them talking? When was this exactly?'

Bill's calm eyes looked up at Bailey, who returned the same placid expression, and added a slight raise of both eyebrows. The man looked back at Halthrop. 'I been fishing here since about two. Took over from Harry, who been here since sunset. Sat on the bridge edge back near the middle there.'

He looked and pointed back between the horses to where three rods stuck out over the water. The railway bridge stanchions both had a small brick platform on each side, which almost looked like they had been designed to accommodate fishermen. 'He told me he seen them up on the other bridge, but couldn't make out what they were saying.'

He turned the long way round, past facing the four with their bikes, to point upriver at the roadway bridge raised on concrete piles. 'It was a calm night, but that'd be too far to hear them. Said they were stopped on the crossing for a bit and then set off down the riverside path. Probably midnight or one o' clock. I'm guessing a bit there, but the night was a bit lighter after midnight. Was strange to hear Vicky was out that late, but I assumed she was with a new fella and they was out for a bit of, well, you know.'

'And they were definitely on foot.'

'Yup.'

'And where does the riverside path lead?'

'Could take you into Gloucester. And then roads leadin' out of Gloucester in all directions.'

Halthrop moved on. 'It was the middle of the night, can we really be sure it was them?'

'Like I said, we known Vicky since she was born. And these two goons as well.' He turned to look up at the twins and waved his hand to indicate them. 'Don't need to see her face close up or well lit to know it's her.' Bill turned back to look straight into Major Halthrop's eyes.

There were a few seconds of quiet. 'I'm not a big fan of hearsay. Where's your brother now? I'd like to talk to him directly, just to check that nothing has been missed in your passing on the info to us.'

'Sorry, matey, he went to visit our old mum in Cirencester Kangaroo. With the armulets broken, we've no idea how she is, and she's not been well the last month or so: kidney trouble.'

Halthrop looked at the time on his armulet and declared, 'OK, they've obviously decided that the most direct road route is going to be too dangerous, too exposed. That will hopefully slow them up. With luck they're at most ten hours ahead of us and we should be able to travel at twice their speed. Let's get back to the bank and follow the riverside trail.'

'Do your navigation recordings, everyone,' Jane chirped.

Bill pulled on the bridles to spin the horses round. 'I'll walk you back to the path.'

Bailey reached his hand down to Bill's. 'Just hang on though – these lot prefer to be in front.' The three from Highnam watched the Bristol Brigade foursome wrestle to turn their bikes around.

Chapter Eleven

Jack woke up with a sunbeam straight in his eye. He and Vicky were squeezed together under a small circular rhododendron bush about a hundred feet from the riverbank. They had travelled nearly five miles along the side of the River Severn, before deciding to hide and sleep under the cover of the dense, green leaves. Sleeping in the daytime was difficult – it was hot and bright, despite the shade provided by their hiding place. Jack rolled over on his side facing away from Vicky, towards the outside of their bush.

Rhododendron was an imported, ornamental species, and not common in the fields about Gloucestershire. The bush they hid in, whilst dense with foliage, stood alone in a large field. Other occasional trees punctuated the flat, grassy land, but it would be hard to approach the hideout unseen.

He felt Vicky crawling through the thick branches to leave. 'Where are you going?' Jack's voice was not wide awake and his question sounded grumpy.

'Need to pee.'

'Quick as you can – don't want to get seen.'

'Nobody comes round these fields. The nearest farm is the other side of the A48. All the ones on this side are abandoned. And with all the irrigation ditches, nobody bothers walking down to here. There's nothing here.'

'Be quick,' Jack repeated. She was.

Neither of them could sleep in the daytime heat. Even in the shade, their armulets were suggesting nearly thirty degrees. They lay top to tail, to minimise the discomfort in the cramped camp, each with their head resting on their pack. 'Tell me another of Ellie's stories from the old days.'

Jack looked at the dark canopy. They were sheltered, shaded by an umbrella of leaves above and below and beside each other, the very definition of interleaved. Each leaf was the size of a hand, thick and waxy, dark green. He looked to Vicky; she was watching him.

He decided that the story of Grannie Ellie's escape from a terrible existence in Brighton, to reach Highnam, would be a good one under their on-the-run circumstances.

Jack remembered his grandmother's face as the one he had said goodbye to the day he left to become a sifter. Her tousled brown hair, the colour of a baby deer, framed a circular face with the lines of a young old woman. It was a cheeky face, vibrant with some secret that you could guess at but she would never tell.

The face he remembered was Ellie Smith at 73, but she had aged well and the visage was much younger. In his darkest moments, Jack had sometimes wondered if the stories she related of his mother, Clara, were made up, and that in fact Ellie herself was his real mother.

She had told Jack that Clara was born into a world in trouble. In 2030, there was little to eat, and danger all around. This was the one story that Jack remembered would always take the light from his grandmother's eyes.

His grandparents had suffered considerable hardship in Brighton, living in a damp beach hut under the promenade. They had never been able to provide his mother with enough food and she grew up malnourished and regularly sick. Grandfather Wayne fought in the Brighton Defence Force to protect the community, but everyone slowly got weaker.

When Wayne was killed one night, Ellie took her eight-year-old daughter and fled west to try and find fertile and safe land. The story of their journey across England was an entire epic in itself, so Jack skipped much of it, sticking with only a couple of stories that mirrored himself and Vicky.

His grandmother had always spoken the same words at the end: 'Once in Highnam, Clara could have all the nutrition that her whole life needed, if only her body could have waited until we got here. But those early years in Brighton set her on a path of skinny undernourishment that she never recovered from. You were just too much for her.'

In retelling the story to Vicky, Jack omitted those ominous final sentences. He instead highlighted the journey from a horrible situation to a land of milk and honey. She smiled and closed her eyes.

Chapter Twelve

The posse faced all different directions at a road junction on a raised section of the old A430. A tributary of the Severn came from the northeast, and the heart of tumbledown Gloucester, and gurgled under the road bridge.

Heat was blazing back off the road surface. The six of them were roughly equally spaced. Each looked off in their own direction, eyes screwed up against the brightness – only Halthrop had sunglasses. Nobody spoke. The water was the only sound except for an occasional snort from the Truvas' sweating horses.

Major Halthrop was repeatedly stroking down his slightly damp moustache, both sides simultaneously with spreading thumb and index finger. 'Though we have heard of stupid haste in war, cleverness has never been seen associated with long delays,' he muttered beneath his fingers.

'Well, what are you lot?' A middle-aged woman in a large straw hat had walked up the road from the south. She had maintained, as best she could, a path in the shade of the decaying warehouses at the roadside. Jane was the one facing south, but had not observed the slight woman's approach and visibly jumped in fright when she broke the humming quiet.

Halthrop turned from looking up the side road and rolled the short distance to stop beside Jane. When the woman stepped out of the shade, she was mostly a silhouette. In the shadow of her hat brim, the major could make out a weathered face that he estimated would once have been pretty. Crow's feet around her eyes were extensive and deep. She was well tanned, and the rest of her face also suffered lines and wrinkles in extremis. He mused inwardly that she was no longer a pretty sight.

'Good afternoon, madam. We're the Bristol Brigade militia posse. We are searching for two fugitives in connection with the destruction of the armulet network.'

As the woman looked at her own armulet, Bailey shouted, 'Whoa,' whilst kicking his horse into movement towards Jane and Frank.

'We're looking for *one* fugitive and our sister.' Truvan also joined them.

Major Halthrop left his bike for Jane to hold and showed the photo of Jack to the woman. 'This is the man we think is responsible for blowing up the Doughnut in Cheltenham.' He turned to the Truvas. 'Do you have a stored photo of your sister?'

Truvan held up his armulet and projected a life-size image of Vicky standing on the road in front of their horses. She was smiling without showing any teeth, and her hand was held up to shade her eyes, although seemingly from the wrong direction.

The local woman did not even glance at the picture Halthrop held out, but pointed at the image of Vicky. 'Oh, yes, I saw her earlier.'

'No sign of this man?' Frank waved the paper in front of her.

The woman ignored the photo and looked up from Vicky's phantom to Truvan. 'Strangest thing you know. I saw her come out of this big bush. She nipped down to the riverbank, squatted down to urinate, and then ran back and wriggled into the bush again. A big circular bush plonked in the middle of a grass field.'

Truvan and Bailey leant forward, hands on their saddle pommels, but Halthrop spoke first. 'Definitely no sign of the man?'

She finally turned to him and said, 'No.'

Halthrop persevered, 'We're anticipating that they're on

the way to Leckhampton, but you mentioned the river; where were you exactly when you saw her? It was definitely her?'

She adjusted the hat slightly further back on her head to look at the major. 'Yes. It was definitely her.' She pointed towards the image of Vicky standing in the road. 'And Leckhampton is totally the wrong direction. I was back there, not even four kilometres. If you go straight on at that junction, following Hempstead Lane, it comes back to the riverbank in about half an hour's walk. A bit further along and you'll see the bush from there.' She was indicating through the shimmering air above the tarmac to a complication of roads in the distance.

'Where are you headed to, madam?'

The woman looked at Halthrop, moved her hat forward again, and said, 'My sister lives in Gloucester.' Without another word, she nodded to the twins and proceeded across the road junction on a diagonal towards the shaded side of the road.

Halthrop watched her walk and then snapped his fingers and called to Darren, 'Map.' Terry and Darren cycled round in front of Jane and Frank. Darren produced the map from the trailer, and the foursome held a corner each to look at the roads shown.

Jane pointed to the map. 'We're here, you see, where the road is over the river. So, she's just walked up here, and that junction she pointed to back there is here.' Jane's pointing shifted between the road ahead of her and the map. Darren tried to twist his head sideways to get the same view of the map as Jane.

Halthrop looked up at the twins, who had edged their horses closer to the group but could not possibly make out the details on the map. 'Do you know that woman?' They both shook their heads. 'Do you think she's reliable? This is the wrong direction for Leckhampton.'

Truvan watched Bailey, who answered. 'I don't think she

could have been offered a better picture to judge, and she was immediate in recognising Vicky.'

Halthrop nodded slowly. 'I agree.' He looked to Jane.

'I've worked out the quickest way to get to the river from here. And it's pretty much a straight line, like she said, so I think it must be the way she came. This means we're looking for an open field with a circular bush, once we get back on the riverside path. The map agrees pretty much exactly with what she said about the distances too.'

'OK. Everybody ready? Let's go.'

'Don't forget your navigation records, guys.' Jane was meticulous. It was thirty degrees in the shade, and they stood in the sun. Darren and Terry both gave her a mean look. However, with Halthrop in close attendance, they both started muttering into their armulets as they set off.

Twenty minutes' ride later, the road turned away from the river. A walking trail continued straight along the riverside. It was overgrown, but not impossibly so. This path was much slower going on the bikes, but from that point they were all on the lookout for something matching the woman's description: a big circular bush.

'Eyes open everyone, a bush to hide in that is within "nipping out" distance of the river. Be watchful, ready to give chase, but also ready to take cover. Remember, we don't know what weapons they might have, and we don't know what state of mind they are in.'

Guns were not common in England. A warlord who might try to enforce control with violence was quickly tracked down by their audiopt feeds. It was impossible for those who would rule by force to monitor all the feeds of those who might want to get rid of them.

Halthrop had only seen guns being fired in videostories from before the end of the Times of Malthus. He thought, *All warfare is based on deception. Hence, when unable to attack, we must seem able.*

Vicky's brothers had stopped their horses. Truvan called to Major Halthrop, 'Our sister is not dangerous.'

Bailey added, 'She's not even involved in this.'

'I don't think any of us know how he may have influenced her. Better to be overcautious and safe. Remember what I said to you this morning, gents. Please do as I ask – you're not trained for a manhunt.'

Truvan responded, 'You take care of Smith, and we'll look after Vicky.'

The major had also stopped. He rode forwards again, shaking his head.

After three hours, they had passed nothing that remotely resembled even the vague description they had of the isolated circular bush in question. The group had passed, by some distance, the expected area that their informant might have had to walk past on her way before meeting them.

The posse leader called them all together for a rest, some water, and a reevaluation of the map. There were plenty of comments about places they had been, and places that might have been attractive to two people on the run.

After the discussions petered out, Frank spent more than a minute looking into the distance downriver. He decided that the two sightings had both been very positive in identifying Vicky, and both had confirmed that the two were following or near the course of the River Severn. Despite the Truvas' intelligence that Leckhampton was the destination, Halthrop listened to his gut instinct, which told him that Jack and Vicky were following the river.

'Right, men, here's what we're going to do. They are following the river course, and they must have left whatever hiding place they were in. As we were travelling slowly, we obviously didn't catch up behind them. So let's continue with all speed and with luck we'll catch them before dark.'

At this point, the overgrown pathway adjoined an option of a metalled road, which could increase their pace significantly.

'That's only two hours from now,' Bailey countered. Everyone looked to Halthrop to see how he might react to this.

'Right, let's go then. We will be wasting our time to continue this pursuit in the dark – it'd be too easy for them to hide when they hear us coming. When night falls, we will have to stop. Unless we get any better leads by then.' There was no further comment from anyone.

With their renewed purpose – to travel as much distance as possible in the two hours till sundown – the posse made quicker speed along the old country lane. In most places, trees and other vegetation on the banks made it difficult to actually see the water, but they were never very far from it.

As the sun's lower edge approached the horizon, they emerged onto a small open field, skirting unblocked views of the river. Orange light reflected brightly from the smooth, wide water surface. A large, white building occupied the far side of the field, fronting onto another road, which curved back at this point to rejoin the riverside path.

The Anchor Inn had been a pub for more than 300 years and was still functioning successfully as one. Most recently, it had reverted back to its original purpose as a travellers' resthouse on the route from Bristol to Cheltenham. The inn held a strong position, being roughly one day's walk from each. It also had a landing for river-borne traffic, although there were no boats tied up as the posse approached.

Major Halthrop stopped the party between the building and the boat mooring and announced that this would be their campsite for the night. Darren, Terry and Jane proceeded to set up their tents, and Halthrop went inside with the Truvas.

The twins opted to stay in a room inside the inn, whilst Frank organised with the landlord that the Brigade members would camp on the lawn. He did agree to them taking a cooked meal in the pub; he knew well that this would boost morale.

The Kangaroos paid expenses on top of the reward money, but he did not cover any of the costs that the twins incurred. Truvan and Bailey made no argument. There was some discussion as to how payment would be made. Electronic money transfer was rendered impossible by the lack of armulet connectivity. Major Halthrop invoked the importance of the Bristol Brigade and agreed to vouch for the integrity of the twins too. The landlord accepted that the debt would be paid later, and Truvan and Bailey returned outside with the major.

Once the tents were erected and the horses tied on long grazing ropes, the six sat around one of the big outdoor tables. The idyllic scene was slightly marred by the temperature, which, without a breath of wind, was still too hot for comfort and brought an unpleasant fishy smell from the river.

Truvan made Darren spread the map on the table so they could see how little the deviation would have been for Jack and Vicky, if they had turned away from the river and taken small roads to the east, in order to return to a route towards the various areas labelled with the name 'Leckhampton'.

A dark-skinned man walking south along the road turned off onto the pub lawn. 'Ho there!' he called, waving, and walked across the lawn to stand at the head of the table between them and the building. 'I saw you lot arriving – up there, where the road comes a bit close to the water. Then it cuts away again and then comes back here.' He pointed a stubby, brown finger upstream. 'Quicker going than me with your bikes and horses, I guess, even if I hadn't gone the long way round.'

Terry was at the end of the bench nearest and replied,

'Where are you headed?'

'On my way back to Thornbury. It's just outside Bristol, but I'm going to stop here the night.' He was an average-looking fellow, carrying an oversized rucksack.

'We know it.' Terry explained, 'We're the Bristol Brigade militia. We're on the hunt for the Doughnut bomber guy.'

'Oh, the armulet destruction thing. You chasing him, eh? Yeah, I'm not quite sure how I'm going to pay my night's stay here. Been coming here often enough, though, I hope Artur inside will accept my credit is good.'

Frank passed the photo along to Terry, who held it up to the man to view. 'Sir, have you seen anyone today? This is the man we're looking for. And he's travelling with a woman.'

Truvan jumped in. 'He may be forcing our sister to go along with him. This is Vicky.' He tapped his armulet for the life-size projection to appear.

Terry carried on, 'We were told this morning that these two were on the riverside trail back near Gloucester, but we've not seen anything all day, and we've travelled all the way from there.' The man laughed, a knowing chuckle. 'Sir?' Terry pushed forward the picture.

'Yes, I saw them.' The moon was rising, large and orange behind the stranger, over the roof of the inn behind him. 'Probably an hour ago, walking the riverside trail. But I'm not surprised you missed them, they're across the water on the other bank.'

'Upstream or downstream?' Halthrop interjected loudly.

'Sorry?'

'Were they headed this way, or were they going upstream?'

'Oh, this way, but like I said, if they come this far, they'll be over there.' The stubby forefinger pointed again, this time directly across the river to the opposite side.

'And you're certain it was them?'

Frank examined the man's face during his answer. 'I guess. I was on this side of the river, and back up there they would have been, what, thirty metres away. It was up in Elmore, there's a little bit like here where the road goes right by the water's edge, and it's much narrower than here. But I wasn't really paying attention to them. They were a little bit in front of me, so I can't say I got a good look at their faces. Hair colours were right.' He pointed at the image of Vicky. 'And she matches well with the girl I saw. Although it was from behind. He had a rucksack as big as mine, and she had a little daypack.'

'That's them,' Darren exclaimed, and his grin puffed up his rosy cheeks. He spun sideways to look at their boss.

Halthrop held up the palm of his hand. 'Did you see anything else, Mr... ?'

'Covell, Sam Covell. I probably only saw them for half a minute before the road I was walking turned away again. She was walking behind him, and then he turned and they stopped. I think they were arguing.'

'I knew it,' Bailey hissed, turning to Truvan. His brother nodded vigorously.

'OK, thank you very much for your help. Sounds like we have more to go on now.' Halthrop then dismissed the man. 'If you need any help convincing Artur inside about the money, ask him to check with me.'

'Right. OK.' He looked around the faces at the table, picked up his pack and wandered into the pub.

'She's obviously not happy about going with him,' Bailey immediately proposed.

Halthrop held up his palm again. 'Whatever the situation, we simply need to apprehend them. We, by which I mean Kangaroo, can work out who's guilty of what later.'

Truvan opened his mouth to argue but no words came out as Halthrop issued new orders. 'Right, this will work well for us.' He pointed at the map and traced along the loops and curves of the river to their location. 'If they're going to walk the riverbank all the way, and we can't second guess any other course, then that will take them some time to get to here. From Elmore, it's a good fifteen kilometres and slow going if they're arguing along the way. And some in the dark. That'll put them here, I'd say, at 2300 at the earliest, but it could be much later if that side of the river is as overgrown as ours was. So, we'll utilise the time to get some sleep.'

Again Truvan made to interrupt but was silenced. Major Halthrop pointed up at the moon. 'That will allow us to see them.' The daylight had faded significantly, but he pointed across the Severn. 'You can see that there's little cover over there.'

'Frank... ' Darren was looking further downriver as the last rays of the now hidden sun shone up from below the horizon.

'Quiet, Darren, let me finish, I'll take questions at the end.'

'No, Frank, look!' He pointed to the middle of the river down from their position, level with the end of a raised brick pathway by the road. A very large wave was sweeping slowly up towards them. 'What is that? Is there a whale in the river?'

Jane looked briefly at the wave and then stared at Darren, silently mouthing the word 'Idiot'.

Terry shoved Darren in the chest from across the table and laughed, 'Haven't you ever seen the bore?'

'What?'

Halthrop interjected calmly, 'It's the Severn bore – the big high tide wave you get up here. We don't see it down in Bristol, but up here it can get really quite large. If you watch after it has passed, the incoming tide will really rush upriver behind it.' His comment was timed exactly as the wave passed, and the river did as it was commanded: the flow raced up behind the wave, a tremendous surge of water that carried floating branches upriver.

Bailey looked at Truvan and said, 'Wow. I've often heard about that, but I've never seen it.'

Truvan eyed his brother sidelong. 'Really? We live right near where it peaks. It goes all the way up to Maisemore. And it goes three or four days in a row, every month.'

Bailey shrugged. 'I'm hardly ever by the river. You know how I hate the water.' Truvan nodded.

The major resumed, 'As I was saying, there's little cover over there. Anyone walking the path will be easily visible from here. Maybe only as silhouettes, but it should be clear enough that it's them. I'll make sure the landlord turns off all the lighting over here. So we'll take turns on sentry duty and watch for them to arrive.

'Unfortunately, there's no boat here, so this is going to be more complicated than I'd like. However, they are now entering territory I know well. I've worked in this area for twenty years. When we see them, we'll head down here to Sharpness. There's a ferry across the river there.' He traced his finger further downstream on the map to point at the marina in a place at a bottleneck of the river, which was by then more than a kilometre wide.

Terry volunteered, 'I'll take first sentry duty.' Jane dropped her eyes and shook her head.

Chapter Thirteen

He woke in the late afternoon to a sweet oily smell, like nectar. The sun was not quite low enough for Jack to see it through his ground-level tunnel in the leaves, but the shadows showed him that it was near.

They ate the fresh fruit he had brought along, sitting up as best they could inside the low rhododendron hemisphere. They would have to wait at least until their next stop in the night before cooking would be possible, so he repacked the remainder of the stolen vegetables, trying to do so without Vicky seeing them. She smiled at his efforts and offered up the bread and cheese.

The sun was cut in half by the horizon of the trees lining the river in the west. Jack and Vicky cut across the shortest distance to the footpath adjacent to the riverbank.

Jack insisted that they should wait for dark before walking on. They discussed it briefly, until she agreed. Jack stole down to the water's edge and refilled their bottles, and they waited on a rock near the slow moving river.

He watched her peach-smooth face in the gloaming: the hazel eyes appeared bright, alert to the movements of insects buzzing around. In the half-light, once the sun had dropped completely, they scanned all around for the silhouettes of people who might spot their flight. In all directions, the land was vacant.

The moon poked up from the eastern horizon. Over the ten minutes it took to rise, a gigantic orange ball was revealed, a harvest moon in full, fiery glory. Jack was distracted by the spectacle. He had worked the noon-to-midnight shift for all of his sifter life. With a west-facing office window, he had not seen the full moon rise since he left Highnam. He was spellbound, both by the scene, and the memories of seeing it from Grannie Ellie's garden.

A rushing sound rose over the slightly diminished insect buzz. Jack grabbed Vicky by the wrist and pulled her off the old earthwork flood defence into deep grass nearer the river. He looked every which way but could not see what was causing the noise.

She shook her hand free and physically turned his face towards downriver. 'Look, it's just the Severn bore.' She also had to point for him to spot the approaching bulge of water, as it splashed along the banks in the dim light. 'Haven't you ever seen it before?' Open-mouthed, he made a single, slow nod as it surged past, and let Vicky lead him back to the pathway.

In places, the grass was knee high, some bits ankle deep and a few sections were just packed mud. Sometimes they had to wend a path through clumps of thistle and nettle, often waist high. The path traversed field after field, and most boundary fences were incomplete. An archaeological history of cattle grazing was on show in the rusty gates and rotten fenceposts they passed every couple of hundred yards. Trees edged the old pastures in places, and their creaking in the wind added to the ghostly foreboding that Jack suffered. Disturbed birds took flight in noisy flurries.

Jack questioned Vicky about her route plan. 'Everything is coming together for good progress tonight – cooler and light enough. You're the local geography expert, how long do you reckon before we reach the island you have in mind?'

They walked one behind the other as the path was narrow. She was behind him, and he had not turned around. Looking at the back of his rucksack, she was hesitant. 'I'm not sure I can answer that too accurately. Um, coming down this way, my brothers often used to ride to Thornbury market and back in a day. But that was on roads, which go in a pretty straight line. As we're going to be going round all the river loops, walking, and maybe on some slower ground, that far is probably two or three night's travel. Then I don't know quite when we should get on to the river. It'll be quicker travelling on the water, but more difficult to hide up in the daytime. Especially if we've stolen a boat that people will recognise. But to walk all the way to Cardiff and then row from there will be much longer. It's pretty random, but I'd guess at a week from here.'

'A week?' Jack did stop and turn. His voice had almost shrieked his disbelief. Vicky had to stop suddenly and they ended up facing each other at very close quarters, under the shadow of a large tree. 'We can't be on the run in the open for a week. They'll catch us for sure. And how are we going to eat for that long?'

She faltered and took a step back. 'I did say it was a guess. The islands I remember from that armulet flightview are past Bristol, and that's a good two days walk from Highnam on the straight roads. So I reckoned on another day for the extra distance, and then double for travelling at night along the river course. And then a day in the boat. To be honest, I don't know anything about boats and how long that might take, but... '

'Right, we need to get on the water now. We won't get so tired, and the water flows fast. Where can we get a boat?'

He saw the shadow of Vicky's arm raise to point. 'Nobody lives in Minsterworth any more. Maybe there's an old abandoned boat there, although I doubt we could trust it for seaworthiness. But Newnham will have boats – it's the main source if you want fish in Highnam.'

Jack remembered his conversation with Aluen. His face developed a scowl. 'It'll have to be Minsterworth. We can't risk going through a Kangaroo. And it'll be less delay.'

'Delay? Are we on a schedule?'

Jack faltered a moment. 'No, not exactly. I just don't know how long it'll take the infotechs to get the network back up and running. As soon as they do, then they'll find us straight away through the audiopts. So we need to be difficult to find or at least to get to by then, and we mustn't get caught beforehand. At worst, I reckon we've got two more days.'

'Two days? Jack, I don't think we're gonna make it.'

He put out his hand to take her free one, but in the darkness missed at first, and in a second attempt only caught her on the wrist. He took that instead. 'Two days before they fix it. They then have to come and catch us. So if we can aim to make the island in two days, I think that's the best we could hope for. And remember, you sent them on a wild goose chase to Leckhampton.'

Vicky was twisting her hair in small circles on her temple. She remained silent for several seconds. 'What will happen when they catch us?'

'I assume I'll be taken to Kangaroo for trial. That's where everyone will realise that I've shown them how we can have privacy, and they'll be able to decide to change our system so that the audiopts are not publicly available.'

'Do you really think people will agree to that?'

'It's not a case of agreeing, they'll want it. After these few days of being free to do things in private, they'll see what I'm talking about and understand what a powerful and important step it is towards happiness.'

'Really? Are you sure?'

'Well, nothing in this world is certain, but how could they not want it? They don't lose anything, because they can still have the feeds available for the sifters, but it means that we're only using them when a crime has been committed, not just for snooping.'

'What's snooping?'

'Oh, Malthus.' Jack shook his head slowly. 'If you watch what other people are doing, then that's called snooping. It means spying on people who either don't want you to, or don't expect that you're doing it.'

'And snooping is bad?'

He slipped his hand lower to hold hers and gave it a squeeze. 'Yes. This is what I'm highlighting to people. They should be able to feel confident that their private activities are exactly that – private.' He held up their hands. 'Like this. Nobody will ever know I've been holding your hand tonight. This private moment will be ours, and nobody can snoop on it.'

She looked at their hands. 'OK, but I can't see people being that worried about it.'

'No, and neither could I. That's why I had to turn off the feeds and force people to experience it. You'll see, once they get to understand how important this is, there will be no going back.' He grinned, 'We're changing the world, Vicky.'

She raised her eyes to his face again, but it was barely visible in the tree shade of the moonlight. With a shake, she extricated her hand from his grip. 'Well, hadn't we better get on with it then?'

'Yes, you're right.' As he turned to proceed on the path, Jack added, 'New plan: hike the river trail tonight, camp before we reach Newnham during the day tomorrow, and take a boat from there tomorrow night. Aiming to reach the island by sunrise the next day.' After half a minute, he asked, 'Am I right that we'll make that far before morning?'

'Yes, I think that's about exactly right, actually. It's something like ten kilometres by road from Highnam, so if we're going slowly and twice the distance like I'm guessing we are, then that's a night's walk.' He nodded vigorously but knew it was invisible to her behind his rucksack.

Jack guessed the river beside them was fifty yards wide

along this stretch. After an hour, a road tracked in from their right to parallel the river. It left a corridor of land that varied from ten to twenty yards wide.

In the initial corner as the road arrived, a group of large, old trees made the path very dark and they were able to halt in the shadows to observe a farmyard. Vicky was confident that the farmhouse was abandoned, but of the half-dozen other farms along the riverside strip she was sure that at least one was occupied. She could not remember which one.

A rank smell from the tidal river surprised Jack. It was a normal river smell, but he was not used to spending time by such a major watercourse. They proceeded slowly along the flood defence dyke, constantly watching the buildings for any sign of activity. No lights were visible, and there were no sounds other than the splashing of the river against the bank.

A dog started barking, and they caught sight of a shape moving swiftly across the ground towards them. Without a pause, Jack and Vicky set off running along the ATV ruts in the bank top. The sound of the dog became louder and was accompanied by a second barking.

They could hear the animals occasionally crashing through a bush as the dogs ran along at a lower level on the farm side of the dyke. The barking continued to get louder, but they could no longer hear the passage of the beasts through the undergrowth. Jack glanced back and saw that they had mounted the ridge and were gaining on Vicky, who was barely ten feet behind him.

Suddenly pain coursed through his foot, and the world rotated slowly through ninety degrees. He landed flat on the solid ground, the weight of his rucksack slamming him hard down. Vicky did not trip on the same rock, but she could not stop herself before she tripped over Jack's prone body, landing beyond him but much more safely as she had prepared to cushion the landing with her arms out forwards.

The noise of the two dogs became very loud and Jack looked back to see them complete the remaining short distance to him. They were large and noisy, but he could not make out any details in their dark faces. Occasionally a fang would show up bright white, reflecting the moonlight in contrast to their dark fur.

Jack flinched at the impending attack, but the animals stopped a few feet from him. The barking continued louder. He cowered with his arms wrapping his head, deafened. It seemed like an eternity later when he felt Vicky's hand pulling on his. The dogs were still barking violently, but they had not come any closer. She pulled hard to make Jack understand that he must get up and move on. They backed away slowly, Jack still prepared for an attack. Vicky kept pulling him.

A lamp lit up in the farmhouse, which was now some fifty yards back. This shook him and he turned to follow her closely. The dogs did not follow but continued their noise.

'I don't think they'd have attacked us, just acting as sentries, telling us to move on.'

'I hope you're right, they're damned frightening.' He struggled, limping.

She let go of his hand. 'Yes, but we're OK, they're not following.'

'No, but they woke their people up, I saw a light go on. We need to get a move on in case they follow.'

'They won't follow. If there's nobody around their place, they'll just shout the dogs to shut up and go back to sleep.'

Jack looked back as they walked on, now at a normal pace. The initial rush of pain had quickly subsided; he was not properly injured.

After a few moments, they had to stop and step down into the trees on the side of the ridge. Another farm was up ahead, and a light was shining in the window. The trees finished at a high, stone wall edging the farmyard. They waited for a few minutes, watching to see if anybody came out. A face appeared at the illuminated upstairs window a couple of times. 'Do you think they saw us running along?'

Vicky shook her head. 'I don't know, but I'd have thought they'd be outside by now if they saw us coming. Don't forget that these people aren't the ones chasing us.'

'Unless they recognise us,' he retorted.

She turned her head to look at him, but could only see a black outline on the ground. They lay against the back slope of the flood defence, peering over the top. 'Do you think everybody in the country will know who they're looking for? Remember the communications centre is destroyed. I don't believe that people are circulating printed pictures of you for everyone to look out for.'

The dogs either got bored, or lost scent of Jack and Vicky. They stopped barking and there was silence. Jack answered in a whisper, 'You're right, but I don't want to give people unusual things to remember. That will tip off any posse very quickly.'

It was a full ten minutes before the light was extinguished. There was no sound during that time. As the silence prolonged, they both took to shuffling and fidgeting in place. No sound or apparent presence of the dogs was detectable. Vicky touched his arm. 'I don't think we'll be able to get around the wall – it goes right down to the water's edge.'

He could not see her pointing in the darkness, but looked in the right direction anyway. He also pointed, aiming at a portal in the wall, visible as a lighter space in the solid darkness. 'We'll have to go through there and quickly across their yard. We'll have to hope they haven't got dogs as well, but I still think it's safer than the chances of being seen on the road.'

'OK.'

Neither moved for another thirty seconds, but then Jack pulled at her arm and they crept down to the doorway. It was a simple gap in the stone, with a lintel overhead. The place looked like it was used as a recreational garden, opening on to the river at the rear of the house.

They walked briskly through the open space until a voice halted them stone cold. 'Are you guys lost?' There was no light on, but the moon just illuminated the shape of a man on the threshold of the back door to the house.

Jack's hand found Vicky's and he tugged to indicate they should flee. She tugged back and responded to the unknown householder. 'Sorry, I guess we are a little lost. Apologies for disturbing you. We're going to Newnham for tomorrow's fish market, but we figured on making a romantic moonlit stroll of it and wandering along the riverbank all the way.'

'Ha. That path gets a bit tricky in daylight, let alone at night. I'd suggest you just follow the road from here. It's right out front if you wanna just cut down the side of the house.'

'Yes, good idea.' Her voice was cool and light and she pulled Jack up towards the road. He followed with faltering steps, needing repeated tugs on his hand to continue.

The man called after them, 'If you do want to be alone, take the railway line when it crosses the road. It also goes to Newnham but everybody walks the road. And it won't keep tripping you up like the river pathway.'

'Thanks,' Vicky called back as they were already in the alley beside the old stone building.

As they mounted the roadway, Jack pulled her to a stop. 'We can't travel on here.'

She waved up to the window of the house, leant in to Jack's face to appear to be kissing him, and hissed in his ear, 'Can we discuss this in a hundred metres please, he's bound to be watching us head off.' Without waiting for agreement, she turned and pulled him along again. After a tense and taciturn few minutes of brisk walking, she turned and stopped. 'OK. How do you want us to proceed?'

Jack did not have an immediate answer. He looked up to the grey-white disc of the moon. Looking back to her face, the features a slightly lighter leaden colour than the night sky behind her, he asked, 'I'm not sure, what do you think?'

'I'm thinking that actually the riverbank path may be much slower than we anticipated. There's another section with old houses beside it further on, and then quite a long stretch like that again on the way into Newnham. In fact, most of the houses in both sections are unoccupied, we could camp out quite nicely in one of the ones outside Newnham. The way I remember it, the road isn't so straight either, but it is easy going underfoot.'

'We can't risk being seen again. We'll have to go by the river, and we'll just have to work harder if it's difficult going.'

As they progressed, moving quickly, Jack kept turning to monitor the path behind. He saw nobody. A number of houses became visible on the left-hand side, skirting the river's edge. Jack grabbed Vicky's forearm, right around her armulet, and dragged her back to the relative invisibility of the tree cover just before the embankment ran out and the houses came close.

She stumbled in the movement, and shook her arm free quite violently. 'Just tell me if you want me to come back.' Her voice was quiet but her tone was angry – a whispered shout.

'Sorry. Didn't you see the houses on the left?'

She continued in a quiet voice, and her tone lost only a little of the venom. 'Of course – those houses are all empty. I can't think what they call this place, but everyone anywhere near here lives in Newnham.'

'How far away are we? If these are all empty, one of them would be perfect for us to wait for tomorrow night. There might even be a boat around here somewhere.'

Vicky's voice had returned to normal, and she had taken a step into the open so that she could indicate things with her hands. 'Yes, this might work. I think this might be Minsterworth. I had in mind another house on the edge of Newnham – a lovely white one. From here it's still several kilometres to there; taking this route is an extra long loop.'

Jack looked at her face, which was now easily visible in the growing dawn light. 'The out of town one sounds like it should work. But we should hurry, as the light is coming fast. Show me the way.'

'I reckon we should still go round any houses on the way and see about a boat though. I don't remember one at the white house – it's on the other side of the road, but these here mostly front the water.'

'OK, let's be quick about it. The light's going to bring people out on to our route, for sure.'

Chapter Fourteen

In less than sixty seconds, and in the first garden they entered, Jack and Vicky found a boat sitting on a trailer. The trailer's tyres were flat, and it was attached to the back of an old car that also stood on four flat tyres.

Neither Jack nor Vicky knew anything about boats, and they walked around inspecting blind. Vicky stood back looking at it. Jack's fingers were trailing along the hull trying to decide what, if anything, could be determined from the sensation. He felt a fine roughness; the small craft seemed intact. It was dirty like the car it was behind, but it was all a dry dust, which rubbed off easily. There was no apparent damage to the underside.

It was a bit less than twenty feet long, with a covered front third. The back end was squared off and had a mounting for a motor, which was not present. Along the rear of the starboard side, the boat was named *Severn Bore Inn* in big gold lettering. The four glass panels, framed in the same dark wood as the rest of the boat, which formed a low windscreen, were all intact.

When Jack rounded the back end and stopped next to Vicky, she said, 'Firstly, how are we going to get it off this cart and into the river? And secondly, how do we know it won't sink?'

'How about we put it in the river, tie it up, and sleep in it for the day? Then if it sinks we can jump off to the shore, and if not we're all set to go at nightfall. And also, if somebody finds us we can just set off straight away. What do you think?'

She looked at the hull some more, and then looked at him for equally long. 'Yep, good plan. I can't believe my dream home bites the dust again.' At that, she punched his arm lightly. Jack grinned, and Vicky followed up, 'Right then, Mr Clever Sifter, how do we get it into the water?'

'Yes... I haven't quite solved that part of it.' He walked around the area, looking at the available materials that they might be able to use. In the meantime, Vicky wrestled with the towing hook mechanism – the trailer was attached to the car. She cursed, shaking her hand and dancing from toe to toe. 'Are you alright?' he called from the far corner of the overgrown garden.

Vicky was sucking on a finger, and it was difficult for Jack to understand her reply. However, as she mumbled through one hand, she used the other to lift the trailer handle up to shoulder height, pivoting the boat about the axle. At the same time, she looked at him and pointed at the boat with her skew little finger, sticking out from the hand in her mouth. There was a loud grinding sound from the boat and it shifted very slightly on the supports that held it. Vicky quickly put the handle back down.

He came back to her side and rested a hand on her shoulder. 'Good work, Miss Clever Farmer.'

She looked at his face and smiled. 'Well, I've established that, if we want to, we can make it fall off onto the ground behind where it is now. I'm not sure how much progress that is.'

The ground behind the boat was ankle-deep grass. After about twenty feet, it banked up a couple of feet, and behind that the garden dropped at a steep angle through vegetation down to the edge of the River Severn. Jack walked over, stood on the small bank and looked at the vegetation. He beckoned Vicky to join him. 'You know what, all of these branches and leaves and stuff are just bushes. There's nothing solid on this little part of the bank.' He looked back to the boat and then back again at the sloping, bush-clad riverbank. 'If we can get those wheels moving, we could run it up this little bump and let it roll itself down the bank into the water.'

The drop from where they stood to the water was another twenty feet and down at an angle of 45 degrees. She looked at him. 'You're nuts.'

He looked down the bank. 'Don't be so sure. I've seen really old videostories showing huge ships being launched by sliding down a massive slide from the place they were built. They have to make boats pretty tough – the forces in the water are surprisingly large.'

'Don't make it sound like you know what you're talking about. The only reason I'm going to agree to try this is because we can't sail the boat from where it is.'

He smiled at her. 'Agreed. Shall we give it a go?'

They walked back, and Vicky took the handle she had released at the expense of cutting her finger. She lifted it up so the trailer was slightly higher at the front end. She pushed backwards to see how easy their plan might be. There was no movement of the wheels at all. It was like pushing against a pivoted boulder.

Jack stood on the other side of the trailer handle and put both his hands flat against the hull at the front end. He arched his back and bent his legs.

'Wait, wait, wait,' she said, lowering the handle to the ground. She walked forward and inspected the area around the wheel on each side, kicking a scrape in front of each. A few small rocks flew off to left and right. 'OK, it looks as clear as we're gonna get. Let's give it a try. But I think we should push on the strut of the cart so we don't just slide the boat off the back right here.'

He smiled. 'Agreed; again.'

They strained and nothing moved. 'I can feel it wants to

go,' Vicky offered. 'I tell you what, let's try rocking it into movement. First pull back, then push forward, then back and forward and so on until we free it up.'

Jack shrugged. 'OK, you call out the actions.'

'Pull! Push! Pull! Push! Pull! All you've got, push!' The whole trailer ground forward a foot and came to a halt. Vicky lost her footing and fell. The handle swung to the ground with a crash. They both looked at the wooden boat. It stayed in place.

'Are you OK?'

'Yes, thanks.' Vicky stood up and dusted her hands together. 'It's working. Ready to go again? I reckon we'll make it this time.'

Jack was breathless. He barely answered, but it was affirmative. They had a working system, and Vicky was correct in her expectation. On her third shout of 'Push!' they hurtled forward, the trailer bumped up and over the little ridge and went crashing down through the vegetation. As it flew away from them, Vicky followed up the rise to watch, and Jack fell face down onto the ground behind.

He wobbled slightly as he got up, and asked her, 'Zhit bruk?' She stared at him. His face was white and covered with sweat. As she watched, he wobbled again, and then Jack's legs collapsed beneath him. He crumpled to the floor. Despite Vicky leaping forward, he was unconscious on his side when she reached him.

She stroked his short, black hair, which was wet with sweat, and he roused. Jack held a hand forward to the space in front of him. 'What happened?'

'I don't know. You collapsed unconscious.'

'I don't remember anything after we shoved the boat. Where is it?' He shook in her arms, head twisting left and right, looking all around.

'Shh. It's OK. We got it over the edge, and it clattered

down to the river, but it's stuck on the mud bank.' She smiled brightly. 'You should have seen me chasing after it down the slope, shouting: "Don't float away! Don't float away!" But it's stuck fast; I can't budge it.'

Jack smiled vaguely but was distracted. 'My vision is... I don't know. There are little black dots flying around everywhere.'

She continued to stroke his hair. 'You know, I think you must have fainted. When was the last time you exerted yourself like that?'

He turned his head to look up to her face. 'I don't know. Can that make you faint?'

'Seems like it. If you're getting back to normal, I'll get you some water and show you what we managed. Can you see OK now?'

'No, but it's improving. Water would be good, please.'

She retrieved a bottle from his rucksack and helped him to stand and drink some. She held his hand, which was also clammy, led Jack forward to the ridge and pointed. 'See, it's stuck fast in the mud. Which I actually think is perfect. The mud is pretty squishy, so I'm thinking that the tide is out a bit and will come in up to there.' She pointed at the place where the vegetation gave way to the river mud. 'Let's get our stuff on board and see if there's a rope to tie her to shore.'

Vicky helped Jack over the side and he slid through the opening under the little windscreen and looked around inside. 'Don't seem to be any leaks in here – everything's dry.'

'That's good,' she called to him. 'You are on the mud bank though. But everything back here is dry too.' She stood and looked over the back end, which just sat in the water, forcing the flow to swirl around it. 'And I don't see any bubbles coming out in the water, so hopefully that means something good.'

'Well, there are lifejackets in here, so we won't drown.'

She joined him in the cabin. They looked through all the cabinets, which were equipped with bedding for the benches they lay on, four lifejackets, and nothing else. Vicky made him lie down with the bottle of water. She fussed over making the best meal they could from the collection of vegetables they had left. Jack just shrugged. His face was still pale.

The temperature in the small space was climbing rapidly, and there was no movement of the air in it. Vicky forced open a small hatch at the very front, and propped it so a delicate breeze came through. She positioned him up on the life jackets with his face in the draught. 'Tell me another of your grannie's stories.'

The thought of his grandmother perked Jack up. He saw Vicky smile at him and decided to recount something that he hoped she could connect with. Grannie Ellie told a tale of Jack's early years. She had always begun with her own daughter's death in labour. She spoke of this like an automaton, as if reciting a prayer. At the point where Jack was born, her voice would rejuvenate – Ellie's storytelling would then become animated and lively.

He began at that point, 'She said I was always strong and well-nourished, bundling around our smallholding without a care.' He told of tree-climbing antics, running and tumbling displays he gave Ellie.

After several minutes of tales, Vicky gave a little nod and a chuckle. 'Really, Fainter-man? Is this true?'

He ignored her. 'Of course, the audiopt feed also meant she could always tell where I was and see what I was up to. So there was never any reason to be worried.'

Vicky looked at him, but did not speak, and he said nothing further. She passed him a plate full of chopped raw vegetables. She had cut them very small, worried that they might be difficult to digest. They both grimaced at the food as they mechanically ate through everything. When he'd finished, Jack complained, 'I don't feel so good.'

Vicky leant forward and he felt her cool hand on his forehead. She asked, 'Do you think you're still a bit faint?' She removed her hand and put it on his.

'I don't know, I feel a bit wobbly. Yes, kind of like earlier.'

The entire boat rocked violently. Vicky had to brace herself against the side wall of the cabin. She lifted her hand from his brow. 'I feel it too. That's not you, it's the boat.'

She rose through the tiny entrance to the cabin and scanned over the side. Jack watched her long, narrow bottom move away. They had entered the cabin as the sun peered over the horizon, and the light outside was now very bright. Once she moved away from the doorway, he had to close his eyes against it. She called down to him, 'The tide has already come in – we're floating. That was fast.'

Shading his eyes with a hand, Jack saw Vicky leap across the width of the vessel, making it rock excessively. 'Whoa, what are you doing?'

'I'm trying to see if we're completely clear of the mud, and I'm pretty sure we are.' Her almond-shaped face appeared at the cabin threshold. 'Do you think we should set off already?'

Jack stared at her, his eyes tracing the outlines of all her facial features. Everything was smooth and each part melded perfectly into the next. The curve of the eye orbits led seamlessly down to the slightly larger-radius cheeks edging the fluted nose. The small smile was warm and happy. He stumbled over a response. 'Um, I don't know. What do you think?'

'Well, I really feel like we're watertight. And the tide came in so quickly, I wouldn't want us to get caught here when it goes out again equally fast. I say "Yes".'

Jack was following the curves on the sides of Vicky's caramel neck. They led his eyes downwards to where they entered the open collar of her white shirt. He was startled from his reverie by the sudden internal question, *How has she kept that shirt perfectly white?* He realised she was waiting for a response. 'OK, yes, let's do it.'

He struggled up off the lifejacket cushions and emerged blinking onto the deck. They looked around the boat together trying to work out how it was controlled when in motion. The small steering wheel turned a rear mounting for the absent motor. 'That's no good,' he pondered.

Vicky lifted the seat of one of the side benches on the deck and removed a long oar. 'Do you think we could use this to steer? I wonder if we might even be able to tie it on to the mounting so the wheel would turn it.'

They worked together, hanging over the back rail of the small boat. It was possible to tie the oar vertically to the little metal strut, but they could not get it to be turned by the steering wheel. With some pressure directly applied to the oar handle, it would move off centre and twist slightly. No marine engineers, they agreed that it ought to function as a rudimentary rudder.

'What about power?' she asked him.

He shrugged. 'I'm assuming, hoping, that the river will just carry us down there.' He pointed downriver, and then moved his hand to point at the middle of the channel where they were moored. 'It certainly looks like it's moving pretty fast.'

She put an elbow on the side rail and leant her chin in the hand. Jack watched her ruminate silently. 'What?' he demanded.

Vicky pointed to the flow that he had previously indicated. 'It's going the wrong way.'

'Eh?'

'Look, the water is flowing upriver.' Jack followed along

110

her slender arm to look at the river. She was right, the water was flowing fast, in the wrong direction. Where he had pointed was the opposite direction to the way they needed to go.

'That, that's physically impossible.' He looked across to the rising sun, which was perhaps ten degrees above the eastern horizon. Jack turned to look around at the bank, then across the buildings to where the road became visible again behind them. Up and down the river showed the bends that they had passed and those that were to come. 'We haven't become disoriented by travelling in the night, maybe?'

She shook her head, watching the flow. 'I think this must be the tide coming up again.'

'The tide. Yes, I do remember Ellie saying that it's big on this river. Does this mean we'll have to wait six hours?' He turned to look at her. 'It does mean we could get some sleep. Although we don't want to miss it, so we'll have to take turns staying awake. But I'm also thinking that actually the flow may stop and turn much sooner than that, 'cause the tide is battling the current, so when they're equal might be the perfect moment. The water will have to kind of stop then, and we could use the other oar to get ourselves into the middle before the ebb restarts. What do you think?'

'I think you're a genius.' Her hair was tied back in a simple ponytail so, without having to move hair out of the way, Jack put his hand on her shoulder as he spoke.

She remained leaning on the rail but turned to smile at him. 'Right, you get back in that cabin and get some sleep. I'll wake you if it happens soon. Otherwise, let's say two hours' sleep and then it'll be my turn.'

He lingered for a moment and then nodded. From within the cabin, he heard her call, 'And have you got a T-shirt? That one is dirty, sweaty and smelly. If you throw it out to me, I'll rinse it in the river, but you'll be better with something cooler

111

anyway.' Jack's planning had not considered that he would need to look good whilst on the run, but he knew he would feel better in clean clothes. He did as instructed, putting on his only other shirt, a navy blue T-shirt.

The vista from the cabin bed showed only Vicky's beige trouser legs, vaguely camouflaged against a background of wood of a similar colour. He balled up the dirty, blue and white checked shirt and threw it out to hit her legs. As she stooped to pick it up, she cast a glance in through the small doorway and grinned.

Jack lay back to try and sleep. The cabin was stifling and he did not expect sleep to come. It seemed like only a moment later when he woke. Vicky had shaken him and said, 'Time to go.' Although it was her normal speaking voice, the tiny cabin amplified it to sound as if she had shouted. The sudden reveille was a shock and he took a moment to get reoriented.

She threw the mooring rope off and the boat immediately slid back from under the west bank canopy of trees. Jack staggered to the back and grabbed the rudder. The boat seemed insistent that it was going to face the wrong way. As he strained to hold the tied-up oar at full lock, Vicky leapt down, picked up the second oar and tried to wiggle it over one side to reorient the little craft. After five minutes wrestling in vain, they accepted that the journey would be on a backwards-facing boat. He adjusted the oar handle to keep them straight and she stowed the spare one.

Vicky wore the broad straw hat he'd only seen her carry up to this point, but she moved it onto Jack's head and insisted that he wear it. The temperature was already in the high twenties, and the water flow quickly built up to push them downstream, heading eventually for the Celtic Sea.

Chapter Fifteen

The Truvas carried out a cup of insipid tea each to join the rest for breakfast. Major Frank fiddled with his moustache and tried to spot differences in the denim threads hanging from the hems of their shorts.

Halthrop had been up since dawn, and the lack of urgency in the posse had been obvious all morning. He looked around the faces at the picnic table. 'Let's get going, people: we should first gain reports from everyone on their sentry observations.'

He looked around the faces of Jane, Terry and Darren. Darren was busily spreading butter on bread; the other two were attentive to their commanding officer. He proceeded, looking at notes on his armulet. 'I'll start us off: I was on watch from 0200 to 0400, I was awake the whole time, and I observed no movement on the far riverbank. I further observed no activity anywhere. Jane, you next, please.'

Although the major had delivered his report seated, Jane stood up to speak. She also referred to notes on her armulet. Continuing round the table, including the twins, covered the entire night, and only the first shift had activity to report. Terry explained that four unknown men had arrived on two ATVs, parked in front of the pub, entered, and then left again an hour later.

Darren presented his report for the final shift, including that he'd seen the big wave coming up the river again, bringing a rush of water behind it. Only Bailey showed any interest in this. As soon as Darren stopped speaking, Truvan leapt in. 'So, where does that leave us? Are we going to wait here forever until they pass? Or head to the ferry and cross over anyway? Do you think Mr Covell really did see them?'

No one spoke. Whilst Halthrop considered, he spotted Jane also stroking along her upper lip. He stopped and put both hands around his enamelled metal coffee cup. 'We clearly need to be on the other side of the river. That will be why we never saw the circular bush that the lady informant described yesterday – we were looking on the wrong side. Thinking back through what she said, it was an easy omission for her to make. The nearest crossing point is the ferry at Sharpness. So, we will make all haste to there, cross over, and come back along the river trail to intercept them. My expectation is that they slept as we did.'

The twins looked across the table at each other, both squinting a frown. Truvan twisted in his seat to ask Halthrop beside him, 'How long are you expecting it to take to get there?'

The map was open on the table and Frank pointed to their position. 'There's no quick, direct route, but if we follow the road here...' He waved behind himself at the road adjacent to the river. 'It's about another ten kilometres to Sharpness, and the ferry journey is around an hour, depending on the wind and the current. Across the water by lunchtime. Does that meet with your approval?'

Truvan shrugged and looked at his twin.

As Darren and Terry pushed the bikes with trailers through the gate onto the road, Jane instructed them to make their navigation records.

From the back of the group, Truvan shouted, 'Vicky!' Everyone turned to look at him, mounted on his horse, facing the river. They all then turned to follow his gaze and saw a wooden boat moving quickly down the middle of the river.

It was cruising backwards, and the person furthest forwards, up to the boat's stern, wore a large straw hat and was looking ahead. They could not be observed in any detail as the low hat brim hid the only parts of the body that were visible.

They maintained a braced leaning position, as if it was all they could do to hang on to a wooden pole that stuck up at the forwardmost end. The second person was a woman, facing the group on the shore.

Major Halthrop took binoculars from a thin storage case suspended between the frame struts of his bicycle. The magnification showed the gold-lettered '*Severn Bore Inn*', and then revealed the face of the sister that the twins had been showing from their armulets. She had a long, lightly tanned face, and her brown hair was tied in a ponytail. Vicky Truva was wide-eyed, frozen; she gawped at the posse.

Halthrop estimated the boat to be moving at twice walking speed, although he knew it was difficult to gauge on the water. He had noticed the tide movements and reckoned that they would be running with the tide for another couple of hours at least.

He looked at the time on his armulet and barked out an order. 'Let's go people, at that rate we'll be hard pressed to get to Sharpness ahead of them. Go, go, go.' He waved forward to Darren and Terry, who were standing at the head of the convoy.

They responded immediately and surged away along the smooth tarmac road. The going was good; the three kilometres of road travel was easy and took less than fifteen minutes. It cut off a meander of the river, around which Jack and Vicky were going to travel ten kilometres.

They transferred onto the towpath of the old navigation canal at Shipton Mill, and this was equally fast going. At times, the twins had to canter to keep up. In another hour, the group arrived at the marina at Sharpness.

The old canal-boat marina was enclosed as part of a harbour built between the main river and the canal proper. To access the river from the marina, boats had to negotiate several harbour areas, via three locks, past old warehouse buildings, before reaching the final exit gates.

There was a giant concrete silo, a temple to the forgotten industrialism of the past. Most of the warehouses had been built of thin metal and were falling down in places. The wide concrete dockside had avoided much of the regrowth of nature, but plants were making inroads in many corners.

The posse stopped at the back end of the final lock before the river. In its heyday, Sharpness Docks had serviced large ocean-going vessels. The final water space was almost eighty metres long, empty, and the water in it was higher than the river level. There were several boats in various states of disrepair in the marina area, two locks further back. Halthrop cursed.

Bailey and Truvan had stopped their horses at a grassy area on the towpath. Bailey called to the major, 'What's up?'

Halthrop pointed to the empty pond beside him. 'The ferry must be on the Lydney side – it leaves from here, but the landing point on the other side is further downriver. It's a couple of kilometres to the southwest.'

The twins looked from their vantage point across the main river and then back to each other. Truvan turned to look upriver, whilst his brother responded to the major. 'I think we can see it over there.' He pointed across the Severn. 'It's pretty hard to tell though. There's something that looks like a boat, but it's a long way away.'

The view of the wide expanse of river extended south into the hazy distance, as far as a giant suspension bridge straddling it. At twenty kilometres' distance, it looked like half a dozen matchsticks stuck together to make a model bridge.

Halthrop turned back to Jane, who was waiting on a small, wooden bridge over a side canal. 'Corporal, two jobs. First, go to the harbourmaster's house and ask the ferry captain's husband if he knows when she's coming back here. He's a Brazilian guy; if I remember correctly, his name is Ricardo.

116

Come back and let me know the answer, and then take the binos back up there and keep watch on the river for our fugitives' boat.' The group watched her cycling away, each person ensconced in their own thoughts.

The major was interrupted by Darren. 'What do you want us to do, Frank?' He became aware that everyone was watching him, waiting for the answer. Even the wind dropped in anticipation. In hot sunshine, he insisted they all wore the Bristol Brigade uniform caps. Halthrop removed his own and wiped sweat from his brow and face using the top of it. He fanned his face with it and looked around the marina at the half dozen watercraft abandoned there.

Across the water of Sharpness old docks, there was a large amount of scrap metal and parts of boats, and a large metal scaffold that once held a crane on top. He looked up to the twins, whose eyes bored into his.

'Ideally, we need to commandeer the ferry and her crew – well, the captain – so that we can intercept Smith and Miss Truva when they get here.'

'If they haven't already gone past.' Bailey's comment was heavy with sarcasm.

Major Halthrop shook his head. 'By river, it's at least twenty kilometres from the Anchor Inn to here. It's not been ninety minutes since we saw them, and their boat was not powered, it was just drifting in the current.' He waited a moment, eyeing up the twins' reaction. They appeared accepting. 'Now, the problem will come if the ferry doesn't return soon.'

He spotted Jane cycling back the short distance. A stocky man stood watching from beside the corner of his house. He wore only shorts and a backwards-facing cap. His skin was a dark colour, and Frank expected that he had little problem with the strong UV rays from the sun.

117

He replaced his camouflage cap to receive the answer from Jane. 'Ricardo says that the tide is very strong at the moment, so the ferry is not scheduled to come back until late afternoon when the tide is coming up, maybe as late as 7pm. He says the electric motors are not very strong against the flow, so they have to go when the waters are with them, and the Lydney landing is quite a way downstream.' Halthrop nodded to her, and she turned to cycle back to the end of the promontory. The short Brazilian had disappeared from view.

'Right, men, we're going to need to sort out boats of our own; we can't rely on using the ferry. I anticipate they will be here in an hour or two, so we need to be ready to take to the water in sixty minutes from now. I want everyone to search one of these boats each and see which ones are seaworthy.' He shouted, 'Jane!' She stopped, stood over her bike frame and twisted her head round. 'Can you ask Ricardo to come down here? We need his help.' Jane waved a thumbs-up sign and carried on.

He stopped shouting, but continued in a loud, authoritative voice, 'Take one boat each – I want a report from each of you in ten minutes. I'll take the furthest one back there.'

Major Halthrop was standing by his bike when the others returned. The twins' light blue T-shirts had large dark stains under their armpits. Only Terry appeared unaffected by the heat and the sun.

Two boats had solar panels and electric motors. The others were without any power. The ferry captain's husband, who also acted as harbourmaster, had informed Halthrop that they could not exit the harbour until two hours before high water at the earliest. They would need to be ready to go at 7pm.

'7pm?' Truvan's voice was a high-pitched squeal. 'We can't wait that long – they'll be long gone by then. You saw how fast they were moving.'

Bailey added, 'Surely we'll be better off chasing downriver on the land and catching them further down? Then we'll be where they are at the high water launch time.'

'Sorry, but we know we have easily accessible boats here that will not sink. We could get scuppered down at those other places.' Frank allowed himself a small smile. 'If you'll pardon the expression.

'Also, with the two boats that have power here, we should be able to catch them easily.'

After a brief glance back to each other, they turned to Halthrop and the other two. 'OK, let's get everything ready.'

One of the boats was called *Top Dog* and Terry had insisted that he would captain that one. Jane was tasked to pilot *Skinny Jean*.

Chapter Sixteen

'How come the locks are still working? What powers them?' Darren was standing on the wide grass strip on one side of the lock that would take them from the old canal marina into the Sharpness Docks rear harbour.

'You do,' Halthrop replied from the deck of the nearer of two narrowboats sitting in the water in the lock. The canal and the harbour area waters were at the same height. 'The locks are mechanical, worked by hand. You'll need to crank that long, white handle round and it'll open the gates. Why do you think I sent you over there?'

Darren grabbed the handle and wound it rapidly. The gate slid open much more slowly than he expected, and after a minute of ferocious turning, he slowed significantly, cheeks red and puffing. 'Come on,' Terry shouted.

For craft that had been abandoned for two generations, both the narrowboats were well appointed. Halthrop assumed that Ricardo and his wife had kept them in good order, although he was unsure quite why. The roofs of both were half-covered in solar panels, and he touched the shiny, smooth surface of the nearest one – at least they would be navigating the Severn with power. The silvery square was hot, almost enough to burn.

Once the gate was fully open, the two boats pootled forwards into the front harbour, and the waiting area for the final exit that connected to the river. Darren bundled along the concrete expanse beside the water.

The harbour had historically taken much larger ships, and the two boats looked lost in the large waiting area. As Ricardo closed up the final lock behind them, Halthrop stood at the bow of the *Skinny Jean* and looked, as best he could, over the gates in front. There was a drop of several metres down to mostly mud in the river. A puddle-deep rivulet of brown water connected the river proper up to the space between two ramshackle wooden piers to the harbour entrance. The gates formed a V shape pointing into the harbour, so the weight of the high water behind kept them closed, although they leaked a significant trickle.

Halthrop looked at his armulet, which informed him it was approaching 3pm, nearly low tide. 'I'll come back when the tide's high enough.' Ricardo wandered away, leaving the posse staring at each other.

'So what do we do now, Frank?' Terry called across. The major frowned and continued his moustache-stroking, left side then right side, over and over.

'I'd say it's gotta be lunchtime,' Darren put in. 'We haven't had anything since breakfast.'

Truvan turned to the major. 'We should watch for their boat coming past.'

Halthrop looked at his armulet again. 'We'll cook for you and Bailey, if you two take it in turns to watch the river.'

Halthrop watched them clamber off the boats and flop down on the ground, leaning against the shaky wall, chatting too quietly for him to hear. Truvan looked over his shoulder, and he and Halthrop caught each other's eyes for a few seconds before the twin returned his gaze to the river.

'There they are! I see them!' Truvan's shout reverberated around the long cabin of the *Skinny Jean*. Halthrop leapt up in the bed and hit his head on the low ceiling. With his head bowed, he quickly felt his way out to the front of the narrowboat and climbed up on to the harbour gate walkway to join the others.

His dozy head cleared as the breeze filled his nostrils and tickled his neat blond haircut. There was a small black spot in the distance in the centre of the river. The course through the low tide mudbanks approached Sharpness by the opposite bank before crossing most of the width to pass close to the harbour's entrance piers.

The small boat was probably still over a kilometre away, and it was difficult to perceive it moving at all. Holding up the binoculars, Halthrop still struggled to make out its occupants. The vessel's general shape and size appeared identical to that which they had seen earlier. Two passengers were visible.

'Jane, go and get Ricardo. The rest of you, let's have everything packed away onto the boats right now, please.'

There was no visible mud between the exit piers now, but there was still probably only a few centimetres' depth of water. After a quick glance upriver at his quarry, Halthrop turned to take a closer look at the water outside the harbour gates.

'It's still two hours till you can get out there.' Ricardo had joined him at the threshold of the long wooden pier into the river channel. His cap was facing forwards now to shield his eyes from the bright sun. 'Wishing the tide up won't bring it any quicker.'

Halthrop looked into the shaded eyes, which stared him out. He put his sunglasses back on, paused, and then turned and pointed upriver. 'The fugitives are on that boat, and we mustn't lose them.'

'If I were you, I'd be much more worried about these two boats surviving the open water. They're underpowered against the rushing tide we'll get today. And are any of you sailors?'

'How quickly can you get us into the river? Forget about seven o' clock, I want to go as soon as is humanly possible.'

Ricardo looked up at Halthrop's face. 'I don't say 7pm to hold you up. We can't open the harbour gates more than two hours before high tide. Quite apart from the difficulty for you of navigating out as the water escapes, the water that is in here holds the gates shut.' He pointed at the expanse of harbour water and the angled barriers. 'This is not a lock, we can't drop the water level so it matches outside, we have to wait till the river is high enough, or the gates are impossibly heavy. I'll come back then.' The man swaggered away.

Terry advanced along the walkway atop one gate and, beyond him, the major could see the other four standing on the decks of the two boats. Terry turned his skinny body to look at the departing harbour-master. 'We're all set to go, Frank. What's the story?'

'Stand them down, Terry. There's nothing we can do till 1900. We'll just have to monitor the progress of Smith and the girl, and hope they're still in sight when we get on to the river.'

Terry's eyes flicked back and forth to different spots on the river. He looked back at his boss. 'There's no way. If the river is full, and it's dark, we'll never catch them. The spotlights on the boats are puny, and we could just motor right past them without even knowing it. We've got to get onto the river sooner than that.'

He walked over to the buildings that had shaded their lunch. Beside them was the shed for the winding mechanism. Terry looked at the giant crank handle. He was thin but, even so, the handle was as thick as his arm. He hung on it so that his entire weight was pulling on it, but there was no movement. Halthrop watched him wiggle his body to try and free the system. It didn't take long before Terry gave up and stepped back outside to look at the approaching boat. It had drawn near enough to be identifiable as a boat with the naked eye.

After Terry spoke to the two crews, they all came and stood on the pierhead to watch the passing of Jack and Vicky. It was torturously slow and much as they watched the river level beside the harbour, it did not seem to be rising at all.

Halthrop noticed Truvan's hands gripping the fence so

tightly they had gone white. He was staring down to the water by the harbour gates. It stubbornly refused to increase in depth, and Halthrop could feel the same tension emanating from all the members of the group. Terry was pacing up and down on the walkways, his eyes never leaving the exit route between the piers.

Bailey broke the peace, 'We've got to get on the water. We've got to catch them before dark, or we'll have no chance. Are there any smaller boats we could drag over the top and drop into the water?'

Halthrop stared at Bailey. The boats they were about to take on to the river were dangerously small, and they had all seen all the boats that were here. He mumbled, 'He will win who knows when to fight and when not to fight.'

Bailey looked into the hut that housed the gate operating mechanism. After a few moments examining it, Frank watched him walk across to a tumbledown warehouse at the side of the docks. He disappeared inside and emerged moments later carrying a couple of metal poles. As he returned, he called to his brother to help use the poles as levers on the winding mechanism.

'Hold on there, son,' Halthrop imposed. 'Ricardo is right. If you open the gates now, you'll just ground the boats as all the water escapes.'

'Yes, and as soon as the tide is high enough, we'll be able to go. The way we're planning at the moment will lose valuable time when the exit is deep enough but we keep on waiting 'cause we're not sure.'

'He's right, Frank,' Terry interjected. 'Also, I reckon that if we move the boats back a bit, we may be able to ride out on the escaping water once the gates are wide enough. When we crack the gates open, the escaping water should help us to get them wide enough, and there's enough water in the harbour maybe even to take us all the way out there to the main river channel.'

From her spot a little way out along the pier, Jane shouted, 'Don't be stupid, Terry, you'll just smash the boats against the gates. We'll never open them enough.'

Terry paused, looking at the boats. 'No. What we can do is move the boats back a long way. As the water level drops, the gates will become easier to open, and when there's enough clearance we send the boats through the gap and the people winding should have a chance to jump on as they go through. When the water's that low, it won't be moving too fast.'

'How do you know?' she retorted, walking back to the group. 'Have you ever even seen harbour gates before?'

'Look, do you want to catch Smith or not?'

'I don't want to die trying.'

'There's no danger of anyone dying. The whole point of this problem is that the water's so shallow.' Terry's tone was haughty, and the major held up his hand to stop the debate.

With a glance to the lowering sun, he commanded, 'We'll try Terry's plan.'

It was difficult from the boats to see the progress in the wheelhouse, so Halthrop shouted, 'Anything happening?' After about a minute without any response, there was a crashing sound from the winch house. 'What happened?' Halthrop called. 'There's no movement of the gates.'

The twins emerged carrying the winding wheel between them. It had sheared off. Although it had been nicely painted, the metal underneath was very rusty.

Halthrop closed his eyes and cursed in his head. Darren interrupted the quiet. He sat on the front end of the roof of the *Top Dog*, legs dangling and swinging in the open doorway like a child. 'We could pull the gates open with the boats. Tie a rope from each boat onto each gate and then motor backwards. I don't know if we'll have enough power, but we could try it.'

'That's brilliant.' Halthrop sounded surprised. 'Take the boats forward and we'll explain to the Truvas.' It was essentially the same plan, but with a new system for opening the exit.

'Look, look,' Jane shouted, pointing past the twins out into the river. Looking into the main channel, they saw an incredible rushing tide surging upriver. Further down, the fugitive boat could be seen being pushed back upriver on the torrent of water.

'Now's the time to go. Both boats backwards now!' Halthrop felt a tingle in his neck.

The motors were engaged and the ropes tightened. They had chosen the thickest ropes they could find and tied them around the entirety of the boats' cabins. If the ropes held and the cabins didn't shear clean off, then they would either open the gates or burn the motors out.

The *Skinny Jean* squealed as it pulled hard against the weight of harbour water holding the gate shut. Terry was working the *Top Dog* just as hard but it struggled noiselessly.

Beyond the harbour, the inrushing sweep of tide was an incredible flood. The water between the piers was already knee deep. The twins shouted encouragement to the boat pilots, and a definite stream of water started spewing through the tiny gap that developed. Slowly but steadily, the gates opened.

By the time there was a metre-wide opening, the water level inside the harbour had noticeably dropped. The wider apart they got, the faster the gates moved, and the greater the rate of flow of water out of Sharpness Docks.

Halthrop was watching all the movements carefully. He wanted to go out at the earliest chance, but also to make sure that the gates would not close again once the ropes were released. Jane told him she had reached a point where she was backing the boat only against the water flow, rather than to cause any pull on the gate. That was the moment. Halthrop shouted the signal, and the Truvas both released the ropes.

The *Top Dog* moved in front of the *Skinny Jean*, and Darren and Frank gathered in their ropes. The gap out of the harbour was a waterfall, and the height difference had dropped to less than three metres. This meant that the twins would have to jump down a metre or so onto the roof as their boat went through, and then the boats would immediately fly out and down in the water cascade.

Terry steered as close as he dared to scraping the inside of the massive door, but the water flow kept him away from hitting it. The boat was picking up speed and he struggled to control it to go as slowly as possible.

Truvan leapt down and Darren grabbed his arms and pressed him down on to the roof. The front end of the boat fell sharply, and Darren and Truvan lifted off the wooden surfaces. As they landed below, the bow bounced off the submerged mud, and they hit the decks hard. Truvan clung on to the roof rail, and Darren clung on to Truvan.

The churning flow pushed them on out into the harbour entrance channel. After another ten metres, the main tidal rush was surging through the wooden lattices of the piers and slammed the long narrowboat sideways against the north pier. The three crew continued to cling on, but the boat was held fast by the force of water. Waves were splashing up against the side and they were quickly soaked.

Halthrop had seen all this, but there was nothing to be done – they had to go in case the untethered gates decided to close. 'Steer much more on an angle to the left. We need to make sure we don't hit them,' he shouted back to Jane.

She set them on a course to pass close to Bailey and then through the gap heading more towards downriver. He was already hanging from the end of the walkway and dropped down as Halthrop grabbed his legs. Bailey fell awkwardly on his side, but the water cascade was already significantly reduced from only a minute earlier. Their passage out of the harbour was less dramatic, and Bailey managed to roll over and cling on facing back towards Jane. She could barely see over the cabin roof, but Halthrop could see in her expression that she had made eye contact with Bailey and there was nothing wrong.

He heard her increase the motor speed to push on past the *Top Dog*. It was making scraping sounds as the rising tide lifted it ever upwards against the wooden struts. Frank could see that, although they were shipping water, Terry and the other two had stabilised themselves and were in no immediate danger. They were simply stuck. The sound of the water was loud, and Halthrop shouted to Terry as they passed, 'Once the tide settles, it'll let you off there. Come and find us as soon as you can.' Terry nodded but did not reply. He gripped the rudder handle tightly.

Looking forwards again, Halthrop could see that Jack and Vicky had been swept a few hundred metres back up the river. As the *Skinny Jean* passed from over the near mud bank into the main river channel, the flow speed was suddenly different. The narrowboat spun violently to the right and Bailey nearly rolled off the side. The major still had a grip on his short trouser leg, and they managed to maintain an ungraceful position on board.

Chapter Seventeen

After a whole day spent drifting downriver, Vicky was still worried about Jack's health. She had insisted that he stay in the shade of the cabin as much as possible. The boat had been consistent that it would only travel backwards, the flowing water buffeting its streamline shape back whenever the little craft turned out of alignment. They had partly grounded a few times, but it had only ever been a bump – they had never become stuck. The mud expanse under the shallow water wallowed like a gigantic jelly and sometimes rose to take them by surprise.

The water was an ugly brown hue but, when a bottle was left to settle for an hour, the taste had surprised Vicky as very good. It was so hot that they had to cycle their bottles continuously: they drank the water as soon as there was no more settling to be had.

After what seemed like an eternity of steady drifting, filling bottles, settling bottles, and drinking the results, she called Jack out of the cabin. His face was mottled red, and his black hair was wet with sweat. The navy blue T-shirt also looked soaked. Jack's facial expression showed interest, but she thought there was an underlying exhaustion, as if he was pushing his body too much in the oppressive heat. 'Tell me if I'm going mad – I've been watching that tree on the bank for a few minutes now, and I'm sure we're not moving at all any more.'

He looked at the tree and leaned on the rail of the starboard side. After a few moments, Jack murmured and nodded agreement and started looking around at the water and other landmarks. It was difficult to survey to the west as the lowering sun was glaring off the water surface.

Vicky plonked her straw hat on his head and stood beside him with a hand resting on his shoulder. She had been right about his shirt – her hand felt it as wet as laundry day – but she kept the hand there. There was no tactile sign that Jack was ill. His shoulder felt thick, stronger than she would have estimated, and when he stood straight upright, she felt him generally fitter than her initial perceptions.

The shoulder noticeably stiffened, and Jack tapped her hand without averting his gaze from the river ahead. 'What's going on there?' He lifted the other arm to point downriver and Vicky felt it brush the side of her breast in passing. Her eyes looked at Jack's profile, and then along the raised arm and on towards the water he was pointing at. The river surface was heavily ruffled right across its width. There was no longer much visible mud in the estuary in front, and a noticeable wave travelled towards them. Their heads turned to look at each other, and their noses were only a few centimetres apart. For a moment, the proximity caused both Jack and Vicky to pause. 'Grab the rudder!'

She leapt back the metre or so to reach their makeshift rudder and grabbed it with both hands. She looked back at him watching her. 'What is it?'

'My guess is that it's the tide coming back in. You'll just have to do your best to keep us as straight as you can. Let me know if you need any help.'

Vicky stroked her hair back, even though it was already tied. She wondered how wild a ride they were in for. The approaching wave looked fairly simple, but she had learnt that the boat responded in strange ways to even the smallest adjustments in the river current. The wave hit the back of the boat and she saw Jack grip the rail to steady himself. It was only small, but the boat rocked them both unnervingly.

Behind the leading wave, there followed the rush of the incoming tide. It was an incredible surge, and they whipped wildly round through 180 degrees. Despite the huge width of open river space, the water's movement roared like sea waves sucking at a cliff cave. The riffles knocked the boat around chaotically, and Vicky clung on to the oar handle, more for support than to steer. She failed to keep it straight in the current, but as soon as there was a slight imbalance in the angle that the hull cut through the flow, they were slung violently back in to line. The symmetrical shape quickly steadied them to point straight downriver, but they were flying upriver. They proceeded at a frightening pace, and the oar handle rubbed roughly in her grip.

He looked back to her again and pointed at the eastern riverbank. 'Look, it's them again.' A long, concrete harbour wall shored up the bank. At the end of this, two wooden piers – giant matrices of wooden planks – trailed out into the river like ant antennae. Between the piers, where they met the huge wall, was a pair of fortress-like wooden doors. On top of these stood her brothers. Vicky was astounded and stared at them. She could see their gaze following her, but could not work out what their vacant expressions meant.

On the way down, they had been much further out and hadn't noticed any people. Closer in, their faces were now well lit by the sun in the west. Normally, Truvan and Bailey were transparent to their sister, but she could not fathom out their emotional state here. Her ruddy-pink lips were apart. The boys distracted her completely.

'Turn it left! LEFT!' Jack's voice penetrated the roar of the water and the block in her mind and Vicky looked forwards again. They were perilously close to hitting the end of the northernmost pier, as it curved into the Severn's main channel.

She leaned hard on the oar handle and the boat responded

131

well. Their course changed briefly before the current knocked them back into line. The deviation was enough, and they continued upriver away from the wall of wooden trelliswork. As she took a final look back towards the twins, she could see that the doors they stood on had parted slightly and a waterfall emerged between them.

Jack and Vicky moved too far up, so the harbour gates became obscured from view by the piers. She turned back to scan the water ahead for potential hazards, but was relieved to see the depth seemed to be ever increasing. The turbid water was always too murky to see the bottom, but the water surface was less agitated. The tidal flow was still an incredible volume, but it was all somewhat more uniform.

She hoped that this calmer scenario would continue until the next time low tide turned upriver again. The sun was setting and they would soon be running blind, unable to avoid any dangers. 'Not that there's much I can do about it any more,' she chuckled with resignation. Letting go of the homemade rudder with one hand, Vicky stared at the beige water a few metres ahead.

Her trance was broken as Jack shouted, 'Vicky, they're on the river.' She looked round and saw a long low craft emerging into the river channel from between the piers. It entered the main channel, and was immediately rotated sharply to point upriver towards them. Jack turned to look at her. His face was shaded, but she was certain it had lost all the day's colour.

Vicky swapped hands on the would-be tiller, curling her long fingers around it tightly. She stood up tall to look beyond the fugitive with whom she had somehow become embroiled. At distance, Vicky half wondered if it was just a huge tree trunk floating. However, the top surface reflected a silvery glare, as the water would have done if it hadn't been so muddy. The rest of the wide river reflected blindingly yellow. She found it all hard to look at, but the brilliance everywhere highlighted the silhouette form of the boat chasing them. And it highlighted a figure standing erect at the front end.

Jack walked back with care to stand beside her. They screwed up their eyes into the dazzling light, in silence, for more than a minute. It took another couple of minutes for them to notice that the distance between them and their pursuers was reducing. This did not surprise Vicky. She had noticed their reduction in speed as the waters calmed, but Jack was insistent that the narrowing of the river meant that the tide should flow faster further up. They were silent again and watched patches of water to try and work out how the current changed. Finally, her observation of a tree branch that moved parallel with them and overtook another, whilst a third travelled downriver nearby, gave them the conclusion that the river was unfathomable.

The current continued to push the little wooden boat northwest across the river width, the way Jack and Vicky had come earlier. They were approaching mudstone cliffs the height of a house. The tops were adorned with deep green trees and bushes, including long trailing branches hanging down over the edge. With the higher water in the river basin, these huge crags on the west bank now dropped into the water. They had passed within a hundred metres of this same cliff face on the way down, but there had been no danger, as the red-brown rock walls had descended into mud at the base. A heavy scent on the breeze, mostly of river water, had accompanied them all day. Here, it also came with a strong overtone of wet vegetation.

Vicky continued to clutch the oar handle, but hoped that the fuller river did not want to take them onto the rocks anyway. Their speed had reduced to what she estimated was about one metre every second. This still felt fast and, as the river curved, they were pointing straight at the cliff face.

Jack put his hand on Vicky's forearm. Neither spoke, but

he gave a foreboding squeeze. She turned to look at his face, but, at that moment, the water flow sent back off the cliffs hit their hull. The boat rocked, and Vicky clung on to stabilise both the rudder and herself. She squealed in pain as Jack gripped tightly on her wrist and pitched with the boat. He first lurched away, causing the pain, and then the pendulum swung back and he fell into her, thumping his other hand into her stomach and knocking the wind out of her. Vicky felt Jack convert his grip on her into a smothering sort of hug as he recovered himself. There was a tug of pain from her hair being pulled. She was unable to speak or breathe and leaned her head forward, both hands supporting with a grip on the oar.

Through escaped ponytail strands that were now hanging in front of her face, she saw that the wave had knocked their course away from the cliffs to a more parallel northward direction. Jack must have realised she had a problem, as he stood at arm's length asking what was wrong. Vicky remained bent forward and just shook her head. As her breath started to return, she stood up and looked at him wide-eyed, still unable to say anything. She put a flat palm to her chest and sucked in a long lungful of air.

'You winded me.'

'Oh.' He paused. 'Shit, sorry, are you OK?' Vicky stood tall, to help her breathing normalise and to indicate that she was fine, and nodded. A breeze pushed all the escaped hair back off her face, and the last few wisps tickled her cheek as they were dragged away.

Beyond him, she could see the pursuing boat moving more up the middle of the river. It was closing, and she could make out the figure of Bailey standing up on the near side at the back. There was a short girl next to Bailey, and the tall man, who had been like a carved figurehead for the previous fifteen minutes, remained standing at the front. The man put his arm horizontally to the side and the little ship turned slightly away from the cliffs.

Vicky realised that her brothers must have motors. She wondered why Truvan was not visible. He could be inside the long cabin but she was surprised that he wasn't on deck watching the action. Jack still had his hands on Vicky's wide hips. When she told him to look behind, he moved around her so that he could see the others, but only let go with one hand.

It felt excruciatingly slow, but Bailey's boat caught up level with them, at a distance of about three times the length of his canalboat to one side. The man at the prow shouted over, 'There's nowhere to go, Smith, please give yourself up now. I'm Major Frank Halthrop of the Bristol Brigade militia. We've been sent by Highnam Kangaroo to take you back.' He was dressed in a military uniform, lean and tall, and had an upright, confident posture and a thin blond moustache.

Vicky looked to Jack, who was staring at the man. Jack did not respond, but Bailey shouted across, 'Vicky, what are you doing? Come home with us.' She looked briefly at her brother, and then back. Jack was handsome, but not in the rugged way the twins were. He still eyed Major Halthrop like an aloof cat, and his arm remained around her waist.

The wind brought the quiet hum of the motor on the other boat to Vicky's ears. She looked at Bailey, who held the roof with one hand. His head shook very slowly and the palm of his other hand was held out, facing upwards, to reiterate the question. Vicky let go the rudder with her right hand and slipped her arm around Jack. She saw Bailey frown, and smiled at him.

The posse boat continued to motor faster and get ahead of Jack and Vicky, who were still floating backwards upstream. The river took their course close along the shape of the cliffs, which curved away to the left again. This gave Halthrop the chance to instruct his pilot to turn left ahead of the two fugitives to intercept. Vicky could see the name of the boat painted under the major's planted feet.

The water current was still strong, and the profile of the narrowboat was all wrong for the manoeuvre. The flow broadsided them and the *Skinny Jean* tilted. She saw Bailey and the girl cling on to the cabin edges. Halthrop stepped one of his feet back to make a new solid platform and held his arms out sideways for balance. They made some progress across to cut off Jack and Vicky, but were being dragged much faster up river. Water was splashing up and over the angled side and rolling across the roof and the small decks. There was a loud, deep grinding sound, and Vicky saw the *Skinny Jean* drag to a stop. Jack pointed and said, 'They must be grounded. Steer left so they can't reach us.'

The continuing pressure against the hull was turning the stationary narrowboat steadily further over. The stocky girl, dressed in the same black trousers and green T-shirt as Major Halthrop, left the back deck and climbed past Bailey onto the increasingly horizontal cabin side. There was a sudden louder crunch. The *Skinny Jean* jolted to a 90 degree capsize and stuck fast. The short girl fell flat down on the cabin side she had been standing on, and Halthrop clung on with the edge of the deck under his armpits. As it halted, Bailey was toppled completely off.

Even at twenty metres distance, Vicky clearly heard a sickening thud as his face bounced off the boat's wooden roof on his way into the water. Jack squeezed her tight, but she wriggled and pushed him away to take a step closer. She could not see her brother at all and pushed hard on the steering oar. Their boat turned across the water race.

Jack shouted, 'What are you doing?' Their little vessel wobbled as she forced it out of the laminar flow. She felt Jack pulling back on her waist, and he stepped around her to push back on their makeshift tiller.

Vicky shoved him away. 'We must help them, Jack. I can't see Bailey, and he can't swim.' Her voice was urgent, higher pitched than normal.

Halthrop and the girl were now standing up on the stricken narrowboat, their backs to Jack and Vicky. 'You'll ground us too,' Jack shouted at her. He tried to push her away from the rudder, but she stood her ground and was strong enough to keep him back using only one hand.

They were ten metres downriver from the *Skinny Jean* and being dragged by the river at an angle. Much as Vicky pushed on the oar to maintain the angle, the current wanted to push them around the sandbank, in its preferred course. At best, she was able to make them go straight forwards towards the capsize.

Vicky felt the wind get knocked out of her again, and the sky went flying up. As Jack landed on top of her in the bottom of the boat, Vicky realised she had been tackled. Jack held her down, and although Vicky had no breath to scream, she writhed violently, kicking and punching. Jack hugged her tightly in the bottom of the boat. She threw him off, stood up in a stoop, and sucked at the air for the second time.

She leapt back to grab the oar handle. It was too late. As she reoriented herself, the *Skinny Jean* was now behind them. The two militia members still stood still. Everyone scanned the water. Bailey was nowhere to be seen. Halthrop looked at Vicky. His face was inscrutable. Vicky felt her eyes fill and she gripped tightly on the oar. Jack sat on the bench, and he looked across to the man who led the posse.

A loud horn sounded, and they all turned to look back towards the harbour. Another narrowboat was now travelling up the river towards its stricken partner. Vicky could make out Truvan standing on the front end waving at them all. She leaned against the vertical wooden pole and tears dribbled from her eyes. 'We must go back and help them.'

Jack replied, 'We can't. When the tide turns we'll see what the situation is then, but for now we can only watch and hope they're OK.'

'I can't believe you stopped us from going to them.'

'We'd be in exactly the same trouble as them now. Don't you remember this big sandbank that we passed on the way down? Right opposite those cliffs.' Jack waved his arms up towards the rock walls that were now left behind.

'Where's Bailey? Did you see him at all? I can't see him.'

'I'm sure he's fine, Vicky. The water must only be standing depth – look, it's not even three quarters of the way up their boat, and that must be only six feet wide. I bet he climbed back inside the cabin to get out of danger of being swept away. That's why you can't see him.' Jack turned around to look at her. He got up and walked back to hug her.

Vicky's vision was still blurry with tears, and she pushed him away. 'I hope Truvan can help them without getting stuck.' The second posse boat was nearing the *Skinny Jean*, and she could see Truvan and a stocky young soldier talking across the water to the other two militiamen. It was too far to hear any of their conversation, but she could see them all waving towards different parts of the water surface. They threw a rope between the boats, but it took several attempts before it flew far enough for Halthrop to collect it and tie the boats together. The index finger of her other hand gently massaged circles on her temple.

Chapter Eighteen

Jack considered the crunching sound Bailey's face had made smashing against the boat as it capsized and he tumbled into the opaque brown water. He did think it surprising, or perhaps ominous, that they had not seen any sign of the man again. But they could not be distracted by any calamity.

Beyond Vicky, the prolonged view of a tree brought Jack's mind back to their situation. He interrupted her meditations: 'We've stopped.'

Vicky turned to look at the nearest bank and stared for a whole minute. She spun round again and looked back to the narrowboats. 'The tide must be on the turn. How long do you think it'll take us to reach them?'

'I have no idea. It's seemed like really sudden changes each time so far.' Jack eyed Vicky. Framed by the glowing green tree behind, she appeared as a vision of Eve in a Renaissance painting. She stuck to her post, but stood on tiptoes and strained to see what was going on with the others.

As the river flow balanced the tidal flow, their boat drifted aimlessly. It no longer maintained its insistent line, and they rotated slowly to a sideways angle. The front of the boat pointed towards the middle of the huge expanse of water, and Jack and Vicky turned themselves to maintain a view of the posse rescuing each other.

There was a line that tied the unaffected boat to the grounded one, and five figures were visible on the decks of the loose boat. It powered slowly backwards. The rope became taut and then strained. The stricken boat had loosened up since it first grounded, as the tide had risen further. It rolled over onto its keel.

Even from their distant location, Jack could see that the boat was sunk. The water surface was now above both decks, and with a door into the cabin at each end of the boat, he knew it must be filled with water.

The crowd on the other vessel engaged in a conversation, which included some looks upriver to the fugitives. There was arm-waving from the man Vicky identified as her brother Truvan. Finally, a big man, with a haystack of flaxen hair, untied the connecting rope and threw it in the water. All five turned to face Jack and Vicky's direction, and the long thin boat started moving towards them.

As the sun dropped completely out of sight, colour left the scene. The approaching craft and its crew became shadows. It looked like a giant sarcophagus floating across the Styx with a complement of undead mariners. The wind had gone completely, and the still quiet exacerbated the sinister appearance of their pursuers. Jack thought he should shiver, but with the temperature still over 25 degrees, he did not.

'Where are they going?' Vicky's eyebrows were furrowed, and her finger went at 100 rpm. Jack gawped back at the underworld ferry and joined her in frowning. They had changed course to head upriver, just as Jack and Vicky were passing the capsized boat on their way downstream.

Halthrop presided over the navigation from the front deck. Over the course of quarter of an hour, he pointed the directions to turn, and they made a number of zigzag movements, which finally completed a circuit right around their shipwreck. As the posse set off on fresh zigzags, tacking further out from the *Skinny Jean*, it became difficult for Jack to always see them. Silhouetted against the wide river, they were visible, but with the banks behind, they often slipped into shadowed invisibility. The wind came back and there were quiet noises of water lapping at the prow as Jack and Vicky slid downriver, stern first.

Voices reached them but were not comprehensible. The odd word was clear, but contexts were not. '...now...' '...Terry...' '...steering...'

At the sound of the name 'Bailey', Vicky called into the gloom, 'Truvan, are you there? Is Bailey alright? What happened to him?'

There was no clear and direct response. They could still only make out a few words, from various voices: '...water...' '...searching...' '...but you...' '...swim...'

It had become dark enough that Jack could barely see Vicky. He slid forward to stand near her. 'He'll be fine. Don't worry.'

Vicky exploded. 'What do you mean, "fine"? You saw him hit his head as he fell in the water. That could drown anybody. Bailey can't even swim.' Jack moved closer and put his hand on Vicky's on the oar handle, but she shook him off.

'I know, but remember that the water is only chest deep. If he was cut, or even broke his nose, he could still stand up. He doesn't need to swim.'

'What if he was knocked out though? And why are they searching for him? If he hasn't drowned already, he will die in the water overnight. The tide is still rising.'

'They're searching for *us*.'

'What?' Although Vicky was just a presence, a shadow in front of him, Jack noticed her take a step back into the rear corner. He could feel her gaze boring into him. In his mind, Vicky's expression was of confused indignation.

'They couldn't be sure where the river course would take us exactly, and how quickly it would get dark, so they took that spiral course to try and make sure they'd intercept us. I think we got lucky that it didn't work.'

'Lucky?' Vicky's voice was a strangled shriek.

Jack turned back towards the for'ard direction and across the water. The moon rose, orange and languid. He watched it bloat a little more before it shrank back and lost the portentous colour. Despite the extra light, the posse boat had vanished.

Jack was brought back to their reality by snuffling sounds from the back of the boat. He turned and Vicky was illuminated by the full moon. She was slumped against the rear, crying to herself. Jack moved to sit next to her and she continued without seeming to sense him. Her hands were clasped in her lap, and neatly tied hair hung forward at the right side of her face. An occasional falling tear caught enough moonlight to be visible and Jack wondered what to do. 'Are... are you OK?'

She made no answer and her posture did not change.

He tried to comfort with an arm around her sagging shoulders. She still made no movements, even as he pulled her into his chest. Vicky's crying did become quieter, but he could feel her shaking still, and several tears landed on his forearm. He tried to stroke her hair gently, as he had seen men do for crying women in many of the old videostories. Jack felt awkward, especially as she made no movement to help and they were in a squashed embrace, but he persevered.

After a couple of minutes, Vicky's uncomfortable position softened and she leaned more against him. After a few more minutes, he heard her voice croak, 'I've lost him, Jack. Bailey's gone.' Jack did not want to sound as if he was automatically gainsaying her grief, so he said nothing and continued hugging. 'Why did they have to chase us on the river? He knew he couldn't swim.' Vicky's head remained hanging and she wiped her face a little. After a quiet period, she continued, 'Why did I have to come away with you? Bailey would still be alive if I had just let you go on your own.'

'Sshhh.' Jack's thoughts whirled: he needed Vicky to be positive about their expedition; she was the one person that he knew believed in him. He could not lose her support. 'We don't know anything for sure. I'm sure he is with them and they're searching for us. They'll have him inside wrapped up warm and dry to recover from his scare in the water. That's why we couldn't see him.' He felt a distinct stilling of Vicky's trembling. Slowly, she sat upright and looked in his face. They could see each other well in the bright moonlight, and her eyes flicked left and right looking at his eyes.

'Do you really think so?'

'Of course. I know the work of the militias. That Major Halthrop will know very well what he has to do to look after his people, and he'll have insisted that Bailey stay in one of the beds inside that second boat.'

Jack and Vicky looked back upriver where they could now clearly see the posse. The light was again good enough that the boat was plain in the river. Before Vicky had a chance to raise any objection or query, Jack carried on, 'And they'll be hanging back from us so they don't get into any problems again whilst Bailey isn't a hundred per cent.' She looked at him, and Jack felt that his credulity was slipping.

'I need to go back. I can't leave my family, Jack.'

'This isn't forever. We just need to evade capture long enough for people to understand how important their privacy is. Once they've got the hang of it, the people themselves will change our society; I've done all I need to. Except to stay hidden until they've all experienced privacy.'

Jack could see questions and confusion passing across Vicky's face. Too many for her to nail down one question and articulate it. He continued whilst he had her attention, 'You know I want to go back to Highnam and live the peaceful life I left behind. I want to go back and work Ellie's farm and enjoy the fruits of my labours like you do.' He wasn't sure if these claims sounded plausible, but gambled further, 'And I want to go home and have a family as well. Little Smith boys... and, maybe, Truva girls.'

She turned her head slightly on its side and eyed him from that angle. Vicky did not speak, and Jack decided he would not give her a chance to. 'The Times brought us back to small village communities where people really engage with each other meaningfully. You know I love my family heritage the same way you do. I just don't have quite the same extent as yours. Let me tell you more about my mother and father.'

Chapter Nineteen

'Military tactics are like unto water; for water in its natural course runs away from high places and hastens downwards.' Halthrop spoke to himself on the small foredeck of the *Top Dog*.

The moon shone and he could see the dark hulk of the stricken *Skinny Jean* to their rear. He had participated previously in the recovery of two separate drowning victims in the Severn near Bristol. Both of those bodies had had functioning armulets.

When he and Jane had been rescued onto the *Top Dog*, Major Halthrop instituted a spiral search pattern to try and find Bailey. As night had become darker, Terry complained that it was increasingly difficult to steer the *Top Dog* in the barrelling tide.

Once their search pattern had become uselessly far from where they started, Frank told Terry to return to the capsized narrowboat. They manoeuvred carefully and tied onto it.

Halthrop sat on the cabin roof at the bow end, his body facing his quarry. Somewhere in the dark distance, Jack Smith was drifting away from them. The moonlight was superseded by the dawn, and he considered their possible next moves. Everybody else slept.

Frank watched the sun rise and lightly stroked his moustache. As the brightness increased, he could make out differences in the colour of the river. The boat had become very still, and he realised that the tide had gone out and gently left them aground on the mud bank that had caught the *Skinny Jean*.

He looked all around. They were near the southern end of the exposed mud, as the remaining water-filled channel cut across just ahead of them, from hugging the western cliff wall to follow a central path between the banks. The water only occupied about half the width of the entire river, and the mud peninsula they were on connected to the north to a much larger expanse. 'Bugger,' he muttered. The *Top Dog* was high, if not quite dry.

Truvan stepped out of the cabin at the other end of the boat. Halthrop watched him turn through a full circle, looking all around. Without a word, he leapt off the boat onto the mud and immediately squelched to knee depth. He stopped moving and tried to lift a foot out. Frank leapt up. 'What are you doing?' he shouted.

'I'm going to check the boat for Bailey.' He twisted his body round to look at Frank. 'Or at least that's the idea. I'm not sure how I'll go with this mud.'

Halthrop turned to look downriver and held a hand to add extra shade to his sunglasses. 'I've no idea when the tide may come in – we'd better get you out of there quickly.' He bent and banged a flat palm several times on the roof of the cabin. 'Get up you three.'

He turned back to Truvan and walked along the roof to the stern. The solar cells on the roof were fragile and covered it in four groups. It was necessary to jump over each section with great care to avoid damaging them. Major Frank had instructed that everybody should walk along the narrow side walkways, and hoped he would make it to the end before any of his men spotted him breaking his own rules. He realised that the noise of his boots landing hard after each leap was a giveaway, but further hoped that they would think this was more of his reveille alarm call.

Truvan's full extent came into view. His brown, hairy legs projecting him up from the mud bank starting at the knees. 'Tell me about your situation.'

'What?'

'How stuck are your feet? How solid is the mud? Are you sinking? I need to know what help you need.'

'Oh, right. I'm not sinking, I don't think. But I'm pretty stuck. I haven't tried sitting or lying down, but just pulling my feet up isn't getting anywhere.'

Halthrop looked around the mud, and around the boat and then back to Truvan. The twisting was difficult to maintain, so the twin turned back to face the capsized boat that might contain his brother. He leaned slightly from side to side, rocking and tensing on alternate sides.

Darren emerged beneath Halthrop's feet. He looked like a living scarecrow, his trousers and boots incompletely fastened, and his hair a tangled blond mop. When he turned to look up to his boss, his cheeks were rosy and his eyes half closed. 'What's up?'

'Truvan has got himself into a slight spot of bother. We need to get him out of there.'

'Are you stuck?' Darren called.

'Yes, I'm fucking stuck.' Truvan did not turn around. 'Throw me down a wooden board or something.'

From within the cabin, Jane's muted voice escaped. 'I'll get the bed support.'

Darren turned to look briefly in the cabin and then stepped forward to the rope stay where they had tied up the connection to the *Skinny Jean*. He untied it and moved the hawser to a different metal ring at the other side. This served to change the course of the rope so that it passed close over Truvan's head. 'Look up. Above your head; that rope will help you steady yourself.' Halthrop smiled.

Holding the line with his right hand, Truvan used this as a brace to turn his body to look to the posse. Jane emerged with a wooden board a metre wide and two metres long. With Darren's

147

help, she lowered it down to the mud and pushed it so it fell forward, next to Truvan.

He clambered onto the board, held the overhead cable and moved to the end nearest the *Skinny Jean*. Dirt had splattered his face, and the stubbly beard had dark lumps in it. 'I have to go and check inside the other cabin, but I'm just going to sink every time. If I go hand over hand on the rope, can you see any way of helping me if I don't make it all the way and get stuck again?' They all stared at him. 'Bailey may be in there. If he's alive we can help him.'

'Hang on.' Jane turned and disappeared back inside the cabin. From within, she could be heard berating Terry. 'Get up, lazy, we need your bed.' There was a muffled groan and some banging noises. Jane reemerged with another identical board. 'If we use this board as well, you can pass them round each other as moving stepping stones. Terry, come on, you've got a job.'

It was slow going, but settling one board and then standing on it and passing the other around to a new position in front made progress.

Jane was sent to the foredeck to monitor the incoming tide, which had definitely turned.

Truvan and Terry had to assist each other to clamber up over the slippery hull. They came out with a variety of wet bags and set off on the return journey. Once they had made it about halfway back, Darren enquired about Bailey. Truvan shook his head but said nothing. Terry answered that there was no sign of him, but they had retrieved his bag. This brought a hush to the group. Only a gentle lapping of the river around them caused any sound.

Halthrop's eyes on the water at the edge of the mud bank insisted that the level was rising. The change was almost too slow to be observable. Jane stood with her hands on her hips and scanned the water flow downriver. Frank caught her eye as she turned back to him at the other end of the *Top Dog*. She nodded, and there was a pause between them before she shouted, 'I think the water's coming. How are they doing?' He waved for her to come back and join them.

'There's no panic, men, but the tide is gently rising now. Just keep working steadily, and you'll get back here fine.' The two expeditionaries looked wildly all around, and then looked up at Halthrop. Independently, both had taken on sour expressions, hard frowns. They said nothing and went back to the methodical rhythm they had established for moving themselves and the equipment across the mud.

By the time the bags were all thrown up to Darren and Jane, the water was ankle deep all around the *Top Dog*. It posed no danger as Terry was pulled aboard, but then the great rush of the tide surged up. It was a shock to all to see how quickly the depth increased, and the incredible rate of flow. Truvan was pulled up, dripping, and they all sat and watched the swell.

'I'm sorry we haven't found your brother.' Halthrop had squatted down on the cabin roof.

Truvan turned to look up at the major, and then stood so they were nearly face-to-face. He hissed, 'How sorry are you about that? Or are you more sorry to have lost Smith?'

Frank did not shift his position and held eye contact with Truvan. 'We do this job to maintain the safety of everyone in the Kangaroos. There would be no point in sacrificing lives in order to catch fugitives – that is not for the benefit of all.'

Whilst Halthrop's tone had been calm and neutral, Truvan continued with vitriol. 'How could you possibly have been so stupid? Steering over a mud bank was always going to be dangerous. Look at the water flow.' He waved his hand to the side without turning away from Major Halthrop. 'It's obvious where the shallower water is. And you knew Bailey couldn't swim.'

'I am sorry that your brother is lost. When the tide is as high as it was when we got here yesterday, you cannot see the differences in water flow. But the main problem is that these boats are not meant for the open river – they're canal boats.'

'And you insisted that we chase the two of them on the river. We said that we should follow them on the banks and catch them when they landed.'

Terry interjected, 'Hang on, Bailey was the one who was most adamant that we should leave the docks too early. That was the main reason that our boat got stuck against the pier wall – because we left too early. And that meant that our two boats were separated. I bet we could have done much safer manoeuvres if we'd had both boats together to intercept Smith.' Truvan turned violently and raised his body up tall. Halthrop held a flat hand up towards Terry to silence him.

'Enough.' He paused. Truvan took a half step closer to Terry, which was all that was needed so that they were nose to nose. Louder, the major emphasised, 'Enough!' He paused again, and nobody moved or spoke.

Truvan stared up at Halthrop. 'We're not leaving here till we find him.'

Halthrop paused and leant down and forwards, even closer to Truvan. He spoke softly. 'I know you don't want to hear it, but we may never find Bailey. I am certain that the only way he could still be alive is if he's made it to shore. And if not, his body will be travelling downriver; probably at the same speed as your sister, as they're drifting too. If anything, I'd say we have more chance of finding him if we chase our fugitives.'

'Our sister is not a fugitive,' Truvan shouted, his eyes bulging.

Frank held up an apologetic hand. 'Sorry, you're right, we don't know what she's doing exactly.' He let his apology sink in for a few seconds before he broached their departure again.

'Are you agreed that we should continue on downriver and try and find Vicky?'

He clenched his grasp on the cabin roof, blanching the skin, closed his eyes, and finally nodded. Halthrop stepped down, very close beside him on the tiny deck, and put a hand on the man's shoulder. 'We'll find her.' Truvan did not open his eyes, but gave another smaller nod.

'Jane, you stow all the bags, and make us some tea, please.' The water was sufficiently high that the barge was again floating, free of the mud bank. 'Darren, untie us off that line. Terry, make a course downriver as fast as she'll go, please.' He held his arm out to indicate to Vicky's brother that they should enter the cabin.

The two senior men sat down together at the galley table and opened a map of the area north of Bristol, covering several kilometres of the river, down as far as the southernmost road bridge. Looking again at the drained eyes of the remaining twin, he remembered Sun Tzu: *It is only one who is thoroughly acquainted with the evils of war that can thoroughly understand the profitable way of carrying it on.*

Out loud, Halthrop said, 'We're currently here, at Purton, or Waveridge Sand.' He pointed at the map and everybody looked at his finger. 'With the wrong tide at the moment, I expect we'll take a good while to get to the first bridge here.' He slid his finger along a blue river channel to a straight line of darker blue road. 'I'm guessing a bit, but as we head further on, the turn of the tide will then assist us. Essentially, we should have our motor power advantage on Smith, as we'll get the same drift he does, but also power from our motors.' He stopped to think for a moment. 'Let's say we have three or four knots on them, and they have twelve hours on us. Hmmm.'

Jane unfurled another map showing a more northerly section of the river and Gloucester. From behind it, she was not

151

visible, but said brightly, 'Yesterday, they made... about twenty-five kilometres in six hours, with the tide. It only stopped them when they got here.' The area on the table was too small to also accommodate the second map, and when Jane held it vertically, her arms spread wide, she occupied a significant proportion of the dining space. Frank pushed it down, so she folded it up and sat down.

He looked across at Truvan. 'We'll catch them, the question is when. And again, we have the problem that if it's at night we'll miss them in the expanse of estuary. I'm pretty confident they won't be able to land, as their drifting will force the boat into the fastest water, which is the deepest channel, which will keep them away from the river banks. Jane, go and remind Terry to stay in the fastest water current, that way we'll follow their route even when we can't see them. Actually, you take over the piloting and send him in for some breakfast.' She had leapt up and Terry was at the teakettle almost before Halthrop had finished speaking.

'How are the batteries?'

Through a fistful of bacon sandwich Terry replied, 'Full.' He quickly swallowed the first mouthful. 'It's blazing out there, they're charging faster than we're using them now the cooker's off.'

The extra man pointed at the map. 'Bearing all of that in mind, I'd reckon my sister will be somewhere between the bridges by nightfall. Definitely no further than the old M4 bridge, and I'd guess it just depends on how much the current slows up further down. Can we make it there before dark?'

'Touch and go, I think, is the answer.' Frank pointed back at the lower edge of the map. 'Trouble is that when the river is five kilometres wide, it won't be easy to spot them. And there's no telling how wide the main river current will be.'

Truvan shrugged and nodded. 'We'll just have to do what

we can. If it's OK with you, I'll keep watch on deck, just in case I can spot Bailey.'

'Of course. In fact, if you station yourself at the front, then you can warn Jane if there are any hazards.'

Truvan rubbed his fists in his eyes, pushed himself up and stooped out of the rear doorway. Those left in the cabin could hear his movements along the outside to the front of the *Top Dog*.

The day continued to heat up – Frank noted 33 degrees in the cabin. With the front door opened up, they got a breeze passing through, but the atmosphere still became languid. The sunshine off the water was blinding. Those on watch hid their eyes and quickly became bored and distracted.

Chapter Twenty

Jack and Vicky woke in each other's arms, slumped against the back corner of their boat, and still adrift in the middle of the River Severn. Jack blinked against the light of the morning. The sun was not even above the horizon yet, but the sky was again bright and clear – blinding after the dark of sleep.

Once again, the water formed a narrow stream stranded within banks miles apart. Vast swathes of the basin were shimmering mud bank, only slightly darker than the glimmering ochre of the water. The air was filled with a sour fishy stench and occasional passing seagulls. They floated in a channel beside the eastern bank, which was formed of craggy rock walls. The russet cliffs occasionally parted to allow reedy flats down to the water's edge. Although tiny crashing waves hinted at the dangers of the rock palisade, the river's current did not have any interest in pushing the boat too close. They maintained a steady, safe distance without needing to assist the navigation.

Vicky slipped out of Jack's embrace and stood on the other side of their vertical tiller. She leant down to reach the wide straw hat and placed it back on his head. Jack looked up at her face. The sun was just rising behind her, and even with the hat, he needed a hand to shield his eyes. Vicky looked tired. Her long, narrow features seemed wrinkled and there was darkness in the skin around her eyes. He could not decide if they were simply shadows or real signs of fatigue. The main water channel turned westwards to cross the estuary and hug the opposite bank, but they were making virtually no progress.

Jack scanned landmarks all around them. 'Looks like we're slowing up again. I guess the tide is about to turn.'

As she looked all around, her hand moved with her head

so the two never separated. The estuary had become very wide overnight. Everything seemed larger, grander. The river was now a panorama where night had fallen on a vista. 'You're right, you know. It looks like we're set for going two steps forward and then one step back all the way.'

After several stationary minutes, drifting aimlessly, the boat spun slowly to face downstream and they began to move back upriver, tail first, past the long rock embankment. 'I don't see the boat chasing us at all, do you?'

He looked up at her, but Vicky's head was turned so that the straggly ponytail was all he could see of her head. 'Could you take the rudder, please?' Without looking at him, she let go of the tied oar handle and walked forward, ducking into the cabin.

He stood and took hold himself. Through the little doorway, Jack saw her curl up on the lifejackets with her back to him. It was reassuring to feel the wood in his palms. The steering was trouble-free, but it gave him something to concentrate on. It kept his mind away from the soft sobbing that emanated from Vicky.

He maintained a vigilant survey of the water ahead and of the proximity of potential hazards. No such hazards existed, but by watching carefully for them and assessing every slight ripple on the water surface, he successfully avoided looking back into the forecabin.

Monitoring the time on his armulet, Jack saw 47 minutes go by before the major rush of incoming tide hit them. The armulet thermometer said 26 degrees. He pondered how hot it must be in the little cabin where Vicky remained in a foetal position. Her body was now still, and he hoped she had stopped crying and gone to sleep.

Jack considered how he himself had responded to Grannie Ellie's death. The way he remembered it, he had made a point of getting on with things and not letting it get to him.

The Times of Malthus had been caused in part by excessive human longevity, which exacerbated the overpopulation in the early part of the century. Every day of the Times had inured people to death and suffering. Society reverted to a naturalistic approach to the cycle of life. People would grieve, but it was much more positive than prior to the 2030s.

Through the small square opening, Vicky's drawn shoulders and messy tangle of hair were motionless. Jack considered which aspect of grief she might be feeling. His memories of her, crying in the snow, seemed as clear as if it had been only last winter. She had spoken to him of her mother's death clearly and succinctly, as if she were recounting one of their sheep getting stuck in the snow and succumbing. The tears rolling down her cheeks as the snow blew around them had seemed to be incidental. Young Vicky had not tried to wipe them away, or stop crying. She simply let it continue as part of normal physiology, like heavy breathing when running.

Jack had both hands clenched around the oar handle and had to consciously relax the grip.

He pushed the straw hat a little further back on his head to survey the entirety of the river. Jack's short but thick brush of hair had built up a sweat under the brim, and exposing this to the air brought a sudden itchiness.

The Severn had filled to the sides; no mudbanks were visible. Jack could observe different rates of water flow, which intimated the presence of the shallower areas that had been exposed mud less than an hour previously. There was no sign of anyone in any direction. A number of landmarks were visible – in the southerly distance, the huge, hanging road bridge – but he could not see people, nor any boats.

'Where are we?' Vicky's face was framed by the dark

wood of the cabin doorway. It looked as dishevelled as the tangled head of hair he had seen lying inside the cabin minutes earlier. Possibly her appearance was rough from being still half-asleep, but Jack thought there was something deeper. She looked raddled: pale, hollow-cheeked, dark eyes.

'Just on the turn again. The tide took us back along that long cliff, so we'll be starting again from the back end of that. No problem though, back and forth as before.' There was a pause as Jack watched Vicky clamber through the little portal and stand unsteadily. She turned slowly around to take in the full scene. Jack gambled: 'There's still no sign of the others. I'm wondering if maybe they had to take Bailey for medical attention. That'd be the only reason they'd give up the chase.'

Vicky stared directly at him, and Jack squirmed. He kept a stoic thoughtful expression, not daring to allow anything else to show through. She turned and stared downriver at the old suspension bridge. 'Maybe we could land for a while. Find something to eat and drink; and I could do with a wash. I feel really sticky, and I expect I stink.' She looked back and gave a watery smile.

'I'd rather we keep going. The tide's about to give us a big push, and with its to-ing and fro-ing all the time, we need to keep going as much as we can. I'm keeping my fingers crossed that the islands you talked about will be far enough offshore to be a problem for the audiopt feeds when they get them back online.'

'Is that likely? I thought you had to be quite a long way out to sea before you lost them.'

'Yes, that's generally true, but I'm hoping that the infotechs are prioritising the more important locations if they only get them back online a bit at a time.

'There's a bucket in the bench storage box.' Jack pointed to the long plank they had lifted to find the oars. 'Perhaps you could pull up some water and wash on board?' His tone made this a question. 'And I don't know what food we have left, but I am starving, so perhaps you could get it all out and we can work out what we can eat and what we should save.'

'There's nothing. We ate the last of it yesterday. We won't starve just yet, if you want to wait till after this tidal push before landing, but we will have to get more food soon.'

'I tell you what, there is some fishing equipment in the other storage under the bench on that side.' He pointed to the seat along the starboard side. 'I've never fished before, but we could give it a try.'

'I'll wash first.' Vicky nodded. 'But fishing is a good idea – we're gonna need to do it when we're on the island, so we should definitely make sure we have the equipment we need before we get far enough from the shore to make landing impossible.' She paused and looked up from the water surface to his face. 'And you should wash too.' Vicky grinned, and Jack felt his mood lift significantly. He gave a closed-lipped smile back, trying not to give away too much of his happiness.

She released her hair from its bonds and it sprawled around her shoulders, separate locks having running battles with each other. Having tied a rope onto the bucket handle, she stripped off all her clothes and made a neat pile on the wooden roof of the front cabin. There was a mild camber to the roof, and she placed the clothes carefully in the exact centre so they wouldn't fall.

The boat drifted back end first, so Jack should have been monitoring the water in the opposite direction to Vicky's naked body. As they moved quite fast, he mostly did so. However, he told himself it was important to keep checking that she had not fallen in; she sat right on the point of the prow to gather water and undertake her ablutions. Generally, he only caught sight of her smooth back. The water quickly tamed her hair and streamed down the pale brown shoulder blades and the small of her back. A pool puddled around her bottom before gravity got the better of it, and the water returned to the fluvial mass.

He saw her methodically rinse each item of clothing, and then spread all the clothes on the cabin roof and lay down fully flat in their midst. Jack felt his breath catch in a constricted throat at the sight of her soaking up the sunshine. He turned and focussed on the watercourse ahead.

Vicky spoke and Jack turned. Her eyes were closed and she remained basking. 'If you carry on navigating until my clothes are dry, then I'll take over and you can wash. I tell you, I feel a thousand times better now. The water's pretty salty this far downriver, but although it looks muddy, it doesn't seem to leave any dirt behind. And that sun feels so good on my skin.'

Jack was breathless and could think of nothing to reply. He tried to say, 'OK', but it came out as more of a croak.

They headed towards a small rocky promontory with an old light tower on the top. The current turned south before they reached any danger from the rocks, which quickly gave way to flat grassy banks on Jack's right for as far ahead as he could see. These brought a smell of farm meadows, and a gentle breeze cooled his skin in the shadow of the hat. In the distance, the land jutted into the estuary in front of them and the giant bridge set off across the river towards the eastern bank. The two white pillars of the bridge were clear against the blue sky, although they still looked no bigger than Jack's fingernail.

He stole another look at Vicky Truva. Her eyes remained closed, and she had her right hand up beside her head. The hand was motionless though, and Jack assumed she had either fallen asleep or become distracted. His eyes were drawn to her breasts, and after following the outline up and over each of them, he turned quickly away again.

When the bridge towers had grown from fingernail size to

the height of his hand, Jack felt Vicky touch his shoulder. He got a start and turned violently. Now reclothed, she smiled and put the hand onto his cheek. 'Just me, scaredy-cat.'

The tension left his body and he smiled back. 'You must be the cat, moving silently like that.'

'Time to switch over. You get washed now. And I'm sorry, I forgot all about trying to catch a fish. Why don't you see if you can manage it while you're up on the front there.'

Jack did not comment. He stepped around her and strode for'ard. Without a pause, he boldly stripped off and clambered onto the wooden deck over the cabin. Jack turned to look at Vicky, but she was watching the river ahead. Her ponytail was neat again and draped over the collar of her white shirt. She had started their journey with a delicate, yellow scarf adorning the shirt. This was now tied beneath the ponytail and around her brow as a headband. The ribbon it left dangling at the back flitted occasionally in the gentle wind.

The rush of the water through his toes felt cold and it tickled. Jack sensed the breeze, warm on his white skin. He surveyed his own naked body: short limbs with dark hairs, which highlighted the paleness of the complexion. The torso was oval, an African leather shield shape. He wasn't exactly skinny, but Jack did not carry an athletic musculature.

The bucket of river water poured over his tight, black hair was staggeringly cold. He took a sharp intake of breath and placed the other palm flat on the deck. As the air returned to his lungs, Jack found that the rays of sunshine on his body were delightful. Moments earlier he had felt hot and sweaty, and the sun had made these discomforts seem endless.

Every minute or so, Jack repeated the dousing, and extended it with rubbing of his skin in an attempt to effect some washing. He was unconvinced that he would become any cleaner, but the whole experience was invigorating. He followed Vicky's lead: after rinsing through his clothes, Jack laid them out across the wooden surface and lay himself down in the middle. He twisted his head around to look at her at the tiller, but still saw only her back.

After some time drying out, Jack felt his stomach gnawing for sustenance. He estimated it had been nearly a whole day since they last ate. The noise he made retrieving a fishing line from the bench storage attracted Vicky's attention.

'You'd better put your clothes back on if you're going to sit in the sun for very long.' Jack looked up from his bent over position and caught Vicky's eyes for a second. Her look backed up the appeal to protect himself from the sun. He did not speak and went back to rifling through the junk in the store. When he stood and closed the lid, fishing rod and tangled line in hand, she was again on watch to their front. Jack laid the rod on the cabin roof and pulled his damp clothes back on. They felt sticky as the wetness redissolved the salt on his skin.

It took ten minutes to untie the knots in the line. Vicky confirmed that they had eaten absolutely everything and had no bait of any sort. The hook already attached to the line had a colourful ribbon, and Jack hoped this lure would be sufficient. He practised working the line in and out and ascertained how the reel functioned. Vicky added that she too had no angling knowledge and that he should try his best guesses at what might be the most successful approach.

The preparations had accelerated Jack's hunger and he paused for a moment to let a stomach pain pass. He supported the rod between his legs on the cabin roof and pulled out a few yards of line, which he draped into the water to dangle behind the boat. Almost immediately, he had a bite. The reel rattled out fast. Jack grabbed the handle, and the line became instantly taut and started to bend the pole and pull on him. Jack gave a tug on the rod, but everything was fast becoming dangerous. If he did not get pulled into the water, the line would break.

He shouted to Vicky, who reminded him that they could not slow the boat. Contradicting this, she steered sideways out of the main river flow, and they did reduce speed slightly.

The line was still at breaking point, and they had not completely stopped. Jack released the spool so that more line played out. He blocked it again and pulled back hard on the rod. This merely served to put him in the same position but with a greater length of fishing line out.

Within thirty seconds, the same situation was reached again, with the rod heavily curved and the nylon cord utterly strained. He gave another big heave and fell backwards. The line went slack as the empty hook and yellow ribbon lure flew back over his head and landed at Vicky's feet. There was a tangle of green weed around the line. She looked up from the hooked leaves at him sprawled on his back and laughed. Jack clung to the rod and twisted his head to look at her. He saw the riverweed that he had caught, laid his head back, and dissolved into laughter as well.

The second attempt did not generate any immediate excitement. Nor did it offer up any fish. Jack tried a few different techniques: waving the rod slowly back and forth, and then slowly sideways, holding it dead still, winding the hook in and casting it back out again repeatedly. None of his efforts were rewarded with even another catch of weeds.

They switched roles, and Jack realised that he felt quite weak from hunger. They finished the last of their fresh water – the river water was now too salty to drink, whether settled or not. Vicky insisted he put the hat on. Jack sat at the rear and spent more time watching Vicky fish than he did watching the river.

By noon, the temperature was 33 degrees. Jack leant against the vertical oar handle, his eyes closed. 'Wooooh!'

Vicky squealed. He opened his eyes to see her reach out and grab the line just above the head of a fish at least a foot long. When she looked at Jack, her eyes were ablaze and her smile looked unbreakable. Vicky carried the whole lot down onto the main deck and wrestled the writhing fish off the hook and into the empty bucket. It leapt about so much that the bucket flipped over and it lay flapping on the floor. Jack and Vicky looked at each other, still smiling.

Neither of them knew the type of fish she had caught, but it was large enough that they would both eat well. Jack remained notionally manning the rudder, and Vicky searched out his big knife from the rucksack. She cut off the head to kill it, and maintained that they should eat it raw to keep as much of the water in its flesh as possible.

It was a slow process, but she cut off pieces and fed them to Jack as he steered. He found the flesh very chewy, so Vicky started him off with some bite-sized organs she found in the guts. She did her best to catch the blood in a cup, but there were other fluids of varying colours. They agreed that maybe they should throw away the potion of mixed liquids, as some of the green and yellow hues looked decidedly unsafe. Jack could not deny though that the little red and black sweetmeats Vicky found in the organ collection were delicious. However, when she dug around in the head and pulled out the little pink brain, Jack insisted that he could not eat it. Vicky grinned and made a meal of lowering it into her mouth and chewing noisily.

The food perked Jack up no end. He smiled and joked with her about the struggle to land a fish and her innate talents. He sent Vicky back to catch them some more and, with a grin, she bowed her head to him in mock subservience. She spent over an hour at the prow, whilst Jack monitored their progress under the giant suspension bridge that carried the old M48 road.

He marvelled at the immense size of the structure,

guessing that its length was probably ten times the diameter of the Doughnut. The two main towers were taller than anything he had ever seen in real life.

Vicky caught another six fish, three of the same type and three of differing types, including a tiny one the colour of cinnabar that they both gaped at. Once the fish had all expired, she wrapped them in a plastic sheet from the bench locker and stuffed them into Jack's rucksack. Although the day was very hot, they anticipated eating the fish before they could go rotten.

She came and stood beside him as they looked towards the ever-widening Bristol Channel. The tidal effects were much reduced here, and Jack hoped that beyond the next bridge, they would find Vicky's islands.

Chapter Twenty-one

'Wow.' Vicky's face was bronze in the rays of the setting sun. Her head strained up, basking in its glory. Jack Smith was slumped at her feet in the base of the boat, where he had hidden in the shade for most of the afternoon. She leant gently against the oar handle that was trussed up as a rudder. He clambered up to sit beside her. The two leaned close, shoulder to shoulder, eyes closed, and their faces pushed up to the west.

They were a half-mile away from the southernmost and largest Severn bridge, the old M4, and the current took them towards the right of a large rock outcrop in the middle of the water. It had been exposed as the tide went out, and the highest points had already dried completely. The rufous, flat slab was textured with bumps and pools. The temperature was high, and the sun bright, so only the rock pools remained wet. The rest had dried off to leave a heated stone field in the river. Even from a distance of several yards, the heat emitted from the stone was perceptible on the skin. Jack could feel it, warm on the back of his neck, although the direct sunlight on his face was hotter. Their course aimed under the central bridge span connecting two vermicular viaducts.

'From my desk, I've watched virtually every sunset over fourteen years. But in that air-conditioned constancy, you never get the beauty of it. You can't feel it.' His eyes spent their time flitting from the sun to Vicky's features and back again. Her face moved downwards, to see that they were holding hands, and then looked back into Jack's face. He gave a wan smile. They stared at each other for several seconds; neither spoke.

Vicky's eyes suddenly widened. Before he could worry, he spotted that she was looking past him. Vicky loosed her hand from his, stood up and pointed upriver. 'Is that them?' she squealed. The pitch of her voice surprised them both, and she pulled her hand back to cover her throat.

Jack held his left hand up the side of his face for shade. He saw the dark shape she had pointed at. There was definitely something in the river a mile or two behind them. He felt Vicky pass the shared hat onto his head, and dropped his hand. He could not be sure what the object was, but the size could easily be that of the narrowboat of their pursuers.

She wrapped both hands around his upper arm and leant close. 'Do you think they've found Bailey? Do you think he's alright now? They wouldn't come for us otherwise, would they?'

Jack could not answer. He stared at the little silhouette and wondered many things. He turned 180 degrees, his back to Vicky, and looked down the Bristol Channel. To the south, the shore jutted into the estuary, but the other bank sidled away faster, so that the river widened dramatically in the visible distance. They were headed for the sea. He looked back to the shape and ahead again.

The eastern shoreline was illuminated beautifully. Although the boat was drifting towards it, he fully expected the flow to move further west. They would be kept in the middle of the huge channel. For the first time, he considered the possibility of being marooned in their little boat. Thirst tickled Jack's throat.

He took another look at the boat behind and then turned back to Vicky. She watched him, and her forefinger turned little circles at her temple. He noticed that she sometimes caught a strand of mousy hair, dislodging it from the yellow scarf headband. She must have spent her life repacking her hair and then slowly stripping locks back out, before resetting the whole lot again.

'I can't promise they've found Bailey; but you're right – their coming after us is a good sign.' Jack put his hands on her upper arms and squeezed. 'Everything will be alright.' He gently turned her to face downstream.

The bridge hovered high overhead, with the brutal white columns at each end rising a further 500 feet. The cat's cradle of cables hung down all along the bridge deck, connected to the edge every ten feet. They approached the shade of the overpass and Jack looked through the picture frame it created to the open water beyond. 'Where are the islands you told me about? You said they were after the second bridge, right?'

Vicky put both hands on the rear rail and leant forwards. She peered into the distance and scanned across the river. She looked at Jack briefly and then scanned a complete circle all around the boat. She moved a hand upwards, and Jack caught it in mid-air. 'The islands?'

A brief look of fear crossed her face, and the other hand rose to trace circles on the side of her head. She looked again at the southern vista between the bridge stanchions. They were almost passing underneath and heading into much more open water on the other side. She faced Jack again; her expression had become perplexed. 'I'm not sure exactly. I don't think it was these rocky patches I was thinking of. I remember two really green-looking, proper islands. Classic islands, maybe a kilometre across. There was grass and trees and seabirds and cliffs.' Vicky's hazel eyes disappeared behind ochre eyelids for a long couple of seconds. 'There were buildings. Definitely buildings. Although maybe only on one of the islands.'

'But where?'

Vicky closed her eyes again. This time she scoured her memory for many seconds. Jack was still holding her left hand in mid-air, and he squeezed it to bring her back. 'The drone flightview I watched came past this bridge. I remember all those

167

pillars on each side. And the islands were the last part of the story. There are definitely two, near each other – it looped round the edges of each, one after the other. So they must be further than here. You couldn't see any mainland shore in the images of the islands. But the view was quite low, so that doesn't mean they're right out at sea. I'm sure it can't have been much further than here. But we're definitely going the right way.' Jack nodded slowly, his face serious.

The sky became grey, the clouds black, and Jack felt the stickiness in his clothes. A day of sweat, the salt from his bath earlier and the increasing humidity all combined to create discomfort. Vicky watched as he tugged slightly at the lower back of the T-shirt. She looked back in the expected direction of her islands, and bent lower to look at the sky emerging above the other side of the bridge deck.

'If it rains, we need to catch as much of the water as possible.' She stepped away from him to open the storage lockers. The lids had a depression in the undersides, so she upturned them onto the floor of the boat, next to the bucket, to catch any rainfall.

The rain came quickly and heavily, carried on a strong and swirling wind. There was thunder, but they did not see any lightning. For an hour, the water gushed from the sky. The southerly wind was hot, but the falling water absorbed much of the heat. The rain refreshed: it directly cooled everything, and the air temperature also dropped. The wind blew raggedly around them, whipped through Vicky's hair, and ruffled their clothes. Although the air spun wildly, the storm was only a small size – it dragged water off the river surface, but generated few real waves. The squall also brought dark night. The lighter outlines of the bridge structures began faintly visible, but faded quickly into the murk. Land, sky and river became united in blackness.

Using light from their armulets, Jack and Vicky bailed the collected water from the bench lids and from the storage lockers into all the containers they had. Both also drank a large amount as they worked. The sweat of the day was washed off their skin and was replaced internally. The deluge halted as sharply as it had started.

Jack felt Vicky wrap her hands around his upper arm and move in close again. He leaned back slightly and stared over the rail trying to distinguish the water from the air. They were still seamlessly opaque. 'This black night reminds me of the death of my grandfather.'

'What?' Her voice was a case study in confusion.

'Sorry, what I mean is, it reminds me of the story that Grannie Ellie used to tell me about it. He was a militiaman in Brighton, and was killed in fighting on a boat on the sea there. The story has a lot of blackness in it – I usually picture the scenes looking a bit like what we can see now.'

'You mean nothing at all?'

Jack smiled into the gloom. Ellie's histories of the Times of Malthus included some portrayals of grandfather Wayne's exploits for the Brighton militia in defence of their seafront part of the town. Jack had never known how much to believe of her narratives of these combat clashes. She had recounted the things her husband had told her, and the opportunities for exaggeration, or indeed simple error, were extensive. He was killed in 2030, before the invention of the audiopt feeds, so Jack could not check on the facts directly by watching the feed annals.

In the absence of verification, he chose to relay the story to Vicky exactly as his grandmother had delivered it to him so many times. 'The militia's little fleet was based in Brighton Marina, and Wayne's squad would speed out and back, repelling marauders on a weekly basis. As the national famine

169

worsened throughout 2029, the frequency of attacks dropped. Looting bandits were not very successful and, as they died, or at least weakened, they became less and less capable of launching missions against the citizens of Brighton. Although the resident population were also weakening in numbers and individual strength, a defending force always holds the upper hand against insurgent attacks. The defence force requested those they protected to move their abodes, and their stores of supplies, at least fortnightly or, preferably, every week. Returning raiders could then be caught and killed or repelled before they found the new hiding places.

'However, in the end, the raiders became more desperate. His entire squad was lost that night, and she never received a detailed report of the exact circumstances. Perhaps as Wayne had intended, she imagined what must have happened based on his previous accounts.

'Wayne would tell Ellie of hand-to-hand fighting on board the small boats that each side used. Whilst there were a lot of close quarter shootings and stabbings, most deaths occurred when people were knocked unconscious and overboard.'

At Jack's mention of this in his recounting of Ellie's tale, Vicky gasped. He paused, realised his insensitive mistake, and tried to twist his head to see Vicky's mood. She pressed her face into his bicep.

Jack wanted to help but his arm was pinned. He used the other hand to touch her head gently. Without any vision, this became a patronising pat on the head.

He put his hand back down and waited a minute. Gently, he whispered, 'Vicky?' His already wet sleeve felt a little warmer.

She snuffled, dragged her eyes across the arm of his T-shirt, and croaked back, 'I'm sorry, go on, I do want to hear.'

The uppermost arc of the moon was pushing up from the

eastern horizon, and he could make out the outline of the foredeck. He slid carefully up on to it and stood to take a pugilist pose. 'Imagine a night like this, my granddad dressed all in black, standing on the front deck of their boat, punching out the lights of a nasty piece of work, bent on stealing the boat and then invading to take everything they could find in the homes of Brighton.'

Jack related a version of the history Ellie had told his younger self many times. 'Shot in the thigh, Wayne Smith repelled boarding members of the Essex Raiders militia. Despite a bullet-shattered femur, he knocked the first and largest Essexman back into his dinghy, with a single knockout punch square on the nose.' Jack hurled a fist out at the air ahead. 'The big man was immediately replaced by two screaming women, who leapt up, either side of Wayne. One had long and wild black hair and waved both arms around with a short knife in each fist.' Jack imitated the woman in the story, whooping loudly as his arms circled vertically.

'The old man in Wayne's squad crouched in the middle of their boat and shot her through the side within a second of her boarding. She slumped to the floor gurgling, the mess of dark hair dangling over the side.

'The other woman was tiny – short and petite – but she was lightning quick. She wore a blood red Lycra bodysuit, and a wide, black plastic belt highlighted the tininess of her waist. She also carried a blade in each hand, bound in place by studded dog collars wrapped around each palm. Almost too fast to see, she had sliced across Wayne's forearm before her partner even hit the deck. She left Wayne briefly, bounced down into the centre of the vessel to slice the old man's neck artery and leapt straight back up. He turned as fast as his damaged leg would allow, but she had already stabbed into his left kidney. Wayne crumpled under the pain and attempted to roll onto his back to be in a position to protect against raining knife blows.'

At one moment, Jack was his grandfather, holding his thigh and collapsing onto the flat cabin roof. An instant later, he had switched to be the stabbing female warrior.

'Like a lizard's tongue, her right hand repeatedly flicked out and back again. Wayne struggled to follow the speed of movement, but felt every thrust with a new spike of pain in another part of his body.

'The remaining members of his squad were each involved in a skirmish in their own corner of the boat, but on that night every Brightonian out there lost the fight. The iron tang of blood filled the salty air. Before he had expired, the little assassin rolled my grandfather to the edge of the deck and gave him a vicious kick to send his bloodied body into the black water.'

As none of the Brighton Defence Force ever returned that night, Jack knew Ellie had invented this fight scene. But it was as good a history as they had; any story was better than none. An empty not-knowing would surely have sent the young wife Ellie into harrowing despair. So many people simply disappeared during the Times of Malthus. Jack had always been willing to suspend his disbelief when she claimed that the little knifewoman had later been captured and spilled this story.

He returned to Vicky, who was sitting up straight. The sky had cleared again as quickly as the storm had come, and she looked pretty in the bright moonlight. The illumination whitened her skin and, with her hair drawn back into its ponytail and accessorised with the yellow scarf, her oval face was beautiful. Jack paused, checking on what appeared to be an aura or halo around her head. He dismissed it as an illusion, but the pause pushed Vicky into action.

She stood up quickly and threw her arms around his neck. She gave him a big kiss on the lips and leant back. 'What a great story. Horrible and frightening, but thanks, your acting has cheered me up no end.' He was taken by surprise and just shrugged. She moved around him and walked towards the cabin, but stopped and turned back. After a moment, she said, 'I'm going to get some sleep.'

Jack took a step towards her and then stopped. 'OK.' With the moon behind, he could see only a silhouette. Her arm formed a sideways triangle up to her head; she looked like a pointy letter P. 'Um, one of us had better watch for the islands. Hopefully I'll be able to see them in the moonlight, but we definitely don't want to miss them.' There was silence. Jack continued, 'You get some sleep, and I'll wake you later to give me a turn in bed.' He looked at the time on his armulet but, when he looked back, the letter P had been erased; the deck was empty. He heard a couple of noises from the cabin as Vicky rearranged the equipment to make a bed.

Jack took a deep breath and turned to the rear of the boat. He looked out at the dark and uniform vastness of the river. He could distinguish the charcoal of the banks from the ink of the water, but there were no discernible features in either. No visible islands.

Jack woke and felt her hand on his cheek and looked up. Shadows showed the position of her eyes, but the light behind was too weak for him to make out Vicky's expression. 'Go on. You get some sleep, and I'll wake you up later.'

Vicky clung onto a lone rock in the fast-flowing river. Water kept splashing against her face, muffling her cries. He could hear her steadily more and more clearly. 'Jack! Jack! Come and help me!' Jack woke with a start. The cabin was dim, but light was coming in through the doorway behind him. Although the dream had vanished, he could still hear Vicky calling him. 'Jack! Get up, will you!' She sounded louder, and he realised that it was her real voice. He rolled over on the

173

makeshift bed and could see her back. She was leaning against their homemade tiller, gripping with both hands.

Jack's head was fuzzy with sleep and he crawled into the dawn light. The sun was not yet visible in the sky, but the brightness of the morning still hurt his eyes. He blinked several times and stumbled to his feet.

Beyond her, the grey cliff walls of an island were visible a mile to the southwest. The form looked pretty circular, and Jack guessed that it was about half a mile in diameter. It was exactly as she had described from her memory: cliffs topped with grass and the odd tree, with a lighthouse poking up at the southern end. He looked back, but there was no sign of the posse pursuing them.

He stood next to Vicky and grabbed the oar handle above both her hands. 'What are we doing exactly?'

'I'm trying to steer us to the island. I remember now, this one is called Beaumont Island, and that's Beaumont Lighthouse. It's working a bit, we're changing course, but I'm not sure we're going to get to it before we've gone too far past.'

Jack tried to gauge their progress, but they were moving slowly and there were no landmarks near enough to judge their course precisely. 'I think it's working,' he replied without conviction.

'Well, I don't think we can steer any better than this, so it's in the lap of the gods now.'

'In the lap of the gods, eh? That's an interesting viewpoint.'

Vicky gave him a quizzical look, her long Truva eyebrows scrunched. She looked back at the island and commented, 'Well, it looks like the gods are smiling on us – we are definitely nearer than we were before. If anything, I'd say we're heading straight for it.' They continued holding the rudder at the extreme right position, and the boat continued due west.

At the northern end, the cliffs came down to a gently sloping, rocky beach. The distance to the beach had decreased to about 200 yards when their course altered. The flow could not be observed by looking at the water itself, but they were close enough to the island to see that their direction had shifted almost a right angle to point southerly.

'Push. Push.' Vicky strained, all her weight against the oar handle.

Jack maintained his grip on the wood, but did not add much force. 'Keep it in that position, but we don't want to break off the lashing we tied it up with.' A jetty, implanted in a concrete block at the base of a steep staircase, slid past. They remained tense in fixed positions, but the boat continued to pass parallel to the island's cliffs. It stuck at a roughly consistent separation from them. They could hear constant crashing of the waves at the base of the rock walls.

'Jack, what do we do?'

They had continued quickly and were nearly at the southeastern corner of Beaumont Island. He observed that the distance to the lighthouse had increased. They were perceptibly moving away from the island again. He looked back up the length of the shore. The whole thing was cliffs a hundred feet high. The only landing spots they had seen, even for a swimmer in the water, were right at the opposite end. It would be several hundred yards to swim, and the distance was constantly increasing. And, Jack realised, they would be battling against the current that had moved them past it.

'I don't know. I don't think we can make that swim.' He pointed to the northernmost point they could see – the shingle beach was now out of sight around the top of the island. 'We've missed our chance.'

'What about if we swim the other way round, past the

lighthouse?'

'Well, we don't know anything about the rest of the coast. It could be just the same, more cliffs, and it's then even further round to the beach.' He again pointed directly to where the beach was obscured from sight. He turned to look at Vicky, who stared past him, glassy-eyed, at the cliffs. Jack's attention was immediately caught. Beyond Vicky, in the distance, another island was directly in their path. 'Look!' She turned to follow his pointing finger.

'I remember that now too. It's Steep Holm. Should we try for that one?'

'Yes. It's a much better plan than trying to swim to this one. If we steer hard from here, we should be able to aim straight on to the top and make the flow land us.'

'What if it's all cliffs too?'

'You saw the flightview, was it all cliffs?'

She wailed, 'I can't remember.' She pulled and pushed the oar handle several times to no purpose. 'I don't know, Jack.'

He wrapped his arms around her, with the effect that he separated her from it. 'We'll be OK.' His voice was a whisper. Jack held her tight for a minute, during which her tense body slowly relaxed. Her forehead eventually rested on his shoulder, and Jack released his grip. 'Come on, let's steer for it.' He took up his grip on the pole and pulled it to the left.

Vicky nodded, her eyes focussed in the distance at the receding island. She moved around to view the next island and leant against the tiller to maintain it at full lock to steer southeast.

They kept pushing on the crude rudder, but the course taken kept moving back to more southerly. They wrestled to readjust and alter the course to keep aim at the centre of the north coast of the new island. The river did not pay attention.

Their frustration mounted as the course they followed insisted on taking them close to but west of their Shangri-La. As far as the two of them knew, this was their last chance to escape the sea and find consistent food and water. They had to get to it.

As Steep Holm island came closer, Jack and Vicky observed that it was another cliff-surrounded impregnable fortress. If anything, it was worse than the previous island. The cliffs looked higher, more continuous and uniform, and the waves crashed against them with more force.

As they passed the northwest corner of the island, Vicky took her right hand off the oar handle and gripped Jack's wrist instead. She squeezed tightly, but did not look away from the rock faces. Huge slabs plunged vertically downwards into the water. The rock walls appeared like the bark of a giant tree stump. Dark green vegetation at the top gave way to grey pillars, which passed down through a black region finishing in sandy brown stone, similar in colour to the water that lapped at the base.

They passed disturbingly close to a sharp cliff corner. Built into the top of it was a concrete structure. It was a semicircular building, perhaps thirty feet in diameter, with a large horizontal viewing slot beneath a flat roof. Jack stared in awe at this lookout point, distracted from the desperation of their position.

'Steer round the back!' Vicky shouted. The waves were quite loud, but the volume of her voice was greater. Jack started, and he took a step back with one foot. He looked at her and saw a fiery expression, her eyes bored into his.

He joined her in pushing the rudder hard to the left again to try and turn the boat east along the southern rock wall. Their craft responded and took up a tack due east. Their four hands were adjacent on the wooden shaft, and at the same instant, both armulets lit up. Vicky twisted her head down to look at hers,

177

and Jack let go with his left hand and lifted it up to view. The network was connected again.

Jack looked at Vicky. She was transfixed by the light, but her hands were glued to the oar. He stared at her until she looked back to him. 'We need to lose our armulets or they'll find us easily.'

Vicky's mouth was slightly open, her peach lips dry from the wind. She stared at Jack, her eyes flitting left and right to each of his. 'Are you crazy? They're the only way we can survive: how to build a shelter, where to find water, how to catch food. We need to know what's on the island and how to get food and water. Otherwise we'll die long before any militiamen find us.'

Jack stared at her. 'Not *long* before – they'll find us in days, or more likely in hours.'

'In which case, what does it matter if we keep them?'

'That little extra time could be the crucial difference between changing our society or not. We must give the people as long as we possibly can to come to their senses.'

The sound of crashing waves was relentless.

'It won't be any good if we die trying – what message will they get then? Jack Smith was a crazy man who blew up the Doughnut for no reason.'

'It's not about me. People will realise the benefits without prompting from me.'

Their voices were steadily rising. 'You know that's not true – everyone will wander around lost, and wonder how their ancestors ever lived without armulets. Unless you point it out to them, they won't notice the separation between the armulet infonetwork and the audiopt surveillance.' She paused, staring him out. 'That is the difference you want people to see, isn't it?'

Jack faltered. He looked around at the water surface, and then back to the bright screen, and then back at Vicky's scowl.

'Yes, you're right. I must explain that to them.' He hesitated again. 'But we must hold them off as long as possible so that distinction is there to be made. We must lose our armulets.'

'You're not even listening to yourself now.'

Jack almost shouted, 'We are not going to die.' At that he began unfastening the straps on his armulet. His left forearm was revealed as bright white, compared to his generally white complexion. He let it fall to the floor and glared at Vicky.

She pouted, glaring back. After five seconds, she relaxed her lips again and nodded. 'What should we do with them? Drop them in the water? Turning them off doesn't stop the tracking sig... ' She stopped abruptly and looked sharply at him. 'The audiopt feeds don't only run off the armulets. They'll find us without them anyway.'

Jack shook his head. 'Like I said, I'm expecting that the audiopt feeds will be fixed a bit more slowly than the main armulet network. Only the infonetwork has just come back on, so we may have a few more days before the audiopts can catch us. I'm hoping that we're now far enough out that we'll be in the tower area for the last audiopts to get repaired. But they do have the location tracker through the infonetwork communicating with the armulets. You keep hanging on to the oar, and I'll take yours off.' Jack crouched down and made to unbuckle the brown leather straps that held her device onto Vicky's forearm.

'Wait, wait. Let's not get rid of them if we don't need to. Call up my audiopt feed and see if it's online.'

Jack leant back and nodded pensively. He picked up his own armulet, tapped at the screen and waited a few seconds. He tapped a few more times and waited again. He finally shook his head. 'No, nothing. I'd guess that we've got at least another day before they can catch up with us that way.' As he leant to take off Vicky's armulet, she twisted her arm to assist him, but never

179

released her grip on the tiller. She too had a lighter patch of skin, but it was more obvious than Jack's, as a contrast with her tan colour.

'So, what should we do with them? The water won't stop them working. And I reckon the current movements would keep their batteries charged up as well. Are you going to smash them?'

Jack simply dropped the two large bracelets into the storage locker at his feet. They clattered past the spare oar, a bucket of water, and the fishing gear, but remained illuminated and produced two soft balls of light in the depths of the compartment. She looked back up to him; her greenish-brown eyes glowed like two mini armulet screens. 'We'll go ashore and let the boat carry them away, so that our would-be pursuers chase the empty boat and never know when or where we got off.'

Vicky pushed out her lower lip, with a slight head nod. Then her expression mutated into a scowl. She burned holes in him again with her eyes and then indicated with a flick of her head that he should look behind. 'So, where exactly are we going ashore?'

Their vessel had slowed to a crawl, and they had passed to roughly the middle of the cliffs they could see. The south coast of the island formed a wall even higher than the north side, nothing but vertical stone: a natural, impregnable stockade. Jack faced it, arms folded. He stood with his feet spread apart and moved his head slowly left and right.

Chapter Twenty-two

'Now or never; jump!' They leapt off the forecabin, hand in hand. Jack and Vicky had put on a life jacket each, and had strapped their bags to a third one, which was then tied by a rope to both of theirs. The boat was bobbing idly in the little wave reflections from the crag forming the south coast of Steep Holm island.

They had drifted to the eastern most end of it, and this had revealed a low, flat beach they could swim to. It lay perhaps fifty yards away, forming the eastern end of the roughly rectangular islet. Their armulets remained in the storage chest in the bottom of the boat. Jack hoped that the change of the tide would send their vessel further on its way out to sea, and take the tracking signals with it. He had little idea about the currents in the Bristol Channel, but he did not believe that they would eddy at this point and keep the boat stuck for long.

Seagulls complained about their presence, some squawking from atop the rock columns, and some swooping and circling. The water felt cold; not dangerously, scarily cold, but it was not pleasant. He heard Vicky's voice over the gulls and splashing water sounds. 'Come on, Jack, get swimming, it'll keep you warm. And I'm not about to drag you there.'

Jack was floating on his back and kicking his legs awkwardly. He twisted sideways to look to her. She was already ahead of him and looking ahead as she swam a careful but solid breaststroke. Jack rolled over and tried to mimic Vicky's technique. He did forget the temperature, focussed forwards to the beach. However, he was very slow and she steadily pulled ahead of him, also pulling the floating bags ahead of him.

'Keep going!' Vicky's voice floated over.

181

Again, he made a bigger effort to swim hard. His clothes dragged in the water, and even the buoyancy of the lifejacket did not keep his head as high out of the water as Jack would have liked. He rolled onto his back and continued with leg kicks. Breathing was much easier whilst looking at the sky, and Jack proceeded to get into a good rhythm with his legs only, hands gripping the chest flaps of the red lifejacket.

A large object bumped into Jack's bottom. It tipped him onto his side before the lifejacket rolled him back. Fear gripped him and he jerked his head from side to side to spot the unseen danger. A large, smooth, grey body appeared slightly above the water to his right, but no limbs, head or tail surfaced. As soon as he spotted it, the creature disappeared down again. The brown water was opaque, and his mind whirled with imagined sea monsters. Sharks, whales, giant squid: Jack had seen videostories in which animals of the deep terrorised humans.

He could hear Vicky screaming but could not make out any coherent words: his own splashing confused all other sounds. He could not turn his head enough to see if she was being attacked. Jack started to kick wildly and moved his arms like wind turbines, as fast as he could. His actions were uncoordinated and resulted mostly in water flying around, but little overall movement towards safety.

He felt another bump on his leg, gentler than the first, but still a definite collision with whatever was chasing them. He splashed more violently and made less progress. Suddenly, he had a breakthrough and managed to power through the water. Jack was distracted from the danger of the attack, as he tried to work out why his swimming technique had become so effective. He guessed that the movements of his arms and legs were not causing the faster motion. He panicked again as he realised that the creature must be dragging him, even though he could not feel where it had hold. Pain surged into the middle of his back.

Jack arched, eyes closed, expecting to feel teeth ripping through his flesh. The pain died down, although there was still pressure on his back and he had stopped moving.

'Hey, are you OK?' He opened his eyes to see Vicky standing over him, her face bent down to look at him. 'Come on, get up.' Her hands were together, holding the tether rope, which hung limply down. The pressure in Jack's spine, he realised, was a large rock. He sat up and pushed his hands down under four inches of water onto the pebbles of the beach.

'What was that thing?'

'I think it was a seal. I only caught a brief glimpse, but it seemed about the size of the ones I've seen on my armulet before.'

'A seal? They're not dangerous.'

'No, they're not.'

Jack turned his body to look at her. Vicky was still bent over him, and her face had a perplexed aspect. He frowned. 'Why were you screaming?'

'I was shouting at you to swim properly. In the end, I gave up and just pulled you in.'

He turned onto his knees and stood up gingerly, dripping from every point. The droplets made loud plops as they landed in the shallows.

He looked back at their boat. Jack could not be certain, but it appeared to be further away than the beach had looked when they jumped off.

There was no wind, and the sun was bright. Nonetheless, Jack felt cold. He dropped the lifejacket and then peeled off his T-shirt and threw it onto the ground ten feet away. The sunshine had an immediate warming effect on his white torso, and he looked at the water trails still drooling from Vicky's ponytail and blouse. She shook like a dog trying to dry itself and then started squeezing loose hanging parts of her clothing.

183

The gulls continued their mindless noise. Jack and Vicky had landed at the end of a rocky beach in the shape of a crescent, with a long tail extending off the other end into the sea, away from the main body of the island. Two antiquated buildings sat at the top of the beach. The smaller was a little house, in the middle of the crescent's curve, which sat on a grassy plateau.

Along from that, where the shingle tail met the main section of beach, was a larger building with a big square tower just off the near end. Both were built of huge, grey limestone blocks, with the larger house being built against the cliffs. A path ascended past the rear of the buildings and continued steeply up away from them before zigzagging back to disappear over the crest of the cliff, high above the square tower. There were no signs of humans inhabiting either building, and the path was significantly overgrown. They had seen all sides of the island and were on the only beach where a landing was possible, and there were no boats.

'I'm starving.' Vicky resecured her hair and untied the fishing equipment from the rucksacks. Jack carried everything else up to the natural lawn outside the smaller house. He sat to dry out in the sunshine and watched her find a spot at the base of the cliffs where she could dangle the line into the water. Unlike the day before, she was not instantly successful.

He realised that he should help and got up to scour the area for wood to build a fire. The beach was exhausted after he picked up a few small driftwood sticks, so Jack wandered up the pathway. It went very steep above the larger house, and he had to stop at the hairpin loop and rest his hands on his knees. All available effort had been used in the swim, and his progress became a very slow meander. He crested the top and his heart lifted at the sight that the rest of the island was pretty well flat. Additionally, there was a large group of trees at the near corner

He threw wood over the cliff edge so that it landed on the path halfway down.

The island looked to have a number of interesting buildings they could explore, but Jack's hunger was also urgent, so he went down to build the fire. Of the water they had collected in the rainstorm, they could only bring their bottles on the swim, and after his exertions up the hill, he quickly finished his two pints.

The wood was damp, but only superficially. He had brought a firestarter lens in his rucksack and, after some wet crackling noises, the fire ignited. It quickly blazed – annoyingly hot, as the summer still showed little sign of giving way to any kind of autumn. England's move towards a two-season climate had been rapid; Jack had even noticed a difference during his lifetime. Many of the scenes that he would project on his walls at home were of spring blossoms and autumn leaves. Such sights had become more and more short-lived each year, and with his twelve-hour work shifts, he had seen them rarely in real life over the last decade.

'I hope you found extensive food supplies up top.' Vicky held out a large fish she had caught and looked at Jack sitting some distance from the heat of the bonfire.

He looked at her, curious. 'I didn't explore further than the nearest clump of trees for the firewood. Why, what's wrong with that, it looks ideal?' She held out the fishing rod from the other hand. 'I also caught the line on the rocks and it broke. So we've got no more hooks and only one working reel.'

She was vaguely orange in the firelight, with a powder blue sky surrounding her. Jack looked past to see the discarded second rod on the pebbles near Vicky's fishing spot. 'Well, let's cook that up first and then go hunting for whatever the island has to offer.'

They gutted and barbecued what was plenty of fish for

two, despite their significant hunger. Both sat on a long stone bench set a few metres before the front wall of the smaller house, entranced by the flames. By the time it was all just embers, the fish was cooked, and they maintained the quiet as they wolfed it down.

'What about water?' Vicky asked with her mouth full of her last share of the fish. He just shook his head in reply. She looked around at the house and then across to the larger, greyer place. A sign suggested it had been a pub, but Vicky's interest lay with the guttering. One of the drainpipes fed into a water butt. She jumped up and took the long way around the fire to see if the pipework looked intact enough to still be gathering the roof's run-off. Thirsty, Jack followed. The green plastic barrel had a small tap on the front, but when she turned it nothing happened. She shook the barrel and it moved lightly, obviously empty.

'Here.' Jack pointed to the back where another small pipe exited the barrel, but had no tap and ended open. 'It must all just empty away. Why would you set it up like that?'

Vicky shrugged her thin shoulders, making the white shirt billow. 'If we can find something to block it up, we should be able to collect water. We just need to hope it rains before we die: there's no drinking the seawater.' She pointed vaguely beyond the pub at the expanse of river estuary that led in the distance to the first island they had passed.

Vicky pressed her hand against the warm limestone and moved to enter the open doorway in the middle of the building's frontage. All the windows were broken, and they could hear seagulls in an upstairs room crying to each other about the approaching humans. The large, open main room had a bar across the nearer end, and through the door behind it, they found a kitchen. There were two skeletons in rags lying across each other on the floor. 'Star-crossed lovers, do you think?'

Vicky flashed Jack a smile.

He pointed to the large kitchen knife passing between the ribs of the top skeleton and said, 'I'm thinking not.' She scowled.

The cupboards were littered with rubbish, but effectively bare, and all containers were empty. The taps at the sink did not produce any water. Each skeleton had an armulet, which lay loosely buckled around the left ulna and radius. Jack pressed on the screens, but they had no power. He looked up at Vicky as she rummaged in drawers, left the armulets and moved to the door. 'I think the kitchen was our best bet, but let's try upstairs.'

The remainder of the pub held nothing of much interest. The birds were nesting in the northernmost bedroom and quickly chased Vicky back out. There were beds they could use in other rooms, but Jack suggested that the smaller house, with its windows unbroken, would likely be more favourable.

Vicky checked that no water sprang from the bathroom taps, and admonished, 'It's food and water that we need to worry about, not beds.' Jack nodded and went down the stairs.

The square tower was an entirely separate building, albeit less than one metre from the pub's south end wall. The door sat ajar, and leaf litter and struggling vegetation held it in position. The square stone rooms were all entirely empty, except for the open top floor, which had a built-in fire pit and a wooden chair. The castellations were shoulder high, so anyone using the chair would not have been able to see out. However, the standing view was good, a full sweep from north to south, over the top of the pub roof, and giving a clear sight to the beach at Weston-super-Mare, five miles to the east.

Gazing at the desolate town, Vicky opined, 'We've got no food, no water, no way of getting off the island, and no communications. Great job, Jack. Is this how you pictured revolution?'

He stared at her, as she continued to look over the wall and over the water. Jack's voice was quiet, pathetic. 'I don't want a revolution. I've seen the bloodshed of the Times of Malthus. I just want for the audiopts not to be published for all to see.'

She turned quickly and shook her hands down at her sides, the fingers wobbling loosely. 'That is revolution, Jack. There'll be anarchy if people aren't held accountable for what they do. Nobody knows how your granddad died on that boat because there were no feeds. Don't you see?'

Jack took a step back. Tears streaked Vicky's dusty, brown cheeks and she trembled. He couldn't tell if it was rage, or fear, or exasperation, or desperation. He paused, scanning her stiff body language and distressed face for an indication of what was driving her arguments. After waiting many seconds to give her time to calm, he answered, 'Of course people must be held accountable. But let the sifters do that in response to crimes. If they are acting for the benefit of all, there should be no reason for people's words or deeds to be watched by others. Life is richer when it's secret.'

'But that's exactly what led to the Times in the first place. You told me what the Bitness Revelations revealed. Giving the sifters that power is a recipe for corruption. You're a sifter, do you just want more power over people?'

'No.' He stopped abruptly. Jack lifted his palm to his forehead, squeezed it, and looked at the chair. He hadn't noticed previously, but it had no seat – it was just a chair frame. 'I don't mean "secret", I mean...' he searched for the right word, '..."exclusive". Or "private".' He looked back at Vicky, but her expression had worsened. She looked at him as if he were a demon who had lured her to an awful death on this island. 'And I've had enough of being a sifter. I want us to live in a new way, but I don't want to be one of the new breed of sifters.'

Jack scanned her face, looking for any softening of the fear and anger she displayed, but she appeared frozen. She broke into sobs, put a hand over her mouth and used the other for guidance as she ran down the stone stairs away from him.

Jack watched over the parapet as she ran back to the dying fire and flopped onto the grass beside it. He could hear her sobs clearly. He put one hand on top of the smooth stone wall and wondered about Vicky's distress. He had always liked her calm intelligence. Even as a child, she had rarely behaved irrationally. Whilst she showed that emotions were going on inside, Jack did not think they dictated her actions. This outburst was odd. His mind ran through a gamut of possibilities that might explain such out-of-character behaviour: sunstroke, hunger, thirst. He wondered if she might be fearful of being caught up in Kangaroo's punishment for abetting his crimes; or worried about their survival prospects stuck on the island; or concerned that her brother, Bailey, might indeed have drowned. To some extent, he had seen signs of all of these possible causes. He decided that the best path to a solution lay in trying to ameliorate the things that he could. Food and water were the only options he might have control over.

Up on the flat top of the island, there were many old buildings, which Jack explored. Most were ruins, and some looked like they had never been completed. There were a lot of ancient cannons. Jack was no artillery expert, but even somebody with only a vague knowledge of history could see that many different eras and wars were represented. He stood by one gun, looking out to sea and imagining a team of bombardiers working the cannon to fire at a ship in the water below. With an elevation of a couple of hundred feet, up steep cliffs, the island must have been a formidable fortress.

Jack harrumphed about armies marching on their stomachs and continued to search for any edible plant matter or animals. In every location where seagulls and cormorants were nesting, they had positioned themselves on inaccessible rock outcrops high above the crashing waves. He reckoned that i they got desperate, he and Vicky could attempt to climb out to one of them. But he assumed they might only gather a few eggs that way – the live birds never came within reach.

In two hours of searching, Jack found no evidence o animals, or any standard vegetable crop that he recognised. The island was awash with pretty trees and flowers, but nothing tha he knew was edible. He made a couple of mental notes of the locations of some berries to check on with Vicky. He was sure that she would know about which berries were fit for consumption, and which poisonous. All the buildings had long since been abandoned, if they had ever been occupied, and the only signs of human beings were the two skeletons in the pub.

Raised high up, the island caught the wind, and the plateau had a constant breeze. Occasionally stronger gusts carried a chill from the Atlantic, and Jack shivered when they caught him. The beach was perfectly sheltered, but the upland would always be exposed. The wind rustled the trees and filled the air with the melange scent from the wild flowers. Jack sat by a ruined cottage, shaded from wind and sun, and inhaled the fog of pollens.

He wondered where they should choose to set up to live The house on the beach was the most complete, but there was so much more life and interest on the top. Jack decided that the best way to minimise carrying things would be to live near the water source.

He leaned forward and placed his chin on his hands elbows on his knees. He had not found any water. All the buildings that had at one time had a roof had water butts to gather the rain. Every one of them was empty, and most looked damaged too. He wondered if there was any natural water source. The presence of barrels at every building suggested that collecting rainfall had been important and this did not bode well. The realisation that they had no water increased Jack's thirst, and he was loath to step out of the shadow cast by the tumbledown brick wall he leant against. However, he knew that they must find water, and that doing so might return Vicky to her old self.

An old barracks building had an attached toilet block. This was utterly dry, and none of the plumbing brought forth any liquid. Jack tried to follow the pipework to find a storage tank. He lost track of the pipes in the walls, but climbed into the roof space and found three large copper tanks. One was empty with the corroded green exit pipe snapped off, the largest one was also empty, and the third was completely sealed. Knocking on it hurt his knuckles and gave a booming airy resonance, which sounded empty, although it was large enough that there might still be a low level of water in the bottom. Again, the exit pipe descended into the wall and vanished.

The cramped space was hot, and Jack felt nauseous. He stuck his head down to the hallway to get a lungful of cooler air and returned to try and locate the route of the pipes entering the tanks. He hoped that the source of the water for these reservoirs could be found, and a broken pipe would explain why they were empty. The entry seemed to come up from the walls below as well. Jack dropped back down to the floor and stepped outside for a deep inhalation of the clean, cool wind.

Chapter Twenty-three

'Are you sure we're on course to intercept them? I can't see anything in the water.'

Terry replied to Darren, 'There's still no audiopt feeds from either of them, but their armulets are giving off a tracer signal. We are less than 1200 metres away.'

Truvan Truva stood on the side of the narrowboat, on tiptoes, looking over the roof towards the direction Terry was pointing. His finger indicated the lighthouse at the southern end of Beaumont Island as they travelled along its western shoreline. The island dropped sharply into the sea, with thick, green vegetation covering much of the steep banks. Ash-coloured, dry rock formed the remainder. The lighthouse was bright white, a blinding pencil stabbed into the dull island colours. Truvan held a hand at his forehead to shade his eyes.

Major Halthrop stood at the front of the little craft, large, mirrored sunglasses shielding his eyes, and the camouflage cap perched on his head. He had instructed his men to keep to the western channel between Beaumont Island and the south coast of Wales, as the water was much shallower than in the middle of the estuary. Their motor would be more in control than trying to battle the faster-moving, deep water. As they had moved further out to sea, and after the battering of the previous night's storm, he had become increasingly concerned for their safety. The canal boat was in no way designed for seafaring, and they had already lost Bailey to the water.

'On this island then?' Darren questioned.

'Um, yes, probably.' Terry's face was contorted at his armulet screen. Truvan's eyes were narrowed and continued to move over the island. Apart from the white top of the

192

lighthouse, only trees could be seen above the dry cliffs and the ubiquitous water.

Halthrop asked, 'What's not to be sure of?'

'Well, this says they are more than a kilometre in that direction, but the far side of the island is probably no more than half that, don't you reckon?'

Halthrop looked back again. 'Darren, motor due south a bit faster. They may still be on their boat on the other side.' This was soon confirmed, as the fugitives' boat emerged from obscurity behind the island. On the murky water, with a bright blue sky behind, the little boat was just a silhouette. It grew quickly as they chased, and it appeared becalmed.

There was no movement aboard. Halthrop assumed that they must be sheltering in the shade of the forecabin, probably struggling with hunger and thirst and the heat. As they came alongside, the boat's lighter colours became apparent, but no signs of life emerged. There were no sounds or smells other than those of the sea. The deck was empty, but they could not see inside the cabin.

Truvan took a few steps along the side to be close enough to jump aboard. Halthrop grabbed his arm and held up his other hand flat. Truvan scowled. 'What?'

'Hello there,' the posse commander called, keeping Truvan's dark eyes locked. 'Jack Smith, Vicky Truva? Is anybody there?' No reply came, and Halthrop did not release his grip.

Firstly, he worried that the two might have died of thirst, and the impact on Truvan of finding his sister dead so soon after losing his twin brother would be a significant, perhaps dangerous, situation. Secondly, there was a possibility that, cornered on the boat, Jack Smith might be armed and ready to do violence to maintain his freedom. Neither prospect appealed, and Major Halthrop decided to pause. He indicated silently that

193

everyone should go inside the *Top Dog*'s cabin, and he tied the prows of the vessels together.

'What are you doing?' Truvan demanded. The major put his finger vertically across his lips to muzzle the man and waved him below for an explanation. The brother's thick eyebrows scrunched, and he followed Frank slowly.

Jane was told to lean out and watch the other boat, whilst the posse discussed various scenarios. Halthrop's main plan, which he omitted to mention, was to simply allow enough time to pass that the fugitives would become confused at the fact that they hadn't been boarded. The apparent lack of interest from the posse would distract Smith and put him at a disadvantage if he was planning anything dangerous.

Alternatively, if nothing was heard from the other boat in thirty minutes, they could assume the two were not compos mentis. That could mean dead, unconscious, or simply asleep, but the posse could expect to go aboard more safely.

Frank explained some of the ideas behind their pause, but omitted a number of subtleties that could put Truvan on edge. To conclude, he quoted Sun Tzu again: 'To fight and conquer in all your battles is not supreme excellence; supreme excellence consists in breaking the enemy's resistance without fighting.'

Terry raised his cup of water and toasted, 'Confusion to our enemies.' Halthrop smiled. Jane maintained her gaze out of the door and shook her head slightly. Darren and Truvan looked at Terry blankly.

After they had spent a tense half-hour around the galley table, Truvan put his palms on the tabletop and asked, 'Shall we?'

Major Halthrop nodded and stood. 'Terry, the rudder; Darren, the tie rope; Jane, you bring the cuffs. Mr Truva, you may come aboard with us, but I insist you stay at the stern until Jane and I have any situation under control. I warn you now that we will be putting your sister in handcuffs until we know for certain what her situation is.' He put up his hand to stifle any protest, although Truvan's expression had not altered, and he had not moved. 'You must understand our position. The safety of everybody, including Smith and your sister, is our prime concern. We don't know what influence he may have over her, so I must take precautions.'

Truvan stared at the major's blue eyes. His lips barely moved as he said, 'Understood.'

The boat was empty. After a brief search to confirm the absence of hiding places, the armulets were found. Truvan, Jane and Halthrop stood and scanned the sea in all directions. Truvan spoke first. 'They must be on the island. Let's land and search for them.' He pointed at the tall, skinny lighthouse.

Halthrop leant forwards, both hands on the port side rail, the sun hot on his back. He could see Steep Holm in the distance and took a couple of glances back to Beaumont Island. Turning fully, the major gazed at the island's forbidding cliff surround. It certainly warranted a lighthouse.

'What are we waiting for?' Truvan demanded. 'It's a small island, we should be able to search it in the tide time available anyway.'

Halthrop shook his head, and Jane spoke. 'No chance. If they're hiding, there's no way. Without the feeds, it could take a couple of days for the four of us to search properly.'

'Five,' Truvan interjected.

'What?'

'There are five of us. Don't think I'm not going to get involved in the search.' He had raised his body up straight and puffed his chest out above Jane.

'I was thinking that one person would need to stay with the boat to manoeuvre it with the tides all the time.'

Truvan turned back to Major Halthrop, and his fingers

195

curled and uncurled by his sides. 'Well?'

Jane had placed the two abandoned armulets on the rear bench and was gesturing at her own. The major instructed, 'Jane, check on those armulets where they've been. Use the tracker history on the maps. I think we're drifting away from that far island, not this one.'

She did as she was told and, after a brief pause, compared the diagrams on the two screens. He watched her scrunch her eyebrows and then start to speak. 'Um.'

'What?' Truvan almost shouted.

'They never got nearer than a hundred metres to either island; but they did get that close to the landing places on both islands.'

'That's it!' Truvan's face was alive: his eyes were wide and he carried an excited grin. 'They're on this island.'

Major Halthrop did not turn, but held his arm up behind himself towards Terry showing his palm. The skinny pilot of the *Top Dog* exchanged glances with Darren, at the front of the canalboat. Darren looked confused, shrugged his shoulders, and passed his fingers through his mess of yellow hair. 'What?' Truvan's voice was again loud and slightly higher pitched. 'Come on, let's go! What are we waiting for now?'

Halthrop turned and spoke gently. 'Their boat has no power – it's drifting. Thus, its routing does not follow any conscious purpose. We cannot tell if they went ashore here, or at the other island, after which the boat drifted back here.'

Truvan scowled. 'Right, so we don't know where they are, so let's start searching at the nearest place.'

'He's got you there, boss,' Terry piped up.

Major Halthrop swivelled to face Terry. Speaking through clenched teeth, with a staccato delivery, he answered, 'This is not a point-scoring debate. We need to make the best decision. For the most efficient use of resources. We need to consider all possibilities. And all probabilities.'

'What we need to do,' Truvan interrupted, 'is not waste any more time. We're here. We don't know where they are. The islands don't have anything to choose between them, and the movements of the armulets don't suggest one choice as better than the other. Come on, let's get going.'

Halthrop looked back at Steep Holm. He turned back to Terry. 'Right, head up here to the jetty and take care on landing at it: make sure the water level is right before getting too close. Darren, you spot for him from the prow. But first, untie the boat and move it to the back to trail behind us.' Darren nodded his ruddy cheeks and set to work on the knot.

'Let us back on there first. Hang on.' Darren looked up startled and his hands froze as the team leapt back onto the side of the narrowboat. With all three coming in quick succession onto the same edge, the boat rocked disturbingly and they had to cling on to the roof rail. Jane spilled the armulets onto the roof in order to hold on, and they slipped around but did not fall. Gathering them up, she looked closely. 'Frank, these armulets, they're nearly out of power.' She turned to her boss as he picked himself up. He nodded to her.

Truvan checked his own armulet. 'She's still not back on the audiopt feeds. But her armulet's not much use to us anyway now. We looked through its movement tracking history, and she didn't record anything else that helps.'

Halthrop changed the plan, immediately, without any consultation. 'Let's go. To Steep Holm, Terry.' He pointed at it in the distance.

Truvan started to query what was going on, but Halthrop answered before the question was posed. 'An armulet will last at most six hours without any kinetic energy input from its user. So if these are out of juice now, then they were abandoned longer ago than we thought. I'm pretty sure that puts them on the other island.'

It was after four o' clock, and Halthrop was worried they might not make it there and land safely before nightfall. If the landings were as precarious as Beaumont Island, then they would have a problem. He hoped the low tide they would have would be better than a high tide.

As they got underway, Truvan looked back and forth across the water between the two islands. A gentle breeze rippled the surface and cooled his face. 'How long will this take us?'

Halthrop was in consultation with his armulet. 'The landing is on the beach on the far eastern end, but should be easy as low tide exposes it well. Somebody will have to stay aboard to control the boat as the tide comes in.'

'How long?'

'At current rate of knots, another fifty minutes.' Halthrop spoke as he stared at the information on his armulet screen.

'And what is your plan for searching this island? We'll have, what, an hour of daylight at most?'

'Yes, tricky. I'm half inclined to camp out on the beach till morning and do a full search tomorrow. Otherwise they could move in the night and hide out in places we think we've cleared. Although we aren't really going to have time to do any searching anyway, perhaps beyond the landing beach itself.'

The lowering sun had become obscured by swiftly moving light grey clouds. Another late afternoon storm approached. As Terry motored on, the clouds thickened, and the colour moved closer to slate. The wind picked up in sudden gusts. Spray whipped off the top of each wave swell, and the waves themselves increased in height. All day, the water had been calm, and the posse had almost forgotten that their vessel was not built for the waters they plied. After only a couple of large ups and downs on the storm waves, all hands were scared.

Jane and Darren sat below, whilst Halthrop and Truvan held tightly onto the cabin roof rail. They stood level near the front of the boat and attempted to shift their weight to counter any asymmetry in the rocking of the *Top Dog*. The darkness of the storm combined with the gloaming of sunset made it increasingly difficult to spot the approaching waves.

Halthrop instructed Terry to steer directly into the wind in the hope that this would take them straight onto the wave fronts. A broadside wave would certainly capsize the shallow craft. It was a futile instruction though, as the wind swirled around them. Their progress slowed. With the squally rain beating down irregularly, it was all Terry could do to hang onto the tiller and attempt to maintain his footing and a straight course.

The storm brought night swiftly, and the navigation soon had to be done by armulet. The silhouette of Steep Holm vanished into the dark. 'Brigadoon,' Halthrop muttered to himself.

The weather was coming from the south, and Terry sheltered them on the north side of the island rock plug that stuck up out of the water. Although the wind and rain continued to dance around and poke at them, the waves were much calmer in the lee of the cliffs. He was able to maintain the position without much difficulty, and they were able to shout and be heard. 'I'm gonna keep us here until the weather clears,' Terry called to the two up near the prow.

Truvan looked at his armulet and tried to get some information about the weather. No satellite weather information had been available for more than a generation, but a number of solar powered weather stations on the ground, and on buoys, fed their readings into the infonetwork. The image on his forearm screen was as chaotic a mishmash as they were experiencing.

Halthrop bellowed, 'You won't get anything useful from that out here. The info is only any good in a few fixed positions on land. Out here, the sea affects the weather unpredictably, and the stations giving the info will be quite a way away.'

It continued for much of the night, and the posse took turns sleeping and stationary piloting, until the dawn brought a sky-clearing sun.

Terry was asleep, so Halthrop steered them slowly around the east end of the imposing cliff face. The buildings that welcomed new people to Steep Holm's only landing site came into view. The tide was fully up, and the water lapped right up against the walls that protected the pub and the lawn around the smaller house. It was unclear whether they could approach safely and tie up to one of the walls. No hawser rings or posts were obvious. Halthrop had one hand on the tiller. There was a loud grinding sound from under the hull, and their speed dropped from slow to stopped. Jane was on watch at the prow, and she turned to her boss. She had a scared look and shrugged her shoulders. 'I didn't see anything, I can't see anything. The water's opaque.'

'Right, we'll wade from here.'

Terry took over piloting and stayed with the boat in case it became free.

Chapter Twenty-four

Jack Smith was shaken awake. He had slept on a dingy mattress on the floor of the old barracks building. Vicky was bending over him, and the sun lit her from behind through a large window, which appeared never to have had curtains. Her face was in shadow, and Jack leapt back.

'Easy, it's just me.' Her voice was unclear to his sleep-laden ears and meant nothing to him. It was only because he could see her properly from his new position that Jack sat still and rubbed his face. She waited until their eyes met. 'We must find some water. After last night's rain we should be able to find some puddles to drink for today. But we need a proper system. If it doesn't rain for a few days, we'll die.' Her last word repeated through Jack's mind several times.

'Where did you sleep?'

'In the small house at the beach.'

'And none of the water-gathering things from the roofs held any water?'

'No. I didn't expect the rain, so I didn't try to plug that one barrel in time. It's still empty. The fire pit on the tower had a puddle, so I've had a little water this morning. I think what was left will have evaporated by the time you get there.'

'I'm sure I'll find some up here.'

Vicky shook her head. 'There's some muddy puddles on the ground, but we can't live like that. It's a gamble we will eventually lose.'

'Don't worry, we'll work it out.'

'Stop talking like that, Jack, this is serious.'

He looked at her scowling face. 'I am serious.'

'No, you're not.' She had raised her voice, and continued

loudly, 'Everything you say has blind hope behind it. There's no organised planning.' She let her voice fall to a normal speaking volume. 'Jack, this is not you. You analyse everything. How did you build and explode bombs, uncaught, without careful planning? Think this through. If we are not going to die, we need to find water, or get rescued.'

'I had intended to go to the bunker at Leckhampton, but you scuppered that plan.' As soon as he said it, Jack stopped abruptly. There was over a minute of silence, during which they eyed each other. When they could no longer stand it, they instead stared at the walls and floor of the white, wooden room.

Jack stood up uneasily, clinging to the nearest wall panel for support. 'Maybe I'm suffering from thirst. And maybe that's affecting my thinking. I think I searched everywhere up here and there's nothing working. But there are a lot of plumbing bits and pieces, so there must be a system, we just need to fix it. Haven't you got any ideas?'

Vicky twisted her head slightly sideways and paused. 'I've only just come up to the top of the island. By chance, the first house I went to I found you, so I haven't explored anywhere else. The only thing I know is that the barrel by the pub is the best bet so far, and we need to fix it and hope for rain. But like I said, we need a better solution.'

'OK, let's go looking again. You can check that I didn't miss anything.'

As Jack walked past Vicky towards the hall leading to the toilet block, she did not move. 'We need food as well.' He ignored her.

The taps in the ablutions remained dry. Outside, there was a thick dew of rain on all the vegetation, but it was difficult for Jack to get much in his mouth. The futility of his attempts made him even thirstier. He guessed the temperature was in the low twenties, but it was heating up rapidly.

An old plastic lid offered Jack a puddle that was enough of a drink to sustain him for a while. Vicky had started to follow his meanderings in the immediate vicinity of his sleeping house, but stopped when they went in circles. After he found the lid of water, she asked him to suggest a plan. She concluded, 'I have some ideas, but we need to work together to make the best decisions.'

He had stopped walking and smiled at her. 'This is the middle of the length of the island.' He pointed away from the beach on which they had arrived. 'That way there are a few cannon emplacements, but no habitation buildings.' He dropped his left hand and lifted the other to point towards the rising sun. 'That side of the island has a number of small houses. None as big as this, but I assume all must have had some sort of water supply. I didn't find anything working in any of them, but this is the only one where I really looked in depth at the plumbing.' He dropped his arm to his side. 'Which seems buggered.' After a moment where neither spoke, Jack carried on, 'Although I can't really see how it was supposed to work, or why it doesn't.'

He stood silently again, but Vicky did not join in the conversation. With the sun at her back, Jack had to shade his eyes with a hand at his forehead. He assumed it must be before 8am, but already felt sweat trickling down his spine. Finally she commented, 'I'm hungry.'

Looking past her, he set off on the path to the next cottage. 'I'm not.'

The eastern part of the island had larger bushes and some trees forming its greenery, whereas the remainder was merely short grass, or rocky patches – the parts of the rock isle that had not yet gained any soil. At the edge of the wooded portion, the ruins of a chapel stood beside a pair of gun batteries. Further along the treeline, a cottage appeared slightly less decrepit.

Behind the cottage, and halfway to what Jack thought

must have been an old livestock barn, he spotted, unmistakably, a well. He had walked between the buildings the evening before, and now stopped to look from one to the other to work out how he had not spotted the well before. The barnyard was part-bordered by a stone wall, and as Jack had walked in the opposite direction previously, he assumed the wall had blocked his view. He considered his own excuse feeble, but could not improve on it.

The well did have a water surface about fifteen feet down, but no system for lifting the water out. He turned a complete circle, twice, examining the outside walls of all buildings. There was a tap at knee height on the side of the barn, but it was only attached to six inches of detached pipe.

Jack also spotted Vicky in the bushes beside the priory. He shouted to her and pointed to the low circular wall around the well. She held a cupped hand high in the air and came over to find him inspecting the isolated wall tap. Her mouth was full and she held out the hand to offer him some blackberries.

'Perfect. Thanks.' He took half of them and stuffed all in his mouth at once. Both were incapable of speaking coherently with mouths full of berries. Jack pulled at the remainder of the broken water pipe, which poked an inch out of the ground. It was immovable, but his wrangling made a noise echo from inside the barn.

He handed Vicky a small rock and said, 'Whit hat when Ar whout.' She nodded without attempting to reply, and they smiled at each other.

Jack called for her to knock the pipe with the rock and searched inside for the connecting pipe. There were several rooms built from wooden walls inside the large stone building, and he found the location where he reckoned the noise of her banging was loudest.

The door was hidden behind piles of wooden planks and,

finally, a blanket hanging on the wall. When he cleared everything away, the door was sound, and either locked or blocked from the inside.

He tried to pick up a large stone from the main doorway, but it was too heavy and he dropped it after only a few feet. He selected a slightly smaller one from outside and waved Vicky to join him. As she entered the cooler shade of the barn, he smashed the inner door open by launching the rock at the handle.

The room was open to the high barn roof but had no windows. There was a large stone sink against the outside wall, several wooden shelves on the inner walls, and high on the stone outer wall was a large copper tank, with pipes descending to the sink and into the floor beside it.

Jack hurt his hand trying to turn the sink tap. As he shook the hand and cursed, Vicky pushed a short piece of wood between the handle prongs. It was a poor lever, but enough to allow her to break the crusty seal that held the tap closed. The pipe clunked, some water dripped from it, and then a sudden gush came out. She quickly closed the tap again, and the two looked at each other in astonishment.

Large metal jugs lined one of the shelves and Jack took one for himself and handed one to Vicky. They stood at the sink and drank too much too quickly. As with the berries, it was several minutes before their gasping subsided enough to talk.

'Food and water. We can live here.' He grinned inanely.

She smiled at him and shook her head. 'Hang on, a few berries isn't enough to live on.'

'It's enough to keep us alive long enough to catch some birds, or fish, or birds' eggs. And to work out what other possibilities there might be.'

She took another gulp, chin already soaked, and nodded.

Within half an hour, they had collected the gear from

beside the previous day's bonfire at the beach. They sat in the kitchen of the farm cottage. The plumbing did not work in the cottage, but they agreed that they would prefer to occupy it and carry water over from the barn.

Vicky had retrieved one of the armulets from the bodies in the pub, and after wearing it up the hill and a bit of additional shaking, it had enough battery power to function. It was not her own, so had not learnt her voice or gestures. She used the touchscreen.

The infonetwork was operating normally and Jack asked her to look up any history of the island, with a view to determining what food resources there could be. Vicky had her own idea though. She looked up their audiopt feeds, which also operated normally. 'What do we do? If the audiopts are on, we can't hide.'

'I'm surprised they work here, we must be miles from the nearest infonetwork tower. Actually, are you sure ours are on?' Jack knew the armulet itself also undertook audiopt surveillance, and that the nearest tower must be close enough if the armulet had a network connection. He tried to wish the knowledge away.

She smiled. 'Yes, I can see you're looking at me.' She showed him the image on the screen, of her holding up the armulet. When he looked at it, the screen changed to an infinitely diminishing repeated view of Vicky holding up the armulet, the screen of which showed her again holding it up, and so on.

He turned away to stare out of the window. He looked past the well and beyond the barnyard wall. He continued to stare silently, whilst Vicky's slender fingers tapped the armulet. It struggled for power, and she had to shake it several times. Although the kinetic energy converter was quite efficient, the distance to the nearest towers meant that the machine had to transmit quite strong radio messages to talk to the infonetwork. As it was barely powered up, this drained the energy almost as soon as she imparted it. 'This says there should be rabbits on the island. I haven't seen any, have you?'

'Where's your brother?'

'What?'

'Check on Truvan's audiopt feed to see where they are.'

'No, I can check Bailey's.' Her fingers tapped faster than he had ever seen her do anything.

Jack sat down and put his hand on Vicky's knee. He could not see the screen easily, so just watched her hazel eyes. She leaned back in her chair, gazing blankly at the device, and he saw her eyes bulge with water. Her right hand reached up to place her finger against the side of her head and it started to draw slow circles. The tears rolled down her cheeks, and she spoke to the armulet, 'He did drown that day. His physiology readings say there's no pulse, and the location tracker has him out to sea. He isn't far from here, but he's gone, Jack.'

He gently took the armulet from her hands and shook it violently to rejuvenate the machine again. Jack searched for Truvan Truva's audiopt feed.

Jane interjected, 'No need, their audiopt feeds are back online.'

'Where are they?' Truvan and Halthrop demanded simultaneously.

'Yep, definitely on this island.' Jane pointed over the beach house roof. 'They're both up top, at the eastern end, this end, about 200 metres inland.' Truvan started activating his own armulet.

The posse splashed up the beach towards the house and the pub. They advanced without any concern for being seen or heard. The morning sun had become covered with a high grey cloud, and Halthrop felt the occasional spot of rain, cold on his face.

The major and Darren had their armulets set to track the audiopt feed from Jack Smith, whilst Jane and Truvan had been instructed to find his sister. The two pairings ignored the beach buildings and set off in single file up the zigzag track to the top of Steep Holm island.

The wind was stronger on top, but was still just a light breeze. As they emerged from the thin copse, which bordered the east end of the island, the posse was at a path junction.

They compared audiopt feeds and split up. Jack and Vicky were in the same room in the same building, but they could approach it from two directions. Darren and Frank went around the ruined chapel, whilst the others continued further north to come around the back of the old barn. Halthrop sent Vicky's brother the longer way round, so he could enter the cottage first and secure the prisoners before Truvan could get overly excited and involved.

Halthrop had not banked on Vicky espying him through the cottage window, which Truvan monitored on the audiopts. He hurried Jane into a run. However, even sprinting, their longer journey gave the major time to enter first.

'Jack Smith, Vicky Truva, we are here to take you back to Highnam Kangaroo for trial,' Halthrop called from the porch as soon as he crossed the threshold.

Neither pair could see the other directly, but Darren was fixed on his armulet screen and nodded to his leader, who watched the hallway directly in front of them. He mouthed, emitting barely even a whisper, 'They're sitting in the kitchen.' With his right hand, Darren gave a flat hand point along the passageway.

'Please come in,' Jack called from his seat in the kitchen. 'We won't run, and we're not armed.'

At that moment, Truvan Truva burst in through the back door, directly into the kitchen. 'You bastard! What have you done to my sister?'

She leapt up to block her brother's path to assault Jack. 'He's done nothing to me. What the hell do you mean? I'm here of my own free will.'

Truvan pushed Vicky aside and grabbed Smith by the throat. His pale arms and hands looked tiny and frail, as they pathetically flapped at the strong hands that gripped his neck. Jack could only manage a gurgle of protest, and his dark eyes bulged slightly in his reddening face. Vicky also grabbed one of Truvan's muscular, brown arms and tried to pull him off. He looked around at his sister's face. 'He killed Bailey,' he shouted.

Vicky started to punch her brother's side and back. Her blows had little effect on him, but she continued blindly one fist after the other. Jane had followed him in through the back door, and she also grabbed at one of Truvan's arms to pull him off. Jack's eyes started to roll up into his head. His weak fingers subsided in their attempts to pull Truvan's hands off his throat.

A careering, blond bull charged across the room and tackled Truvan to the ground. Vicky was thrown to the side, and Jane stood looking stunned at her empty hands. Darren continued to wrestle with Truvan. He managed to hold the surviving twin down on the ground, and Halthrop positioned himself between the pair and the unconscious Smith.

'STOP!' Major Halthrop's commanding voice caused everybody to freeze. 'Mr Truva, Darren will escort you outside. Do not attempt to come back in.' He took a step to Vicky and held out his hand to help her up.

Darren carefully climbed off Truvan, who had not tried to move again. Darren pulled him up and shoved the man towards the back door. 'He killed my brother!' Truvan shouted and lunged again for the limp body in the chair. Darren had his path well blocked and was the larger of the two. He pushed Truvan further towards the door, and without actually touching either of them, Halthrop moved slightly to add his weight to the proceedings.

Jane had her fingers touching Jack's neck, and Vicky knelt beside him. She looked at Jane with wide eyes. The young militiawoman reassured her, 'He's alive. Fingers crossed he's just been knocked out. I don't think he was strangled for long enough for any lasting damage.'

Vicky put her hand to Jack's cheek and bent forward to whisper to him, 'Please be alright.'

Halthrop put his hand on Vicky's arm, and she turned her head to look up to him. 'Could you go with your brother back to the boat, please? I'm hoping that you can soothe his anger so that we don't have to restrain him. We do have restraints, but I'd like to avoid him becoming another criminal.' She nodded, kissed Jack on the cheek and walked out to the yard.

'What do you think, Jane?'

She looked at her boss with surprise. 'Um, oh. How about we try splashing his face with water to wake him up?' Halthrop gave the slightest of nods. She took the cup of water that Jack had previously been drinking and threw it into the side of his face, but he did not stir. She checked his pulse again and then tried slapping his cheek. Jack still did not move; only gravity made the water drip from his nose, cheek and short, dark hair. Jane looked to Halthrop and shrugged.

'OK, lift him up a bit, I'll carry him down.' Between them, they flopped Smith's body over the major's shoulder, and Jane guided him to squeeze out of the doorway without banging their prisoner on the frame.

Jack woke up on a low bed in the cabin of the *Top Dog*. Vicky sat beside him and was mopping his brow with a wet cloth. It was delightfully cool and Jack smiled at her, unaware of where they were. Beyond Vicky's slight smile and concerned eyes, Jack saw a ghost. He had seen the man hit his head and drown in the water. He started in the bed and discovered that his left wrist was tied to a pole, which held the second berth up above him. Jack was still groggy, and he pulled hard, looking at the plastic tie. It cut into his wrist and the pain woke him up properly.

His mind filled with a different memory. The same bearded man had also strangled Jack, nearly to death. For an instant, Jack considered that he must have actually died and this was the afterlife. Then he came completely to his senses and recognised Truvan as the second twin, the real, live strangler.

The interior decoration in the narrowboat was red, terracotta and black. Despite the brightness outside, the decor made the cabin dark. The heat was stifling, and Jack was glad that Vicky continued to touch the cloth to his forehead. She put a hand onto his arm with a hushing sound. 'It's OK, Jack, lie still.'

'Where are we?' he demanded much more loudly than was necessary.

Truvan interrupted, 'You're on your way to pay for what you've done.'

Vicky waved to quiet her brother and gave him a sharp scowl. He muted and Vicky explained, 'We're on the other boat, on the way to Weston-super-Mare, from where they're going to take us back to Highnam.'

'Highnam...' Jack mumbled, his brain fogging over again.

She squeezed his upper arm gently. 'It's Saturday, Jack. Kangaroo is tomorrow.'

'Kangaroo,' he repeated, but remained uncertain as to what she meant.

She leaned forward, kissed his cheek gently, and then

211

whispered in his ear, 'Shh. Go back to sleep now, you need to rest.' Without considering her words, he closed his eyes and tried to think through what he had just been told. The cloth was cool, and that was all he could think about. Jack fell asleep, but was awakened again only ten minutes later when they arrived in Weston. Jane came into the cabin, sent Truvan on deck and helped Vicky to prepare Jack to be untied and go ashore.

Terry motored as fast as the shallow boat could manage and deliberately ran them straight onto the flat sand of the main beach. The Spokesperson of the town's Kangaroo met them on the beach with ten horses to loan for their trip back to Highnam.

A few of the townsfolk were with her, intrigued to see the man who had blown up the Doughnut. Most mistook the non-uniformed, rugged man standing at the prow as the likely terrorist, but Truvan leapt off first under no control of the Bristol Brigade members. The confusion was quickly dispelled when Darren helped to pull Jack Smith up from below onto the tiny foredeck.

They were not rough in handling him, especially as Vicky stuck close by him every step. She was not bound, but Jane had been instructed to watch her every move carefully. Halthrop did not expect trouble, but knew that such assumptions could be the most dangerous. 'The wise ones should first look to their own self-protection,' he muttered to himself, last man on the canal boat. He leapt down to the beach and went to shake hands with Weston's head woman.

The posse formed an unlikely looking convoy. Jack and Vicky, as well as Truvan, were noticeably dirtier than the others. Halthrop looked almost pristine. Jack's bonds were cut and replaced with a single tie holding his wrist to the knotted reins.

He could ride safely, but his horse was also tethered to Darren's and Terry's, one in front and one behind, as they moved up a long concrete ramp that rose from the beach to the old roadway. They then rode three abreast to stop the ropes tugging on the horses. This meant that Vicky could not easily get to talk to Jack, and most of the time Jane rode next to her.

The youngest of the militia asked Vicky many questions. Halthrop brought up the rear of the group and listened in to Vicky's answers as much as possible. Often though, she did not provide a coherent explanation for things. At times, her responses were even self-contradictory

Chapter Twenty-five

They rode along the old railway line from Weston to Brigade HQ in Bristol. The sun beat down, and horses and riders al sweated profusely. They arrived at the militia house after lunchtime, rested inside, ate a little, but mostly drank pint upon pint of water.

For the remaining journey, to deliver Jack to his home Kangaroo, Halthrop announced that they should take the ATVs They sat fully charged and would be able to recharge again when they got there. Although it would only take a couple of hours along the old M5, Halthrop told his troops to expect to remain overnight. He anticipated that Lloyd Lloyd would want them to guard the prisoner until Kangaroo met and sentenced him. He stated to Jack, 'I fully expect that we will also be tasked with delivering you to serve your sentence.'

Jack was sitting on the floor with his back to a wall and hands bound, clasped between his raised knees. He asked 'What do you think they'll give me?'

The rest of the group sat around a table on the other side of the room and all ears pricked up to hear what Halthrop might pronounce. He stood silently over his prisoner for a few moments and then shook his head. 'Ours is not to make such judgments. We are just policemen. Moreover, we aren't members of Highnam Kangaroo. You're their sifter, you'll know better than I the punishments that they give out.' Jack continued to look at Major Halthrop but neither spoke any further. As part of his job, Jack had always attended Highnam's weekly Kangaroo. He had always done so via armulet, and deliberately as an observer only, not a participant.

'It'll be OK, Jack. Don't worry.' Vicky looked across

from the table and tried a little smile.

Truvan's head jerked from looking at Jack to face his sister across the table. He almost shouted, 'They need to string him up. He is the exact example of somebody that hanging is too good for.'

Vicky stared at her brother, her eyes full of tears. She struggled to form words. 'Wha... Why would you say that? We are a peaceful Kangaroo. Since the Times, nobody in Highnam has been punished with death. Why would you want to drag us back to that?'

Truvan continued to shout; spittle caught in his beard, and he pointed across the room without breaking eye contact with Vicky. 'He's the one who wants to take us back to the Times. Don't you have any idea what he did? He killed Bailey, Vicky. How can you defend him?'

She reached her hand out to touch the one he had left on the table. Her voice was tiny, barely audible. 'You're wrong. Bailey's death was an accident; Jack had nothing to do with it. And destroying the computers didn't hurt anyone. If anything, it gave us all a bit of peace from the armulets for a few days.'

Truvan lifted his hands to his head and pulled at his hair. He strained, oblivious to any pain. His eyes were wide, showing large whites around the brown irises. At the same time, he bared white teeth in the midst of his brown beard. He then staggered back out of the chair, which fell over. 'I'll kill him now,' he cried as he ran towards the figure on the floor.

Terry and Darren leapt from their seats to chase Truvan, but Halthrop floored the twin before they could take three steps. With a swift swing of his arm, the major planted the point of his elbow hard into the man's Adam's apple. Truvan pivoted to horizontal as his centre of gravity carried on forwards and then crashed flat on his back, both hands clutching at his throat. The two younger militiamen grabbed him, rolled him over and

215

swiftly tied his wrists.

Jane had a grip on Vicky's upper arm, but it had all been too quick for her and she had barely shifted in her seat by the time her brother was face down, bound and gurgling. 'He can't breathe,' she shouted, without any attempt to break Jane's grasp, or get up.

They sat Truvan up and dragged him across the floor to sit against the wall opposite Jack, as he coughed and spluttered to regain his breath. Jane allowed Vicky to leave her seat and tend to her brother. He pushed her away with his leg, and she crossed the room to talk to Jack. He sat still, looked at the threatening man, and wondered if he would get to Highnam alive to face the Kangaroo.

'Are you OK?' Vicky knelt, put her hand on his cheek and leaned her head right down to make eye contact.

Jack thought. 'Yes. He didn't get near me.' He looked up to Halthrop, who stood in exactly the same place as previously. The militia's commanding officer appeared completely unruffled at having just felled a man with a single blow. 'Thank you, Major. I hope you will be able to get me there in one piece.' Halthrop bowed his head slightly but did not speak.

They remained in the building for another hour as the Brigade members organised a second set of expeditionary equipment, strapped to two ATV trailers. Halthrop made a list on a large board of the things they would need to clear up once this mission was finally completed.

There were bikes and equipment at Sharpness docks, to be co-ordinated with the return of the horses, and the need to keep the ATVs charged up and finally returned to headquarters. He looked at the list for a few minutes and decided that the scheduling of the things to be done could not be addressed until they had fully completed Jack Smith's case. Without foreknowledge of the punishment he would receive, they could not guess at the time required to complete the job.

Jane startled her boss: 'It's going to be a big payday, but we'll definitely have earned it.' He turned and asked how the preparations were progressing. 'That's what I've come for – to tell you that we think we're all set to go. Nearly 1600 now, so we should get to Highnam before dark if we leave asap.' Halthrop agreed and they walked Jack out to the bright sunshine, where the others were prepared on the four-wheelers.

The camouflage caps distinguished the posse from their charges. Major Halthrop had now classified both Truvan and Vicky Truva as prisoners. He rode at the rear, alone, whilst the rest had one militiaman driving and one prisoner riding behind. Darren had been assigned as guard for Truvan, and they were sent ahead fifteen minutes before the other three vehicles. Jack watched them whizz off and hoped that being out of Truvan's sight would be enough to calm the man, although he was also glad of the physical separation that Halthrop had engineered.

The sun continued to sap the energy from everybody. Vicky muttered to Jack that they had no hats, but she was beaten to complaining further by a change in the weather. A swirling wind rushed down the street, and brought cold. The sky darkened quickly, and the grey clouds came in thicker and lower with each new gust. The wind continued blowing in random directions and with ever greater speed. They set off along the road and, with his hands tied together, Jack found the blowing of the wind unsettling. He was not convinced that he could cling on to Terry in the event of an unexpected gust. However, it was also very difficult to make himself heard. Heavy rain came.

Even before they passed the edge of the desolate city of Bristol, rivers of rainwater were snaking across the old tarmac. Any hole was filled with water, and cracks in the road surface, formed from years of cold winters and hot summers, became miniature raging torrents.

It was nearly three hours to nightfall, and yet the city streets were very dark. The ATVs had to travel slowly to ensure they avoided the bigger potholes. The problem that really slowed them down was the rain in their faces. Everyone had goggles for riding the open quad bikes, but these became covered in large droplets making it difficult for the drivers to see much in front. Major Halthrop was the first to fall foul of the conditions.

Jack turned his head away from one gust of wind and noticed that the major had stopped well behind them. Jack shouted but his words were blown away, so he banged Terry on the head. Terry turned slightly and shouted something back that Jack also could not hear; he knocked on his head again and Terry braked. He turned to remonstrate to his passenger, but Jack turned his own head to indicate that the young soldier should watch behind for his boss.

Halthrop was astride his stationary bike with the front right wheel in a ditch. They could see he was rocking it back and forth to try and jump back out of the little trench. Terry made to shout to Jane, but she had stopped to wipe her goggles and noticed the hold up. Halthrop escaped with the only damage being very wet mud splattered all up his black trousers.

They progressed further, continuing at little more than ten miles per hour overall. Every minute or two, it was necessary for the drivers to stop and clean their goggles. Jane and Vicky developed a system whereby Jane would just turn her head, and Vicky would wipe the rain from her lenses. Terry never asked Jack for help with it. In all cases, the small cloths they used for wiping became sodden very quickly – it was a case of wiping the water around the mini-windscreens, or at least making it more uniform, rather than actually drying them.

The wind was still howling, a ragged din racing up and

down the road and chasing off up side streets. It brought rain from all directions and everyone was completely soaked, despite rain ponchos that Jane had brought from the Brigade HQ stores.

For people who had spent the summer surviving an average daily heat of thirty degrees, the storm's ambient temperature of just over ten degrees, with wind and rain, made them all shiver. Each time they stopped, driver and passenger would try to shake off the wetness in their clothes. Water did fly off in all directions like drying dogs, but the wind hurled it back mercilessly. Every time he stopped to clean his goggles, Halthrop would also wipe his moustache.

Jack wondered how long such a strong wind could be sustained; it ought to blow itself out quite quickly. An hour of slow travel took them on to the M5 – the Big Road – which had good drainage. The surface still had a lot of water, but it was relatively uniform, and there was less danger of accidentally driving off the road. However, it encouraged them to drive faster, and the holes and cracks in the tarmac, although less frequent, were larger. The wide road was much more open on the sides than the city streets had been, and the wind buffeted more powerfully. Jack became more and more scared as the little four-wheeler scooted along.

They came across Darren and Truvan, stuck. The ATV had its nose down a small crevasse that cut right across the road. Darren was pulling at the handlebar on the right side, but the scar in the road was just the perfect width and depth: the front wheels and the nose were jammed hard. He had no success. Truvan was squatting in the middle of the motorway, trying to gain some shelter from a low metal railing that ran along the central reserve. The others approached slowly, and Jane found a narrower spot to bump her ATV across.

Halthrop and Terry stopped behind the stricken vehicle

and got off to assess the situation. Jack sat shivering and turned his face away from the incoming rain. All discussions had to be undertaken very close to the listener's ear, or the sound was abducted by the wind before anything could be heard.

The final plan had Jane sitting on the seat ready to assist with the motor, whilst the other four men – including Truvan whose bonds had been removed – pulled, one at each corner. Jack could see that Halthrop was careful to ensure that each person understood their role and the potential risks. The most likely danger Jack foresaw was that Jane might engage the wheels whilst somebody's hands were dangerously close especially the two behind that would be outside her field of vision.

He looked across to Vicky, who sat on Jane's ATV. Vicky was watching the activity intently. She had a grim look on her face, and a silver sheet held around her body. Jack's shivering had warmed him enough that it stopped.

He heard a muffled shout from Halthrop, and they all heaved. There was a crunch as the four-wheeler moved back a few inches. It was the sound of plastic cracking, which Jack guessed would be the front bodywork suffering damage. He could not see much, with the bodies buzzing around the bike but it must have been loud to be heard at all.

He turned his face away again, more interested in trying to stop the cold stinging on his cheeks. With his hands tied together, it was difficult to protect every bit of exposed skin.

At the second attempt, the ATV was completely rescued. The nose was broken, with a large piece flapping in the wind but still partly connected. Darren gave it a short test drive and returned giving a fat thumbs-up signal. He jumped off, grabbed the hanging plastic piece and pulled hard to snap it off. The entire front end came off in his hands, including the headlight shrouds.

Terry and Darren engaged in a tug of war with the bodywork to complete the breakage that Darren had attempted. The rain was ceaseless. The plastic broke and Darren fell backwards onto the soaking ground. Terry dropped the piece he held and howled. Jack could immediately see blood dripping amidst the water from the thin white fingers of Terry's left hand. Jane swiftly pulled her small rucksack off and took out a field dressing to stem the flow. It was a large bandage pad with ties that she wrapped around his hand several times and tied off neatly over the pad on his palm.

Jack was knocked hard to the ground to the side of his ATV. Truvan flailed punches wildly. The deluge made it difficult for either man to see the other clearly. Vicky's brother was on top of Jack, so most punches landed somewhere. The bound man held his two hands over his face and squirmed. Through the grim, wet air, he heard Vicky scream the word 'Stop!' Within a second, the weight was off him. Halthrop stood astride Jack, but watched Truvan, who had rolled some distance from the kick that the major had landed in his side.

Truvan got onto his hands and knees. His expression was unclear behind the large goggles, but his mouth hung open for deep breaths. A trail of water ran from the lowest point of his beard. 'I'll kill you, Smith,' he shouted over the storm. 'Kangaroo won't sentence you to death, but I won't let you live. Bailey was a better man than you.' Major Halthrop took a step towards the wolf-like twin to cement his blockage of the route to his prone prisoner.

Twenty feet away, Jack could see Jane perform a similar guard job on Vicky. Jane kept between her and the action and held up a hand to indicate that Vicky should stay put and let things happen without her.

Darren and Terry were waved over by their boss. He didn't speak, but they came and picked up Truvan under his

221

armpits. The two younger men frogmarched him back to the newly released ATV.

They bound his hands together behind his back and added an extra tie to the pillion bar across the rear. He twisted to look back at Jack, who remained on the floor, a layer of water running around his body towards the roadside. 'Murderer!'

Jack's first thought was that the way they had tied Truvan would be very dangerous for him if they went over any bumpy ground. At the very least, the plastic cuffs would cut mercilessly into the man's wrists. Jack did not have time to question his own thought processes.

Major Halthrop grabbed his upper arm and pulled. 'Come on, let's go now.' It was not enough to lift Jack, but enough to force him to make the effort to get up.

With a strong shove, Darren remounted the larger piece of the nose of his ATV. It clipped into place with a crunching noise, and the headlight covers refracted their light into tight beams again.

Terry's injury was painful but not severe. However, with the over-sized bandage, there was no way that he could handle his vehicle. Although Truvan had experience with such machines, Halthrop did not even consider putting him to drive Jack.

Halthrop had to shout to be heard by his team over the wind. 'We'll keep the convoy tight from now on. Truvan is to stay tied to that ATV all the time.'

'I can't drive, Frank,' Terry shouted back.

The major nodded. 'You ride passenger and Mr Smith will have to drive you.'

The weather was so miserable that they left as quickly as possible, Jack's first test being a careful trundle over the narrower part of the hazard in the tarmac. As it required a very delicate touch on the accelerator to maintain movement at a low speed, he gave everyone a poor first impression. It was Jack's first time to control such a vehicle.

'Come on, let's go.' Terry was loud in Jack's ear.

Whilst he understood the theory of how the ATV functioned, the balance between the different controlling levers was sensitive. The electric motor could be engaged slightly without being powerful enough to start them moving. The tiniest movement of the lever beyond this caused significant acceleration. Like any new driver, Jack spent the first few yards lurching and stopping as his grip moved the handle beyond that threshold and then he released again in a panic.

Terry gripped Jack around the waist, but with his weakened right hand, there were two occasions when he thought he had hurled Terry off the back.

'Careful, you idiot. What are you doing? Keep it smooth – I can't grip on properly.'

Each time he turned, he got an earful of abuse from the slight militiaman, who remained on the back seat. He didn't argue, but simply said 'Sorry' each time.

Darren led the convoy, followed by Jane, and then Jack, with Major Halthrop following last. Jack tried to follow Jane's route as exactly as he could, aiming for the wheel tracks left as her tyres part-cleared the water. He figured that he could avoid any hazards that way, as she would have to crash before him. Vicky kept turning to monitor his progress. Her expression was neutral and Jack tried to catch her eye with a smile. He assumed that the grey, rain-filled air made it impossible for her to observe this. She did not smile back, or make any gestures.

The road continued in fair condition for another eight miles, before Jack had to grip the brake handle hard and brace himself against Terry's flying weight in his back. The light level had dropped towards twilight, and the vehicles' headlights were poor. Jack and Terry halted before they hit the back seat on which Vicky was perched.

She craned to look over Jane's shoulder, and this meant Jack could see little in front. His view was almost entirely of Vicky's back, which was shiny in the camouflage-pattern rain poncho they all wore. Ahead, he made out a single narrow beam of light, pointing forwards and at an angle to the right. It scattered from the solid wires of rainfall.

Jack's own headlights were blinding in reflection, especially in combination with Jane's bright brake lights. They dimmed as she switched the motor to parking mode. Darren emerged to the side of his ATV, stepping forward to look in front. Terry pulled hard on Jack's shoulder to leap off and investigate. Halthrop drove forwards past them all and took up a position at the left side, to illuminate the area in front.

As he leant over, Jack could see that Darren had crashed into a fox. The animal was squirming on the ground, but one leg was stuck out of Jack's view under the ATV wheel. Halthrop grabbed hold of the wet head, but it immediately slipped his grasp and the fox continued to writhe. He knelt on the animal's shoulder and took a better hold avoiding the biting teeth. Darren bent down in front and cut its throat. The movements subsided, there was a shudder and then it was still. The two men dragged it out from under the vehicle and investigated underneath for damage.

Jack reversed a little and then pulled up beside Vicky. She was shivering. They had to shout to hear each other. 'You should ask them for more clothes.'

She shook her head. 'I'm OK when we're moving, it's just when we stop that I get cold.'

'I guess concentrating on hanging on probably distracts you when we're going.' Jack gave a little laugh. He looked ahead again. Halthrop was watching him.

Terry and Darren were pointing under the centre of the

crashed quad bike. Their heads were close as they shouted over the wind. Jack could not hear their discussion. Terry stood and relayed the conclusions to the major. He looked down at the single headlight beam and nodded.

He waved a hand towards Truvan, bound to the pillion handle, and Darren used his still-bloody knife to cut the plastic ties holding him. Vicky's brother shook his hands in the air and eased himself off the ATV carefully. He stamped his feet and jumped from side to side a little.

Halthrop continued to give orders, and Jack continued to catch one word in several. The upshot was that Jane moved to the point position in the convoy, with Darren to follow in second place.

Although the sun had not been perceptible since the storm arrived, it was time for night to close in. Jack wondered if there would be any difference. He felt like they had already travelled most of the journey at night.

He wiped his goggles and his cold cheeks, and they drove off. As the light level dropped further, the convoy drove even closer behind each other than before. Occasionally, Jack would steer slightly off course and be able to see the front bike.

Darren was right behind Vicky. If he reached out his arm, Jack was convinced that his chubby hand could touch her back. On a couple of these occasions, Jack would wave at the situation as a message to Halthrop. Given that Darren had crashed twice already, and had only one headlight, he drove very dangerously. Jack wanted Halthrop to tell his man to hang back a little. He pictured Darren's handlebars slamming into the small of Vicky's back. She could easily be paralysed.

There was nothing from the major though. Jack had to hope that, as they were only travelling at ten to fifteen miles an hour, Darren would be able to react. He knew he could see very little though, and Darren would have the same wind and rain in

225

his face. He had abandoned his cap, and the mess of golden hair stood out in the grim conditions. He was a beacon to follow, but Vicky and Jane were enshrouded in dark colours. If they had to stop suddenly, there would be a much more significant accident than the fox collision.

In the end, Jack's imaginings got the better of him. He steered to the left and sped up to come alongside. Darren looked across to him and shouted something that was lost in the wind. Jack waved for Darren to hang back a little, but he thought Jack meant for them to stop. The convoy came to a halt in bits and pieces.

Halthrop drove right up adjacent to Jack to ask what was going on, the same question Terry had been shouting ever since Jack pulled forward. Jane and Vicky did not notice that they were alone at first, but eventually turned full circle to return to find out the situation.

Darren protested, 'I can barely see. This one headlight hardly gives any light. If I hang back any further, I lose the route. I have to go like a baby elephant holding its mother's tail.'

At this, the men stared at Darren, and then at Jack.

Jack shouted back, mostly towards Halthrop, 'If they have to stop suddenly, he'll kill both of them.'

'Rubbish. My front wheels are ahead of my handlebars, we'll just bump wheels if they slow too quickly.'

Jane and Vicky sat just out of earshot, perhaps only ten feet away. Jack looked at the girl who had left her home and family and lost a brother, on his quest to change the world.

Halthrop took charge. 'OK, Darren, drive safely. Whatever is needed to ensure that you can proceed with the minimum risk. The conditions are awful, but you know what you're doing. Let's go, people.'

They lined up the vehicles again ready to go. 'Get a grip

you idiot,' Truvan told Jack through the rain and faced forward again to cold shoulder any response.

Darren drove pretty much exactly the same way. Jack fumed. Truvan's back was right in front of him, blocking any view of Darren or the women. Jack drove closer to the bike in front than he had previously. Instead of the danger to Vicky, he focussed on his own handlebars hitting Truvan.

Inevitably, Jane had to stop suddenly, and so Darren's brake lights lit up, blinding Jack. He swerved slightly and braked hard as well. He came to a halt squashed over his handlebars, Terry on his back, and right beside Truvan. As they all sat up and took stock, Jack cursed that his instincts had saved Truvan from any harm.

Darren had stopped inches from the rear of Vicky's seat, and Halthrop trundled past them all to see what had panicked Jane.

The motorway was up on an embankment, and as it dipped and the adjacent land rose level, the River Frome was flowing across the carriageway. The road had a bridge over the river and then went into a cutting on the other side. There was so much water in the river that when it escaped from its banks, it flowed north into the cutting and formed a wide ford.

The Brigade gathered around Jane, who stayed seated, and Jack could see them pointing forwards and to the sides. The water's edge was still fifty yards away, so it was difficult to make out much through the poorly lit, rainy darkness.

'Hey!' Jack heard Truvan shout and turned to look. He felt the man's gloved fist hit him straight on the chin and Jack flew sideways off the ATV on to the ground. He was not knocked unconscious, but there was an instant where the gloom went completely black, and he only regained his faculties on the ground. He was already soaked, but his left side felt suddenly colder. He could see Truvan leaning over the now vacant seat and expected he would quickly move over it to continue the attack. Jack got up and ran.

He headed back the way they had come and then across the central grass onto the return carriageway. The light was lost within a few yards, and Jack did his best to follow a white line painted on the road. After five seconds of sprinting, he looked back. He could see a couple of figures in the headlights, but could not tell who they were, or where Truvan was. Jack faced south again and continued to run as fast as he dared. It was not long before he was out of breath and slowed to a walk.

Away from the headlights, the night was black. Although the moon was still fat, the thick clouds absorbed all the light it offered. He pulled off the goggles. The wind-whipped rain forced his eyes half closed and made his vision even more obscured. Looking back, Jack could not see any shadows following him, and certainly no lights. The ATVs were getting on for 200 yards away. Although it was difficult to make out anything that happened at that distance in the storm, the small pool of dim light appeared stationary.

Jack looked ahead and on both sides of the motorway. He decided that when they came looking for him he would be easy to spot on the barren tarmac. He was nearly at the end of the raised embankment. Down on the west side, the vague difference in blackness between the land and the sky was broken slightly by a square shape. The lines were so straight, it had to be man-made: a building.

Jack crossed back over the central grass border and the low metal rail and half slid down the muddy bank towards the dark shape. He could not guess at exactly how far away it was. And he could not tell anything about the terrain in between. From his lower angle, the building's silhouette stood out more clearly against the dark grey sky. Jack held one hand out in front of his face to protect against tree branches and walked precariously over squelchy ground.

The field between Jack and the farmhouse lit up slightly, as if the clouds had parted just enough for some moonlight to filter down. He turned to look at the swirling sky behind, and could see three headlights shining down from the embankment. They were quickly joined by four more, and the vehicles were parked in a line glowering down at him.

The bank was too steep and slippery for the bikes, but Jack saw the largest and smallest members of the posse bundle down the slope on foot. He turned to run away, but collided with a fence of metal wires. He put his foot on the second wire up, but it was rusty and snapped as soon as he tried to step up. To catch himself, Jack grabbed at the top wire. Only one hand closed on it, but it was barbed. The pain and the missed grip caused him to fall forwards against the fence. He then slipped in the mud and slid down the front of the wires.

Before Jack could pick himself up, he felt Jane crash down on top of him. She was not a heavy girl, but had launched herself from some distance and hit him hard. He heard her scream and felt Darren's big hands drag him along by the shoulders. The farm boy easily lifted Jack up to his feet, and he saw Jane pick herself up slowly rubbing the top of her cap. She had careered headfirst into a fence post and looked a little unsteady.

'You OK?' Darren asked her.

'Yes. Just banged my head.' She put her hand out to hold the fence, but Jack grabbed it. Darren whipped him back like a rag doll, Jack's feet off the ground. He had her by the sleeve and she stepped forward with the pull.

'Stop. The fence is barbed wire.'

Jane shone a light from her armulet and inspected Jack's claim. 'He's right. Come on, I'm OK now anyway.' Rubbing her head again, she led as Darren half carried Jack back up to the convoy.

When they arrived, the headlights were blinding and Jack had to cover his eyes. Darren stepped him to the side to face Halthrop. In the background, Jack could just make out Vicky stroking her hair. Her mouth was slightly open, and her goggles created an alien appearance.

Halthrop spoke. 'You know the audiopt feeds are back on? Even if you can't see anything in the dark, the locator still functions.'

Jack nodded. 'I'm a sifter, I know better than anyone how they work. But you are going to have to protect me from him.' He waved his hand towards Truvan, who sat as driver of the ATV Jack had been on.

Halthrop pulled a torch from the front pocket of his camouflage pattern jacket. He leant forward and scanned the torchlight over Jack's face. He glanced over at Truvan and put the torch away. 'Darren, retie Mr Truva to the pillion bar and keep him away from Smith.' The hand that Jack had waved had revealed that it was dripping blood, and Jane appeared with another bandage. He didn't find it painful, but the size of the dressing also ruled him out as a driver.

Halthrop looked around and then barked orders. 'Smith rides with me. Miss Truva, you'll have to drive, with Terry as your passenger. Jane, keep yourself and your quad bike between Jack and Truvan, whatever happens.'

Chapter Twenty-six

As they arrived in the village in the middle of the night, Halthrop decided that they would billet in Jack's grandmother's place. There was no jail in the village, and they knew her house was empty. Halthrop took Vicky and Jack inside with Terry. The house was unheated, but simply stepping out of the blowing rain made them all feel suddenly warm.

Darren and Jane were sent on to take Truvan to his house. Halthrop transmitted a video message to Lloyd Lloyd to explain that he had the fugitives and where they were to be kept until the Kangaroo met later that afternoon. There was no immediate reply from the Spokesperson.

They found dry clothes, as best they could. Vicky and Terry went to sleep in two of the bedrooms, and Halthrop and Jack made beds on the two sofas in the lounge. Halthrop had arranged for the doors and windows to be locked, and he untied Jack's bonds.

Jack rarely drank alcohol, but he and the major both recognised that they were in a situation that the old videostories would have insisted merited a glass of whisky for each man. Ellie had maintained a bottle that she had brought from Brighton. It had become a family heirloom, a dash offered up on the various momentous occasions in her life.

Jack had not been born the time she had touted a shot to toast their arrival in Highnam in 2038, and was only days old at Clara's wake in order to celebrate his birth. The only taste he had ever had from the bottle had been fourteen years previously when she had decreed that they should celebrate Jack's appointment as a sifter.

At more than fifty years old, the whisky tasted revolting.

It burned their throats, and Jack likened it to drinking muddy puddle water heated to scalding. Halthrop nodded, and his finger played around the glass as he contemplated the brown liquid. They dutifully swigged the remainder down; Jack resealed the bottle and put it back in the low cupboard.

'Eeugh,' he winced. 'With luck, I won't have something else to celebrate for at least fourteen more years.'

Halthrop raised both his eyebrows at Jack. He rested his glass against his chest and hoarsely asked, 'You have something to celebrate now?'

Jack closed the cupboard door, sat and smiled. 'I suppose "celebrate" is the wrong word. Or maybe not. It's difficult to guess how the people will have taken to their new lives without the audiopts. If they've understood and vote to switch them off then I'll be celebrating later today.'

'Why would they do that? It's against the Covenants of Jerusalem.'

'Actually, it's not. Well, not directly. Indeed I would argue that using the audiopts goes against the benefit of all.'

'How so? I mean using the audiopts goes straight to the heart of both "Nothing will be secret" and "Everyone's actions will be judged by all".'

'Yes, I must get in the habit of being clearer about what I mean on that. I'm wanting that the audiopt feeds be recorded but not published for everyone to see in real time. It used to be that the police would only look for evidence of crimes after they had been committed. People's lives were their own, unless they chose to break society's rules.'

'I'm very familiar with the historical approaches to law enforcement. The problem with that system, and what ultimately triggered the Times of Malthus, was that many, if not most, crimes were never reported or even spotted. They happened behind closed doors. And then, even if they were reported, it was extraordinarily difficult for the police to gather evidence that would have enabled society to pass judgement on them.'

'Exactly. Remember that the audiopts were invented after the Times began. We've never had a justice system in which the audiopt feeds could be used after the fact as evidence for making judgements.'

'Except that that is exactly the system we have now.'

Jack frowned. It was as if Major Halthrop was deliberately trying to avoid understanding Jack's arguments. Both men were seated on the edges of their sofas, looking straight at each other at a distance of six feet. Halthrop's blond eyebrows crinkled in bemusement at the phlegmatic revolutionary.

The room was cold, but neither of them lifted their blankets to wrap around their shoulders. The wind and rain continued to batter the outside walls and windows. Jack could still smell the woody scent of the whisky. He turned slightly to the side and lifted his feet on to the sofa, to lie back supported by its arm. He crossed his ankles, leaned back and turned to look side on at his captor. Whilst most of the Bristol Brigade had treated Jack like a dangerous criminal, at best with disdain, Halthrop had given off much more of an air of reasonable contemplation of the prisoner's position.

'The audiopt algorithms send suspect clips to the sifters as they happen. The system we have now is set up on the assumption of guilt, of crimes being committed.

'Last week, I had to send a clip to Kangaroo of a man and a woman making love in the woods. It was adulterous, but that's not a matter for the whole town. People should work stuff like that out amongst themselves.

'There are virtually no real crimes, but the assumption that we must guard against them has developed a system in which people round on their friends in an instant, decrying the most trivial of social errors as criminal behaviours.'

'But they don't really. Think of the punishments meted out by your own Kangaroo. They usually get people to work for each other as an apology for minor misbehaviours. The system reinforces respect for each other. It brings people closer in the end.'

Jack sat upright, gripped his glass tighter and his voice became uncontrollably louder. 'That kind of tittle-tattle should be dealt with socially between people – it is beyond the remit of a society's justice system. Or perhaps a better word would be "beneath" the remit of the justice system.'

'Look, we collected that young man who killed his father last month and took him to the jail in Bristol. That was the only serious crime I've ever heard of happening in Highnam, and that boy is simply ill. He has to be incarcerated, but it would be a stretch even to refer to him as a "criminal".'

Jack nodded and pointed towards Major Halthrop. His voice remained loud, head nodding wildly. 'This is exactly my point. There are no crimes and yet, every week, we have a court that meets, and metes out punishments. How can you not see the inconsistency there?'

Halthrop sounded calm. 'I don't see it as a court. That is a town meeting in which the citizens agree on the conduct expected in their community. Have you ever been to a Kangaroo session? Most of the business is about organising local activities; who's going to put up decorations for the summer fair, and so on.'

Jack was silent. He closed his eyes and tilted his head to face the ceiling. Without opening his eyes, Jack closed and opened his fists. He responded, 'Then why does it need to surveil the citizens every second of every day? There is nothing to be gained from it.'

When he finally turned and looked sidelong at Halthrop, the major kept his finger sliding along each side of his moustache, and smiled. 'Chicken and egg, Mr Smith. Is there no crime because the citizens are constantly monitored? Or is the monitoring excessive because there is no crime?'

Jack returned the smile, with a snort exhaled through his nostrils. 'You say Malthus, I say Malthoos.' They nodded in unison. Both men stared at the ceiling. 'A Victorian author called G.K. Chesterton summed up what I'm getting at when he wrote, "The most sacred thing is to be able to shut your own door."'

Halthrop tapped his whisky glass on the table. 'As I said, historically, most crimes happened behind closed doors.'

Jack held a finger and thumb to the bridge of his nose, without opening his eyes. It was a rhetorical affectation, and he hoped Halthrop was watching. He enjoyed the opportunity to practise some of his arguments and oratory. When he delivered them at Kangaroo, he would not want the people to be distracted by pauses or repetitions – they must be focussed on the logic.

'The society that led to the Times no longer exists. The crimes against society that were committed by big governments and corporations could not happen now. In populations of less than ten thousand, you cannot organise a conspiracy of any size, as everyone knows everyone. And, moreover, there are no great spoils from any such crime – it is impossible now to become supremely rich or powerful. We used a sledgehammer to crack a nut. The public publishing of the audiopt feeds came twenty or thirty years too late. By the time that was introduced, we had already destroyed the conditions that allowed the great kleptocracies to flourish.'

'Yes, but the breakdown of that society gave way to the anarchy of the Times. The introduction of the audiopts was

235

absolutely necessary to put an end to the banditry and looting that had the whole world in misery in the '30s. They brought stability, and you won't get people willing to risk the peace we have now with the threat of a return to that, for the sake of some notion of personal liberty.'

Jack tried another oratorical gesture. He spread the fingers of both hands and bumped the tips together several times, after which he held the touching forefingers to his lips. He maintained a thoughtful pose for several seconds and looked over to Halthrop. The major held a slightly wry smile.

'Two generations have seen the peace that the Covenants of Jerusalem brought. Food and fulfilment are in plentiful supply now. We are no longer in danger from raiders, bandits or others who would do us harm. Nobody in the world has any imperative now to behave like that. The darkness has been replaced by light. Thus, there is no need to maintain the spectre of the audiopts hanging over us – it is the one shadow that remains in our otherwise sunny lives.'

'Again, I counter that the audiopts bring the light. They shine into the dark corners and send malice scurrying.'

Jack smiled a broad grin behind the forefingers that still pressed on his lips. Halthrop smiled also, but a small close-lipped smile. He dropped a hand, to cup both around the empty whisky glass. He looked back at Jack and changed the subject. 'Tomorrow, we will need to leave here at about noon. I want to get us to Highnam Court without any kind of public parading of you. If we can get there long before the public, that will help. I have asked Lloyd Lloyd to provide us all with lunch in the hall when we get there.'

Jack nodded. 'Of course, that sounds sensible.'

'You will need to be in handcuffs though. The people will expect that a man who caused explosions, and in pursuit of whom one of their citizens died, is likely to be a dangerous haracter.'

Jack sat up and frowned. 'I trust that you can release me rom them when I get the chance to speak in my own defence.'

'I will check with Lloyd Lloyd, but I hope that if I vouch 1at you are no threat they will allow it.' Major Halthrop laid his lass on the table beside his sofa and stretched out to sleep. Jack ooked at the man. He appeared immediately peaceful and, if ot already asleep, he would be quickly. Halthrop clearly did ot consider Jack a personal threat.

Destined to meet his peers in ten hours' time, he lay back) review the plans for his defence. His eyes closed, and Jack's onsciousness slipped into dreaming.

'Sun Tzu once said "Opportunities multiply as they are eized".' Halthrop's deep voice sounded triumphant and onclusive at this. It was the first thing he said.

'Am I in the right place?' A boy sat in the front row next) two girls in their mid-20s. The boy was a similar age, but had 1e soft, pale skin of a young teenager. Compared with the other ive recruits for the Bristol Brigade militia group, Jack did look ut of place. 'I'm supposed to be at a training briefing.'

Frank Halthrop leaned forward to rest an elbow on the top f his lectern, the hand on brow equally supporting and estraining it. 'My name is Major Halthrop, and I am the Brigade commander. This is indeed orientation, Mr Smith.'

Jack blinked like he did when his bedroom light came on irst thing in the morning and he leaned as far back in the chair s was possible, gawping. 'How do you know my name?'

The moustachioed speaker moved slightly as if to shake is head in exasperation, but he stood up straight again. 'As Brigade commander, it's my job to know all of you better than ou know yourselves.' The major's lips moved no further, but ack heard Halthrop add, under his breath, 'Which won't be ery difficult.'

Jack exhaled deeply through inflated lips and looked around at the other new recruits. They were all sitting upright attentive, almost gaping at their new leader. He slouched.

'Thank you, Mr Smith, you have illustrated two very important lessons already.' Jack's dark eyebrows furrowed, and he looked again at his neighbours, who were still watching the major. 'Gain as much intelligence as possible. You did not know if you were in the right place, so you quite correctly confirmed, at the earliest opportunity. Don't let ignorance fester. Well done.'

Jack relaxed and looked at his new comrades again. He couldn't be sure if any of them had moved at all. They were mannequins. He touched the arm of the of the girl on his right and in her fixed position, the mannequin fell over slightly until her arm rested on the empty seat to her right.

The major continued, oblivious, 'And secondly, always be fully prepared. I have briefed myself on all of you, and I was certain I knew your name correctly. You were in the right place but had not prepared for what to expect here. Thus you were not a hundred per cent confident. Your enemy would seize upon that weakness. Luckily, I am not your enemy.'

Jack opened his eyes and found himself lying on his side and looking straight across at the major on the other sofa. Frank lay on his back, in exactly the same position as when Jack had gone to sleep. He made no sound.

'I am not your enemy,' Jack mumbled and closed his eyes again.

Chapter Twenty-seven

'You are living in Elizabethan times,' Jack bellowed.

Lloyd Lloyd pushed his blond fringe slightly to one side. 'Do you see any cars driving the streets of Highnam?' he asked Jack.

At a much lower volume, Jack responded, 'I meant you are living with Elizabethan values.' He swept an arm towards the audience from the elevated stage. 'You gossip and titter and tut-tut about people breaking monogamy when it's not even a natural human state. As a sifter, I have studied human populations all over the world and throughout history. Few of them bother with the idea of monogamy. Many include marriage, but it's not of great interest who you actually sleep with. Everyone takes responsibility for the whole community. Each have roles, and a place where they sleep, but it is all a communal effort.'

Lloyd Lloyd interrupted, 'You are describing our way of life here in Highnam.' There was a momentary interlude in the arguments. The large space was filled with the smell of coffee and wet coats.

Jack shook his head and held his voice at a calm, even volume. 'No, here in England, we have simply adapted to our current situation that same selfish life they had before the Times of Malthus.'

'Do you hear anyone else complaining about their lives?'

'Yes, everyone. That's my point.'

There was some muttering within the assembled crowd, which Lloyd Lloyd muted by raising a hand towards them. 'I mean in a serious way. Everyone knows they have the power to affect Kangaroo. Right here.' It was Lloyd Lloyd's turn to invoke the assembled masses. He waved the hand left and right, indicating the audience. 'Or simply to leave and travel to live somewhere else, perhaps in one of those idyllic Kangaroos you speak of.'

The noise of the crowd increased, with several people calling out 'No!'

He raised the palm higher, stilling the chatter. 'But they don't. We like what we have. Let the Africans like what they have. And the Italians. And everybody. This is what the Covenants of Jerusalem protect – each population defines its own way of life without influence from others.'

'Hear, hear,' a man called out.

Jack moved his body position so he was addressing the crowd directly rather than arguing with the Spokesperson. 'But you know people won't leave their families; or what they grew up with. This is all they know. They aren't free, they are trapped here by their ignorance.'

Lloyd Lloyd also turned his body to present to the audience, although his head remained half-turned to Jack. 'And you would like to destroy the technology that gives them access to that education that would allow them to decide to leave if they found something better?'

'No. I'm not an enemy of knowledge. I want people to have privacy; to find out about it, to talk about it, try it out maybe. We don't have to move to Italy to get the best of their lifestyles, we can have it here. But nobody will experiment with lifestyle changes, because it's all public knowledge. You are all Big Brother: you show them what they did, and then you all glare and shake your heads and tell them, "It's not what we do in Highnam – two weeks building labour, next case please." Privacy would allow people to test things out, free from that suffocating moralising. And then good, new things would be absorbed into our society, and things that don't work for most people would not.' Jack paused to let the members of the crowd mull over the titbits he had offered. 'Critically though, we don't all need to be the same. So, if there's something that some people like and others don't, then we can have a situation where some practise it and others don't. And nobody need know who is doing what, because it just doesn't matter.'

There was quiet for some seconds, and then Lloyd Lloyd countered, 'I think you have hit the nail on the head. People here don't understand what you are talking about, because the whole thing just doesn't matter. We are a tolerant Kangaroo, and allow people to behave as they like. We know about it because of the audiopt feeds, but we don't judge them.'

'I slept with your wife.'

The Spokesperson looked at Jack, and then at the crowd, and back at Jack. 'What?'

'When the feeds were down, I slept with your wife. But it's OK, because you don't judge people or stop them doing things.'

'Now, just a minute... '

'I didn't,' Jack interrupted. He looked at the assembly. 'I did not sleep with Lloyd Lloyd's wife, but maybe now you understand what I'm talking about. If you know about things, you automatically want to punish people for them. But we're getting sidetracked – infidelity is just an example. Maybe in Highnam we do want to discourage it.'

'Yes we do,' the same heckler concurred.

Jack carried on, 'It's just an example. The most important thing is that we don't need to know. I'm not suggesting we destroy the audiopt feeds. What I would like is for us not to use them unless we need to. Don't go looking for problems. If a big crime is committed, like the boy who murdered his father recently, then check up on the feeds and bring the culprit to justice. But if two men argue and punch each other, the village just doesn't need to know. That knowledge is not for the benefit of all.' This was Jack's punchline. He stopped there.

'Well, Mr Smith, I'm glad you bring up the issue of big crimes. Perhaps we should move on to consider the destruction of the Doughnut computers.' Lloyd Lloyd had obviously prepared himself for this encounter, as he was able to move easily around the arguments.

Jack had also spent many hours confirming his logic and preparing it for presentation to the people – to his revolutionaries. 'Yes, let's. I referred a moment ago to the Second Covenant of Jerusalem: "Everyone shall act for the benefit of all." Having established that the audiopts are not for the benefit of all, I was compelled by that Covenant – by our law – to act to remove their insidious effects. My actions were for the benefit of all, and can in no way be classified as a crime. It took a significant destructive act to bring about this change, but we are now in a position to switch off the broadcasting of the audiopts and only use them for reference at a later stage if we have a crime that needs investigating.'

Jack looked aside to Major Halthrop, and they caught each other's eye. Halthrop was flanked by Terry and Vicky, all seated at the side of the small stage. Darren and Jane maintained a protective guard of Truvan at the back of Kangaroo Hall, as far from Jack as possible.

He continued, 'The trivia of everyday social interactions are not worthy of Kangaroo, which should be a town meeting. Let me show you what I mean: each person in the room, turn to the person next to you and tell them of some interesting, shocking, or maybe funny event that happened to you earlier this week. They will not know what you have done in that time, because the audiopt feeds were off, so what would you like to tell them about? Let's spend five minutes, so you both get the chance to relate an interesting story.'

In the first row, right in front of him, Asa and his father turned to each other. Tony stroked his shaggy, grey beard, and they agreed that there wasn't really any tale that they could offer each other as they lived and worked together so knew each other's lives inside out. Jack eavesdropped on them and, in the end, Asa explained a new design he had thought of for the patterning they marked onto the horse bridles they made.

As Jack looked across the hall, he could see all the villagers in small conversations, during which they regularly gave furtive glances to him up on stage. Truvan, arms folded, stared straight at Smith.

Nearby, Jack could see Vicky's father, Marmaran Truva, waving his little, white coffee cup towards a tall, ginger man. Jack recognised the larger man from the KangaReview he had sent through recently but could not remember his name. Jack cursed himself. He expected to know everyone in Highnam, but could only assume that his mind had been heavily distracted in the weeks before the explosion.

The ruddy man laughed heartily and slapped Marma on the shoulder. The shorter, darker man smiled and held the cup down upon the saucer. Lloyd Lloyd turned to Jack on the stage and said quietly, 'What is the aim of this? This is what people do all the time. Most of them arrive half an hour early for Kangaroo for a drink and to catch up about the week they've had. How does this exercise prove your point?'

He looked at the Spokesperson with a frown. Jack's eyebrows scrunched tightly and he turned his face slowly away from Lloyd Lloyd to look again at the crowd. After their early arrival, Jack, Vicky, Darren and Frank had occupied a small room above one end of the stage. It was a round room in a turret built into the front of the hall and was raised on a mezzanine slightly above the bulk of the hall space. When Highnam put on theatrical performances, it was used for the musicians.

243

Jack remembered that there had been a significant buzz from the main hall for a long time before the official 3pm start time. From the tall, narrow window in the minstrels' gallery, he had watched a continuous train of people arrive for about an hour. He had assumed that, as this was the biggest case in the history of the Kangaroo, everyone had arrived early for the show.

Highnam's main man added, 'Sometimes people will tell these sort of anecdotes to each other by armulet video call, but nobody really monitors each other's audiopt feeds. It's not interesting or important enough to spend the time on it.'

Jack stared across the few hundred heads in the room. They continued talking, some in animated conversations, some more concerned with what this turn in the proceedings was supposed to achieve. The snippets he caught ran a gamut of possibilities, from mundane trivia, to questions about the protocol of the accused running the Kangaroo, and a few who were indeed discussing philosophical arguments about surveillance and society and criminology.

He was unsure what, exactly, he had expected the townsfolk to talk about at this point. Jack knew he had wanted to stir up the debate about the intrusiveness of the audiopts – and the option of switching their live broadcasts off – but he was surprised at how few people seemed to be discussing that. He caught some comments about it, but became concerned that only a handful had even realised that the ultimate aim was to make that decision.

To the right-hand side, fat Frances and her skinny sister Amy had loud cackling voices. Jack remembered their inane chatter from the marketplace the previous weekend. He despaired that their only interest seemed to be overtly shaming Marisa Leone, the adulteress who had been exposed in Jack's last KangaReview. They made a point of talking loudly to each other about how Marisa was a 'whore' and a 'home-wrecker'.

Jack felt his throat catch. He wondered if he would ever be able to convince the likes of Frances and Amy that they should vote for a fundamental change in Highnam's society. Quite apart from getting them to understand the sociological, anthropological, and psychological aspects to it, he realised that their lives revolved around rumour and gossip. He scanned further around the throng, hoping to hear more mature considerations amongst his peers.

'OK, enough.' It was Lloyd Lloyd's turn to bellow. 'I don't think there's much to be gained with this distraction. We are here to try this man for terrorism and extreme destruction of communal property. And remember that his crimes reached far more widely than Highnam. We have a responsibility to the other Kangaroos to punish him appropriately.'

Jack interrupted, also loudly, 'We have a far greater responsibility than that here today. This is your opportunity to change all our lives for the better. Who would like their children to grow up in a better world than we have today?' There was a murmuring in the crowd. Rhetoric was uncommon in the localised world of 2089. Nothing was politicised, and the idea of influencing by oratory was unknown to the gathering. Jack thrilled at the response as the atmosphere in the room surged at his suggestion. Lloyd Lloyd's eyes flitted around the faces of his friends and family in the audience. He was probably the only person in Highnam who had ever experienced the possibility of bending a crowd to their will.

'The state of affairs we have now has served us well. The audiopts brought stability in times of great distress. And that peace laid the foundations on which we built a peaceful and successful society. Right now we have good lives, don't we?' Across the assembly there were nods and mutterings of 'Yes'. 'We all have enough food; we all have fulfilling work; and we

245

all have the love of our friends and families, don't we?' The voices were slightly louder and greater in number. Everyone was rapt: all faces looked up at Jack. He could see the only dissenter was Truvan Truva who remained stony, arms folded. Jack pressed on, glad that Truvan stood behind everybody else.

'All great things are simple, and many can be expressed in single words: freedom, justice, honour, duty, mercy... privacy.' As he misquoted Churchill, Jack caught a slight shake of Halthrop's head out of the corner of his left eye and heard the major suck his breath in. The audience below did not notice and were now nodding in unison, with some turning quietly to their neighbour, 'He's right, you know.' Jack knew his moment had come.

'But the most important of those is freedom. As everything is so good these days, we don't take the time to consider the state of our society in fundamental terms any more. I entreat you today to take this opportunity to do so. As you do your duty and administer the justice of this Kangaroo, I ask that you will show me mercy. Honour all our ancestors who died to give us the world we have, and leave hope for a better future for your children.' Jack had watched many political leaders from videostories of times gone by. He waved his arms and stood upright, mimicking the best of them.

'My own mother died for me to live, and my grandfather was killed protecting his community. As I have served you as your sifter, I have no children, so I offer guidance to all of you who have. Will you take this chance to offer your children better than you have had up to now?' There were shouts of agreement, and everyone was jostling. The buzz was becoming excitement, and Jack reached his crescendo, 'Will you give them freedom?'

'Yes!' many shouts agreed, and some added, 'Freedom!'

In a final frenzy, Jack raised both arms from his sides as

he spoke, to finish palms up pointing out across the throng. 'Will you give them privacy? Will we turn off the audiopts' live broadcast?'

The crowd froze. The faces changed from rapture to confusion. People lowered off their tiptoes, and some turned to each other. Big Bearded Bill was in the centre of the room and called out, 'What you on about, son?'

Beside him, a man that Jack recognised as the apple seller from the market followed up, 'How will that help?'

More voices joined in with variations on the same question. The villagers could not see Jack's connection between a better life for their families and the audiopt feeds.

Lloyd Lloyd's big right hand swept up his stack of golden hair on to the top of his head, and it fell back in an unchanged unkempt manner. He beamed and quieted the questions, his arms forward with the palms face down.

'Well, I think the defence has presented everything he wanted to. We are at a good moment to work out what to do with him.' Jack stood frozen, nonplussed. He turned his head slowly to see the Spokesperson continue with the established legal process, which Jack had briefly managed to circumvent. The crowd were now following Lloyd Lloyd. 'Jack Smith,' he waved one hand to the side to indicate the defendant, 'seems to think that there is something wrong with the audiopts system we have used successfully for fifty years. He blew up the Doughnut to destroy them and seems to think that everybody else wants to do the same.'

'He's a nutter,' Bill shouted through his bushy beard. There were heckles of agreement with Bill's sentiment and the crowd, which had hung on Jack's every word only a minute earlier, jeered and pointed at him.

Lloyd Lloyd repeated the calming gesture with his hands and continued, 'That destruction of property was an attack on our way of life, more than just the damage it did.'

'And he killed my brother,' Truvan shouted from the back. Those assembled turned to look at him and silence fell. He ignored the crowd, eyes fixed on Smith.

The crowd turned back to see what their Spokesperson would make of this new impeachment. Talk of Bailey's death had been the gossip of Highnam since the armulet connections had come back on and Truvan had been able to contact his father. The exact circumstances though had been exaggerated and misrepresented right from the source.

Halthrop leapt from his chair at the side of the stage and walked in front of Jack. 'If I may,' he said to Lloyd Lloyd as he upstaged him too. The major did not wait for an answer. 'Ladies and Gentlemen, I am Major Frank Halthrop of the Bristol Brigade. We captured Mr Smith after something of a manhunt across the countryside and out into the Bristol Channel, where we secured him on a remote island.'

Halthrop paused for what Jack found to be an unsettlingly long time. The major was scanning the assembled faces. 'The Truva twins forced us to accept them to join our posse, against my advice, and I was present at the unfortunate death of Bailey Truva. He drowned after the boat he was on capsized. There was no direct action or influence from Jack Smith, which contributed to this tragic casualty – it was just a terrible accident. Bailey was not a sailor, and the boat he was on was not fit for the waters we were in. It was exactly this kind of thing that concerned me when the twins joined us, and which I cautioned them about. They should never have been a part of the posse, untrained as they were, so I hold myself ultimately responsible for Bailey's death. However, nobody was directly to blame for it, and Mr Smith certainly cannot be charged with any crime in connection with it.'

'Liar!' Truvan shouted and was restrained by his father

and George Kendrick as he tried to push through the audience. Darren and Jane stood in front, but allowed Marmaran and George to control Truvan.

Halthrop looked to Lloyd Lloyd. The Spokesperson stepped forward and Major Frank returned to his seat. 'There was no audiopt record of this incident, but I have spoken to the other brigade members, and they concur with the major's explanation. It is a terrible shame, Bailey was a true gentleman, and a dedicated member of our community.' The Kangaroo meeting had begun with a minute's silent reflection on Bailey's life and contributions to Highnam population but, until that point, nobody had known how or even if it would form part of the proceedings. 'Although his body has been lost to the Severn, I'd like to suggest we erect a gravestone in the cemetery.' This was taken as read, and there was no discussion of whether the village as a whole agreed.

At the back, Truvan finally shook himself clear of his guards and sat down in tears, his face angry red. Jack looked to Vicky, ten feet away at the side of the stage. She was seated with her face in her hands, elbows on her knees. He was sure that beneath the hands she was also crying, although her body was still, and she made no sound.

Lloyd Lloyd pointed sideways to Jack and turned his head, but kept his body facing the audience. 'So, only considering the matter of the explosion, we need to decide what to do with him. We have no KangaReview footage to prove his guilt, but he was photographed by cameras at the Doughnut, and he has confessed.'

Jack interrupted, 'I've never admitted being guilty.'

Lloyd Lloyd turned and stepped forward to look past Jack to Frank. 'Major Halthrop, can you please confirm that he confessed?'

The Brigade commander stood and faced the assembly. 'It

is true that he has never said anything along the lines of "I blew up the Doughnut," but he has discussed his revolutionary ideas with me, with an unsaid acceptance that he was guilty of it.' The major remained standing but looked across to centre stage. The sound of heavy rain lashing the building filled the ensuing pause.

Jack stated loudly and clearly, 'I did not blow up the Doughnut, and I have never committed any crime.'

Major Halthrop shook his head and strode across to hand Lloyd Lloyd the printed photograph of Jack entering the computer basement at the Doughnut. The timestamp on the picture clearly stated that it was from a few hours before the explosion. Jack was shown with two backpacks in his hands.

Lloyd Lloyd addressed his people, 'Please do look through my eyes and see for yourselves, but I can confirm that this is a photograph of the accused, entering the crime scene at the appropriate time, and he's carrying bags of equipment.' A few people looked down at their armulet screens, but most watched the stage directly, happy to accept their Spokesperson's evidence.

Jack was inventing his story on the hoof, and his body language and voice tone were unconvincing. 'Yes, I went down to the basement. I was removing a load of old equipment from my office.' Suddenly, the proceedings were not about how to revolutionise their society – the citizens clearly did not understand that imperative – the argument was now all about saving his own life. The biggest crime in England since the signing of the Covenants of Jerusalem could, in the worst case conceivably merit execution.

Highnam's population was an enlightened and peaceful one, but Jack knew that there were a significant number present who had lived through the horrors of the Times of Malthus. There could well be an uninformed knee-jerk reaction. He knew that it would probably only take one person to call for it and the mob would agree.

'I had to do it off shift, because I need to work during the twelve hours I'm on shift every day. If that... electrical fault hadn't blown the place up, I could take you there now and show you the two bags of old computer equipment. All the stuff in my office is cobbled together from old parts; they're decades old. I regularly have to get the infotechs to replace stuff, but they just pile up all the junk and I have to take it downstairs myself.'

People in the audience looked to their neighbours to chat and mutually gauge reactions. There were many raised eyebrows, cynical smiles and headshakes. The mood across the room shifted full pendulum, and Jack's eyes flitted from group to group around the audience.

'Banishment!' Vicky's voice was surprisingly loud above the hubbub. Jack turned to his left. She was standing at the front of the stage, arms at her side and her eyes were wide as she stared out to the crowd. Jack tried to ask a question, but his voice made no sound. There was a long silence, as the villagers tried to process what she had said, and Vicky looked stunned herself at her own actions. Her chest rose as she drew in a large breath. She pointed to the side, at Jack, and spoke loudly. 'Let's banish him. I was on the island where he was caught. It's uninhabited, and he seemed to like being away from everybody. You can see he wears no armulet – he doesn't like being connected to other people. That was the whole point of his destruction of the audiopt feeds, so let's give him his wish and exile him. Send him back to live on the island he escaped to.'

Tony the leather craftsman called out, 'Yes, exile.'

Tony's son, Asa, squeezed his father's forearm and joined in vigorously, 'Banish him!'

Jack could see heads urgently nodding. Some people were staring at the hairless, paler white strip of his arm that had held his armulet. Exile had never previously been used by Highnam as a punishment.

Lloyd Lloyd stepped nearer to Jack and slightly forward of him. The Spokesperson was truly centre stage. 'This does sound like a good proposition. We will be able to report to all other Kangaroos that we have dealt with it proportionately and seriously. But we can also be happy with ourselves that we have found a non-violent and appropriate punishment.'

He paused for a moment and looked at the faces in the assembly. 'Does anybody have anything... sorry, I'm going to have to rule that Truvan Truva has such an emotional bias, that he may not speak on the punishment. You can vote Truvan, but hand up only, you've had your say and we've determined that Bailey's death is not a part of this.'

Many people turned to look at the twin. He was standing, fuming, arms again folded across his chest, face flushed beneath the stubbly, brown beard. Marmaran's free hand was on his son's arm. George Kendrick, the big redhead, stood beside Truvan, watching him carefully. If needed, he could again help father Truva physically control his son.

'So, does anybody have anything to say in support of exile, or against it, or an alternative suggestion for punishment for Jack Smith?' Many people shook their heads, and open faces looked up to the round cheeks of Lloyd Lloyd.

'Make sure there is no boat or anything left on the island, so he can't escape.'

'Yes, and the other sifters should monitor his audiopt feeds to make sure he stays on the island.'

Lloyd Lloyd ran a hand through his blond mane, and nodded. 'Yes, good ideas. Noted.'

Jack interrupted, 'How long is the proposed banishment to last?'

Lloyd Lloyd stared at him. Jack looked across to Vicky,

who had not moved since she first spoke. She looked down to her feet. Her dun hair was not tied back, and it fell forward obscuring her long face. Lloyd Lloyd turned back to the crowd. 'Well, um, good question. I had simply assumed that we meant banishment for life, but we'd better agree on it formally: maybe you don't think it should be forever?'

Truvan shouted from the back. 'Please, did Bailey mean nothing to you? At least let this man's punishment make it mean something.'

'Truvan,' Lloyd Lloyd admonished.

'Please. You will be saving both him and me. If I see the man ever again I will kill him myself.'

'Truvan,' Vicky gasped looking up again.

Lloyd Lloyd took charge. 'Exile for life on Steep Holm island in the Bristol Channel. Hands up, please.' It was not quite unanimous, but a sufficient majority that Lloyd Lloyd did not need to count the hands. He looked carefully across all assembled and then at his armulet screen for absentee votes, and thus the decision was recorded by his audiopt feeds.

Chapter Twenty-eight

Jack was tied to the pillion handle on Halthrop's ATV. The storm had abated, to leave the woods around Grannie Ellie's farmhouse warm and wet.

Vicky approached. She wore a wide-brimmed, white hat with a navy band on it. Her brown ponytail extended behind, and her dress matched the hatband in both colour and the light cotton material.

The sun shone brightly, but Jack's face was in the shade of one of the grape vines. Across the back garden, he could see Frank Halthrop exit the house and carefully close the door, with a check that it had definitely clicked shut. The major turned and stopped. His finger went up to stroke his moustache and he waited.

Vicky paused about six feet from Jack. 'I hope you're not mad with me?'

Jack looked down at her feet, unsure whether or not he was upset. He considered his answer carefully and then looked back up to her eyes, the hat brim casting a shadow across them like an old bandit's mask. She looked beautiful. The contrast of light and shade, her smooth skin, strong yet slender figure, and the combination of her hat and dress made Jack's stomach whirl. He couldn't tell if the dappled woodland sunlight, or his own mind, made the vision appear in soft focus.

'Of course I'm not mad with you. I'm mad with the rest of the population for not having the brains to see a better future. But, it's possible that you saved me from execution.'

'That's what I was hoping. I don't want you to go, but it's far better than you being dead.' She took another step closer.

'Well, Grannie Ellie would say that it's Justice for

Dummies. We're both young. Hopefully, changes will come, and my punishment will be lifted.'

'It's a shame you won't even have your armulet; it would have been nice to talk to you each day, to see how you're getting on and hear more of your ideas. I didn't really think when I said that, I just blurted it out. It sounded like a good extra bit of punishment to really seal banishment as the best idea.'

'I know what you mean. There was a moment when I knew I had lost the crowd and all it would take was someone – your brother probably – to call for execution and they would all have jumped on board baying for my blood. It wouldn't have surprised me if Truvan could have produced a rope at short notice and slung it over the centre beam in Kangaroo Hall,'

'Stop it, it's not fair to say that about him. He lost his twin brother. He's just disoriented right now.'

Jack held his tongue about Truvan. Vicky obviously could not see the same venom spat from her brother's eyes every time they looked at Jack. 'I'm sorry, I didn't really mean it like that. What I was getting at was that the mob mentality could easily have escalated out of proportion, so you really did save my life.'

After a pause, Jack changed tack. 'And I suspect that your proposing my punishment was what made them let you off with no punishment. It sounded like you were against me, and, with Bailey's death, there was no way they could think you were on my side. You must have been forced to go along with me.'

Vicky had looked away, and she turned back again, the glow in her face returned. She gave no answer to his implied question but held a wry grin.

He said, 'You never know, I'm sure we'll talk again in the future.' She tilted her head with a quizzical expression, but said nothing further. They contemplated each other, each with a small, sad smile. 'What will you do now?'

Her eyes opened slightly wider and she looked ove Jack's shoulder. He could tell she was focussed on something far behind him. After a few moments, Vicky's greeny-brown eyes fixed back onto his face. With the slightest shrug she replied, 'What else is there to do? I'll help Truvan and fathe with our crops and hopefully the three of us will be able to work through losing Bailey, and three will be able to manage what four used to do.' Vicky's expression was simple and open.

Jack shifted on the ATV seat and looked through the tree away from Ellie's house and garden. The forest was bright and verdant.

'What about the audiopts? Will you do anything to help bring privacy to the world?'

She stepped close to Jack and put her hand on his cheek He looked up into her face. 'That was never my fight, Jack. love you, and I support you, but that's for you, not for you ideology.' His eyes fell, but Vicky's cool hand remained on his cheek. She bent forward and applied light pressure on his cheek to lift his face to meet her kiss. Her lips were also cool and delicate. She paused. From only a couple of inches away Vicky's bright eyes glinted into his. 'I tell you what. From now on, I'll make sure I never look down when I masturbate.' She broke into a large grin.

Jack shook his face free from her hand and said, 'That's not funny.' His head was bowed to look down at the seat in front of him, but there was a smirk on his lips.

Halthrop's armulet chirruped, and Terry's voice came through it. 'We're all set, Frank. The road is clear – we should be able to drive straight away.' Major Halthrop walked across the garden and closed the gate behind him as he joined Jack and Vicky's final farewell.

She turned around to face Halthrop, a finger twisting the hair that escaped her hat. 'Look after him, please, Frank.'

The major came to attention and gave her a mock salute. 'Will do.' He looked straight into her eyes and added, 'You look after Truvan and your father.'

Jack thought it a little incongruous that Vicky and Halthrop should embrace in a hug on parting, but his eyes were distracted from it. Fifty feet beyond the major, Tony and Asa stood, silently, looking at him. They were dressed in hunting clothes: forest camouflage colours and black boots. The father and son looked similar, apple close to the tree. Both had shaggy hair, one brown, one grey, bushy beards, and looked like they had not been home since the storm, as there was mud spattered all up their legs. They stood either side of a large bush, like three beards in a row, nodded to Jack and then looked at each other. Halthrop and Vicky separated and she stepped aside to the garden fence as Halthrop mounted the quad bike. Jack looked back to the muddy leatherworkers, but they had vanished.

'Right, no use waiting around, let's get on with it.' Halthrop pressed the ATV's power button. It was silent but the headlights came on, barely visible in the bright morning sunlight.

Vicky's voice caught in her throat as she uttered his name, 'Goodbye, Jack. I... I hope it goes well for you.' Tears rolled down her face, but she smiled at him. The major lifted his hand in farewell and steered the four-wheeler away.

Jack said nothing. He kept Vicky's gaze though, turning his head to hold on to it, until the distance made it impossible for his neck to achieve what was needed. He turned forward again and stared at Halthrop's back. In his mind's eye, Jack held a lingering vision of Vicky standing still, arms at her sides. The thing that caught his attention in this memory was the skew little finger of her right hand sticking out at 45 degrees from the rest of her fingers.

The route back to Weston-super-Mare was often flooded. In some parts, the mud was still so thick and slippery that even the so-called all-terrain vehicles found it tough going.

They stopped overnight at the Brigade HQ in Bristol, with a view to taking the horses along on the second leg, to return them home.

Jack lay on a canvas camp bed in the militia building, unable to sleep. Jack's mind became swamped with fearful images of the well run dry and of a hot wind blowing through the cottage. In his head, the sun was beating down and the island's upper plateau was scorched, brown earth. He saw himself as a withered, decayed man, crawling towards seagulls on the high cliff, desperate to grab something to eat. There were no eggs or nests visible, and his feeble hand stretched weakly up to try and pluck a gull from the air. The birds taunted him, cawing and whirling. He struggled to even look at them as they hovered in line with the sun.

Jack sat up on the edge of the bed, and breathed short, sharp gulps of air. Bile-tasting vomit pressed at the back of his throat, and he sweated.

After very little sleep, Jack functioned poorly on the road from Bristol to Weston. He fell off the ATV when they first pulled away from the HQ building. Halthrop had capitulated that he only needed to be bound as they left Highnam, and again when they arrived at Weston-super-Mare. When he fell, he was able to break his fall with his hands, but was significantly shaken, and there were rough grazes on both palms.

There were other occasions during the day when the hot sun and bumpy road made him feel nauseous and worried that he would fall again. Major Halthrop was sympathetic to his repeated requests for the convoy to rest in the shade. Jack could see the younger soldiers muttering to each other each time. He felt so ill that there was no way he could possibly run.

There was no improvement in his condition when they transferred on to the boat. The rocking of the little vessel, along with his hands again being tied behind his back, made the nausea worse. When he threw up over the side, Halthrop stepped forward and cut the plastic tie on Jack's wrists. He was then able to vomit in more comfort. The crew were wary at first, but the Brigade commander was able to convince them that he knew his prisoner, and there was no danger. The boat journey took an hour, and when they walked down the gangplank onto the pebble beach, Jack's gait was a stagger.

Major Halthrop had put together two large duffel bags of equipment that he referred to as a 'New Life Starter Pack'. Jack knew that many of the accoutrements of everyday life would already be on the island – he had seen two fully equipped kitchens and plenty of lounge and bedroom furniture. As he and the major had walked around the Brigade building, Jack had tried to argue for as much food as possible, along with a variety of clothes and powered items, like a solar-charged torch and a rare cooking stove with wax fuel blocks.

'Where will you set yourself up?' Major Halthrop asked Jack for direction. Terry and Jane carried the bags of the New Life Starter Pack, and Darren supported Jack's feeble attempts to walk.

His throat was dry and felt dusty. He waved towards the upper level of the island, and croaked, 'Where you found us. That's the only water supply we found.' Halthrop said nothing further, but nodded and waved the party forward towards the path leading up the hill behind the ruins of the old pub.

With no ceremony, Terry and Jane dumped the duffel bags on the floor in the cottage kitchen. Jack felt that Darren similarly dumped him into one of the kitchen chairs too. The young trio left without a word. Through the wide window, Jack and Frank watched them wandering away across the yard past the well.

The cottage's new permanent occupant looked across the full range visible through the window from his low vantage point in the chair, and then inside around the room. Jack did not have the energy to stand up, so accepted the viewpoint he could muster from his seat. Finally, his eyes settled on the major. Halthrop watched his charge closely, and his face looked serious.

'Is there anything I can do before we leave you?'

Jack's eyes fluttered a bit and the wooziness hit him again. He placed his left hand on the kitchen table for support, and refocussed on the man who had caught him and brought him to Kangaroo. Halthrop's eyes looked gentle and concerned. Jack again surveyed the kitchen in which he sat. 'However beautiful the strategy, you should occasionally look at the results.'

Halthrop's finger dropped, and he replied, 'I always avoid prophesying beforehand, because it is much better policy to prophesy after the event has taken place.'

The two men looked at each other for more than two minutes. No further words were spoken, and Major Halthrop finally nodded to Jack, turned and exited into the farmyard. Jack watched the man's back diminish across the sun-bleached stone space, until he turned out of sight behind the barn that contained the big copper water tank.

Jack spent his first afternoon mostly in the same chair. He made a trip to the water supply room and staggered back with a jug full of water. The heat was not excessive, but Jack felt it so.

He attempted to cook one of the ration pack meals from his New Life Starter Pack, but the solid fuel cooking stove was weak and he was impatient with it. Jack blamed the fact that the vacuum-packed meal was sixty years old more than the fact that it was poorly cooked. He vowed that, from the next morning, he would eat only fresh food cooked on a wood fire he would build himself; and then he extended his vow to making the solar cells and battery packs on the island work so that he could cook on an electric stove.

His lethargy and queasiness led Jack to be unconvinced by his own vow, and he went to bed early to try and shake off the sickness. The first bed he found in the stone cottage was comfortable, although it smelled musty. He lay a military sleeping bag over himself, but the night sweats returned, and he mostly lay awake and uncovered.

The early morning light was beautiful and, as the sun rose, the temperature was pleasantly cool. Jack walked slowly but purposefully around the area outside the cottage he would use as home. The gorgeous sunrise and windless cool lifted his spirits.

Jack knew winter would be on him within a month or two, but decided he had time to get enough procedures in place that he could make a good go of it. He would save the packaged rations for moments of desperate hunger if the winter was severe, but planned to revamp a greenhouse of sorts, so that he could grow food year-round.

With each step across his new domain, Jack felt energy return. In this reconnaissance walk, he did not do or collect anything, but noted numerous points to be dealt with later. There was a rabbit warren, which could likely hold a source of meat. The copse he had collected wood from on his first visit to Steep Holm had suffered a lot of damage in the storm, and there were branches all over the ground. He planned to make a wood store in the big barn.

The tide was low when he descended to the beach. As the sun lifted high enough to flood into the east-facing windows of the old inn, Jack was in the kitchen. He picked up the remaining armulet, shook out the bones from within it, and continued

261

shaking rhythmically for several minutes. He strapped the armulet to his left forearm and walked out to admire the glistening water gently lapping. Jack leaned down and picked up a smooth, rounded river cobble. He felt its weight in his hand and then dropped it to hear the cracking sound.

Epilogue

'Vive la revolution!' the Braille message begins. 'Jack Smith was our inspiration. The visionary began us on this path to a society with privacy. We can achieve it, but we need to work together globally, and in secrecy, if we are to gain personal freedom for all.'

The shaggy-haired man's fingers trail across the page, his eyes closed. His face looks euphoric, like a meditating yogi. 'It is necessary to communicate in Braille, as the audiopt feeds will proclaim publicly everything we see and hear. But not what we feel, or smell, or taste, or think. And plotting to destroy the audiopt sensors doesn't go down too well at the Kangaroo courts.

'One of the Jacksons – the children of Jack Smith's ideas – was sentenced to execution by his Kangaroo in Belgium last year. Luckily, with the populations all running their own affairs so independently, and our cautious approach, we have not yet been discovered as an organisation. The Belgian was considered a solo maverick, probably with mental health problems, and written off to execution. We can bide our time; but we are not so far away from bringing about our private revolution.'

Before opening his eyes, the man turns his head to look out of the window of his small cottage. The view across the flooded River Leadon valley, over Rodwayhill Covert and up towards Highnam, is bright with winter sunshine. He runs his hand through his hair, shaking the grey mane wildly.

The Braille call to arms continues: 'Jack Smith's individual attempt was five years ago now, but a lone strike was never going to be enough to unseat the audiopts' all-seeing eye. As one man acting alone, he tried to foment revolution by blowing up the entirety of the computer systems based at the Doughnut in Cheltenham. It was a fantastic target, but the tentacles of our oppression spread wide and deep. And revolution cannot be instigated through a single revolutionary act or a single revolutionary man. We will need to hit many infonetwork centres simultaneously if we are to succeed. We will need to be a widespread organisation, so that the seedlings of the new society already hold ground in many populations.

'Jack felt that our so-called open and transparent way of life is in reality oppressive and invidious. He pointed out that by being able to live vicariously through anyone, or everyone, nobody has anything to live for. There is nothing they could call their own, and no experience that is unique. Everybody lives in fear of the audiopts. We believe in the truth of this philosophy and the need to upend the existence humans currently suffer.

'Jack was caught by his Kangaroo, and shown in no uncertain terms that society was bigger than him. The hypocrisy of the Covenants of Jerusalem seems to know no bounds. Where he alone was defeated, we together can be victorious. By showing all populations the wonders of unique experience, we will change the way people live forever – we will set them free. Vive la revolution!'

The man's lips silently echo the sentiment, 'Vive la revolution! Vive Jack Smith!'

He stands and leaves the house, opening his eyes only as the door clicks shut behind him. Outside, his son, Asa, is waiting.

Printed in Great Britain
by Amazon